I0517545

STAR SLAVE

by

NICOLE DERE

Published by **CHIMERA**
ISBN 9781780806501

Chapter One

'Hi. Come on in, darling. I'm just about to turn in. I'm absolutely dead. I thought they'd never go!' Felicity Keynes put her hands lightly on John's shoulders and turned her head sideways, offering her cheek to be kissed.

Her cousin paid the expected homage, thinking as his nose touched briefly the fragrant curtain of straight black hair which swung at her movement how beautiful the slender figure was. He never failed to respond to her beauty, in spite of his familiarity with it through all the years of their adolescence.

The brother she never had, she was fond of calling him. They were almost as close as brother and sister, he acknowledged, though his thoughts were often extremely unbrotherly. As now, when, having shut the door of the apartment behind him, she turned and carelessly slipped the black silk robe off to the floor, allowing him a splendid view of her nakedness as she walked through to the bathroom. She called over her shoulder, 'Come and talk to me in the bath. Help yourself to a drink, if there's any left. Those bastards have probably drunk me dry.'

With some difficulty he dragged his eyes away from the sight of her taut little behind swaying ahead of him, and turned into the living room. It was wrecked with the aftermath of a party. Glasses and plates, crumpled napkins and overflowing ashtrays covered almost every surface, and the heavily sweet smell of cannabis hung in the blue tinged air.

'You want one?' he called, hearing the sound of the water gushing.

'No thanks, I've had more than enough. You know I can't drink. I'm well pissed.'

He had to go into the tiny kitchen to find a clean glass.

He poured a generous measure of whisky from a nearly empty bottle, and filled his glass from an open soda bottle. She was bending over the deep blue tub, whipping up the contents to an ice-cream foam. She slid into the water with a luxurious sigh.

He watched her lovely breasts disappear into the clinging peaks of lather. She had slipped a towelling bandanna around her hair, lifting it on top of her head, where it fanned out in a rich plume. 'God, that's better!' Her head rested on a small foam cushion, and she closed her eyes. The eyelids were dramatically shadowed, the make-up increasing the appearance of exhaustion. Yet the tiredness only seemed to add to the air of youthfulness. It was hard to believe she was, at twenty-two, nearly two years his senior. She looked no older than when she was sixteen or seventeen.

The eyes, when she opened them, were startlingly large. 'Well, bro? How's the world treating you? I don't blame you one little bit for steering clear of the party. Such a bore, most of them.'

'The price of fame,' John quipped. He perched on the small cork-topped stool. He was not joking. Felicity was already making something of a name for herself as a stage actress, and now this deal for her to star in a television drama, which was the reason for tonight's celebration, would make her face and name familiar to practically every household. He sniffed exaggeratedly. 'Been smoking the weed, have we? You can smell it from the car park.'

She gave him a wrinkle-nosed grin of comic guilt. 'Well, I had to do something. You know I don't drink. Thank God we had some.' She assumed a clownish dolefulness. 'It's not much fun with Michael away up in the wilds of Scotland.'

As always, when she mentioned her fiance's name, John felt that tiny quiver of jealousy, even though he knew it was absurd. Mike was a perfectly decent sort, if more than a little stuffy, and certainly a good counterpoint to Felicity's sometimes volatile temperament. And she swore she loved him. 'I want to have his babies,' she'd told John, soon after they'd started going together. But not for a good while yet, her cousin suspected.

Felicity was extremely ambitious as far as her career went, and it was going to go a long way. In fact, this latest leap might well cause one or two problems in her love life, John surmised.

'Have you told him yet?' he asked, and saw a swift but unmistakable flash of genuine guilt pass across her lovely features.

She knew at once what he was referring to, and shuffled uncomfortably in the warm embrace of the water. Her role in this telly pic, which was to extend to six hours of viewing, was one that Michael would not accept with equanimity, she guessed - no, knew, she corrected herself gloomily.

She was playing the part of Kathy Weldon, the junior partner in a female pairing which emerged from nowhere to take the fashion world by storm. But Stella Mann - the surname carefully chosen by the writer - was the senior partner in more than a business sense. Their lesbian relationship was the central theme of the drama, and the clincher which would gain them the highest ratings of any of the channel's productions yet, the independent backers assured her.

She had been hesitant about taking the role on - but not for long. Yvonne Lightman, her agent, had stared at her in disbelieving scorn when she'd voiced her doubts. 'It will make you, darling. And the fee!' She was right. It was astronomical compared with anything she had earned so far. But the nudity clause was to be exploited to the full.

'We're practically doing it on camera!' Felicity had squeaked. Though when she thought about it, she didn't really mind all that much. It was really what Michael would think of it all that was disturbing her. Optimistically, she decided she could persuade him that it was all for art's sake. However, she had not succeeded yet. She'd not even broached the subject, which accounted for her guilty look at John's question.

'It's just a question of getting him in the right mood, darling,' she sighed. 'Anyway, I'm all signed up. We'll have our Rolls yet, my pet!' She sat up, and he watched the suds sliding off her breasts. The nipples were small, scarcely bigger than his, and very pale. 'Do my back for me, will you? This is a rare treat these days.'

He knelt, and pushed up his sleeve. He took the sponge and began to gently rub at the flawless shoulders and the curve of that exquisite back. He felt his prick hardening against his clothing, and his anger at her returned. They had grown up together. As a child, he was used to seeing her naked, to sharing nudity with her. Their fathers, who were brothers, had been close then, and John and Feely - the unattractive epithet he had bestowed her, to her initial chagrin and their parents' amusement - spent a great deal of time together, especially in the long summer holidays, abroad, or in the country. Their habit of bathing together had gone on until well past propriety, until parents tardily realised it was no longer seemly.

Felicity remembered now, as she leaned forward, enjoying the sensation of the sponge moving over her skin, the trickle of water as he held it above her. She giggled. 'Why don't you get in? It'll be like old times.'

Suddenly, he felt his heart racing. He tried to match her lightness. 'Don't be such a prick teaser, Feely. I might just take you up on it.'

'Beast! You haven't called me that in ages. Anyway, I'm not teasing. I meant it. Bath night's nowhere near such fun as it used to be.'

He was sure her voice sounded catchy, too. He stood, and started to pull his shirt over his head. He half expected her to shriek out in dismay, but she didn't. Hastily, he slipped down slacks and underpants, tore them off, and dragged off his socks. His penis was swollen, elongated, stirring, though not yet erect. She gave a squeal of protest as he leapt in and splashed down opposite her, his feet touching intimately against her limbs under the foam. 'Hiya,' she sniggered, leaning forward towards him. 'Long time no see.'

'What are you referring to?' he asked, and she chuckled wickedly.

She splashed water over him and flung the sponge. 'Here, wash yourself you mucky pup. And don't forget to do behind your ears.'

'Bossy as ever, Feely,' he grinned, and complied with her orders. Suddenly he felt her foot brush against his prick, her toes waggling, to stir the throbbing column to excited arousal.

'Whoops, sorry.' She gave a dirty leer. 'Feely by name and nature, eh?' The foot touched him again, the big toe grazing the underside of his balls and gently lifting the stiffening shaft. 'Now who's a prick teaser?' she murmured huskily, those huge eyes holding his.

Suddenly he looked almost frightened. 'Don't,' he said tensely. 'That's not fair.'

'Why not? It's just a bit of light relief. Nothing wrong with that, is there? Or is it too incestuous?'

'Yes,' he answered. 'Too dangerous, too.'

'We should've done this when we were kids. All that time - I thought you didn't fancy me.'

'I don't,' he said, trying to smile. 'I'm not really into girls - if you'll pardon the expression. Or hadn't you heard?'

She nodded. 'Jeremy was saying something about you being gay. Mummy and daddy didn't want to talk about it, of course. Is it true then?'

He could feel himself blushing. His shoulders moved in a shrug. 'What you might call a grey area at the moment.' He suddenly caught hold of her dainty foot, digging in hard with his thumb and fingers, keeping it away from his beating prick. Everything was still hidden beneath the creamy surface. 'Anyway, what about your beloved Mike? He wouldn't exactly be chuffed if he could see you now.'

'Wouldn't he? Are you so sure? He's not quite as uncool as you might think, bro. But the point is, he isn't here right now, is he? He's miles away.' A slow, siren smile spread over her face. Her eyes smouldered as she gave him a superb vamp's look. 'Mary Ann always makes me randy. P'raps you should try some, instead of booze.'

Her foot squirmed, but he held onto it. Then she gasped as he reciprocated her movement, and she felt the pad of his foot press firmly against the soft flesh of her mound, the toes pressing against the dark patch of her pubic hair. They broke the surface, at the base of her belly. 'See how you like it,' he grinned. He moved again and she shivered, her thighs opening a little. She thrust back against his pressure. 'You like it,' he said. 'Hmm, that's nice.' His foot was working now, moving against her silky softness, and she was alight with excitement. 'It's like walking in a mossy stream.'

4

'Guess we both like it,' she gasped. She leaned forward, searched under the water and seized his prick, her fingers gripping it tightly. She began to move, firmly, slowly, drawing the foreskin up and down the column she could feel throbbing under her touch.

'Don't!' he cried, but she didn't let go, and he made no effort to escape. She worked him harder, the water swirling about her arm. The dark red helm of his penis reared up out of the bubbles.

'Just a bit of relief,' she panted. Her face reddened. 'It's what we both need, I guess.' He was fully erect now, his column jutting, hotly filling her hand. She was jerking him faster, feeling the potent surge of him, triumphant in her power over him.

'No!' he cried out tightly, in real alarm, and reached to seize her slim wrist. Her fingers closed like iron about the base of the helm, which purpled, hugely swollen. With her free hand she pulled off the towel swathed about her hair and tossed it over the side of the tub onto the floor. Then, in a welter of foam, she knelt up, dipped her head forward and, with a delicious shiver of fear, lapped at the shiny dome and tasted the tangy flavour of the emission from the tiny slit. Her lips parted, stretched wide, and she sucked dizzily at him, taking his throbbing strength deep into her throat.

His hand fell limply away from her, and he gave a moan of pure surrender. She lapped and nuzzled, worrying his rearing prick until his body stiffened, his belly heaved upward, and he gave a shrill cry, his dark head stretched back against the deep blue of the tub. Instinctively, she jerked her mouth clear as the great surge of his come erupted thickly over her chin and throat and the fist which was still holding him captive. But then she bent once more, eagerly, and lapped with an ecstatic shudder at the residue of his fluid, which oozed thickly from his already wilting penis.

She hastily sluiced herself clean while he lounged back, his eyes closed, his face pale. Savouring the feeling of triumphant power she could feel stirring within, she quickly and competently washed his shrunken, satin soft prick, the helm already concealed once more beneath its hood, the size cutely diminished.

'There now!' she said, the amusement evident in her tone. 'That'll teach you to get cocky with me, little bro!'

Chapter Two

'Are they twins?' Lord Burnopside gazed with appreciation at the slim figure of Felicity Keynes across the large room. She was bending close towards her companion, one slender arm raised to his shoulder. They were almost the same height, and his build was scarcely less delicate than hers. Their facial characteristics were strikingly similar, enough to make Lord Burnopside's question a valid one. Felicity was wearing an insubstantial wisp of a dress, of a lacy fabric which was semi-transparent. A thin strap held it over one shoulder, the other was bare. Her breasts, innocent of any other cover, showed mistily through the material. The dress ended around the upper thigh. She wore no stockings or tights, and the tiny black V showing at her loins could well have been her pubis, though it was, in fact, a black satin G-string. She was laughing heartily, and turned now to the burlier figure on her left, whose features were altogether more conventionally handsome, in a masculine way.

The woman at Lord Burnopside's elbow chuckled deeply. 'No. I told you. They're not even brother and sister. They're cousins.'

'Are you sure?' His lordship did not take his eyes off the trio. 'Same surname, isn't it?'

'Their fathers are brothers. Keynes. One of them - hers, I believe - is supposed to be a writer. No one's heard of him, though.'

Stella Priest nobly smothered the stab of irritation she felt at the attention her fellow actress was claiming. Attention stolen from her, for she was the real star of the show. It was her name and reputation which were going to put this enterprise at the top of the viewing and money-making lists. Money which would go mostly to the charming, gravelly-voiced rogue beside her. Fair enough, she admitted. After all, he'd put up the lion's share of the production costs, and both she and that cute little ingenue over there would make a sum which, though smaller, could undoubtedly be classed as a fortune.

They were perfect together. Some people said it was his lordship who'd envisioned them thus, though he didn't seem bothered about taking any credit. Stella's golden voluptuousness and Felicity's dark, almost adolescent youthfulness, were predicted by David Allison - Ally, as he preferred to be known - their camp director, to be the greatest sensation since Baird's first flickering images appeared on screen seventy years before.

Stella and the others had stared in awe when, after they had run through the rehearsal script several times, Ally had described in graphic detail just how far he wanted the love scenes to go.

'You'll never get away with it,' Stella had breathed, already damply excited by the prospect.

'Lord B has friends in high places, dear,' he told her confidently. 'You'd be surprised. Stand by to be infamous overnight, girls.'

Felicity's smutty giggles had endeared her to Stella. 'We'll be just about doing it in front of millions,' she marvelled.

'Maybe we ought to get together, try a few private rehearsals,' Stella quipped, her heart thudding at the prospect, but was sharply disappointed by Felicity's flip reply.

'Thanks but no thanks. I'm straight as an arrow, darling.

Sorry to disappoint you, but I'm a strictly butter on one side only kinda bird!'

In spite of the younger girl's peeling laughter, Stella had privately wondered whether she'd heard any of the rumours that were no doubt about to be resurrected concerning the star's catholic tastes in sexual gratification. Never mind, she resolved philosophically. Early days yet. Wait till they got down to the nitty-gritty. For all her bravado, the kid had done no public shedding of her kit so far. And this would be, by all accounts, one hell of a hands-on initiation. She might well make the cute little bitch eat her words - as well as other things - one day. It would certainly be fun trying.

Now, though, young Felicity was stealing more than a considerable amount of her thunder. But the wide-eyed innocent approach didn't fool her one little bit; not wearing a little number that was more like a naughty nightie than a cocktail dress. Cock-tease, more like. It was working on Lord Burnopside, that was for sure. The craggy, ruddy features, with the thick silver-white moustache and the thatch of carefully styled matching hair, were aglow with admiration and veiled lust.

'Who's the other fellow?' his lordship asked.

'That's the boyfriend - sorry - fiance,' Stella answered. 'He's been promoted to officialdom, apparently. They plan to marry soon.'

'Living together?'

'No, not as far as I know. I don't even know if they're sleeping together. She's a funny little thing. Very hard to read sometimes. Sometimes I think she's been around, other times I wonder if she's even lost her virginity yet.'

'How intriguing,' Lord Burnopside muttered, one crooked finger rubbing thoughtfully against his moustache. My God, Stella mocked inwardly, all he needed was an opera cloak and silver-topped cane. 'We must have her down to the Han,' Lord Burnopside continued. 'And her cousin, too. Delightful, perfectly delightful. '

'Which one do you fancy the most?' Stella teased. 'He's very pretty too, isn't he? And not much use to me, I fancy.'

Felicity could see that Michael, in town from north of the border for the weekend, was finding it hard to take the amount of attention she was getting. Just as he had found it hard to take her dress when she first appeared in it back at the flat. That was why she had insisted that John be there. She and her cousin were closer now than they had been, even as kids. The pleasantly teasing, unfulfilled attraction he had aroused in her during their adolescent years was something she had missed when she went off to drama school, and then to a series of lowly acting jobs up and down the country, while he loafed at university. Meeting up again in London, after an absence of well over a year, had been a great bonus. Then the other night, disturbed by the sudden vast changes taking over her life, and stirred by the dreaded weed, which she had discovered to be a powerful sexual stimulant, she had revived that childish, half innocent sensuality they had shared. When she invited him into her bath she'd had no idea other than that vague naughtiness of former days, enhanced a little by the unconfirmed rumour from a mutual friend that John was involved with the gay fraternity at college.

Even when, spurred by a sudden devilment, she had begun the sexual stimulation, she had thought to go no further than masturbating him. And he'd seemed even more shattered by the experience, so that she'd savoured even more the feeling of power over him.

She had curled up naked with him under the sheets and fallen asleep. Next morning she succeeded in taking the initiative once more, capturing his squishy prick before he was awake. She manipulated it to a pulsing hardness, pushed him onto his back, spread her hair over his warm belly and thighs, and licked and nibbled at his seeping prick until it was purple and ready to burst. He lay there, stirring and whimpering like an overwhelmed virgin, his helplessness thrilling her, until his body spasmed and he gave a shrill cry and came, fearfully, excitingly, all over her fist and his palpitating belly, while she stared in fascination at the pumping seed.

'We can't do this,' he said, when, after they had shared another bath, they were sitting still naked at the worktop in her tiny kitchen, with coffee and toast.

'Don't be daft,' she answered, her mouth full. She picked off a crumb from between her breasts with a finger pad. 'We could marry if we wanted.'

'Do you want to?'

'Eh?' She gazed at him blankly. 'Marry me?'

'Don't be daft,' she said again. She grinned at him, her cheeks pouched as she bit into another piece of toast. She reached out and put her palm over his limp prick, and gave it a friendly shake. 'I'm glad I've done you, though. Just think what we've been missing all these years.' She hesitated just a fraction. 'Come on, John. You can tell me now. Are you really gay?'

'You just want my body,' he said, and slid off his stool to kneel between her knees, which he pushed gently apart.

He let his fingers pluck at her dark pubic curls, teasing them out, lifting the white skin beneath. One finger found the uppermost folds of her labia and stirred lightly. Her thighs moved. He saw the long muscles bunch, and her legs came together, holding his forearm.

'Don't,' she sighed, squirming on the plastic stool. His fingers moved more boldly, pushing against the plastic, opening her up until he could feel the dampness. He dragged her forward by the hips until she was straddling the stool, her legs stretched out wither side of him, her toes touching the floor. Her vulva was more exposed now, hanging over the rounded edge of the stool. He bent forward very slowly, puckered his lips, and kissed her, drinking in the delicious tang of her aroused body.

'Jesus!' she gasped. 'Don't, please!' She shivered, not sure whether she meant it or not.

'I'm just answering your question, coz,' he murmured, his breath warm against her most secret flesh. He lapped steadily, his fingernails pushing aside the sticky tissue, revealing the raw redness of the inner surface, and her hands cupped his head, stroking his short hair, holding him in to her.

'Don't!' She was begging genuinely now, squirming, wet, unable to keep still. 'You're not... you can't...'

He raised his wet face, grinning up at her from between her thighs. 'I like it like this.'

Felicity was overwhelmed by her own drumming need. 'Moo - make it happen,' she panted.

He lifted her, once more surprising her with his strength, seizing her about the middle, and planting her roughly on the edge of the worktop among the debris of their scratch meal. She sat blatantly, her genital area thrust at him over the hard edge, her thighs gaping, and he worked his tongue up and down again, then slid two working fingers deep inside her, feeling the slippery walls grip them in welcome.

The plates rattled softly as she began to jounce, her buttocks clenching and unclenching while she sobbed. Just as she felt the approach of the climax the fingers and mouth were snatched away, and she gave a sharp cry of torment. But then he was upright, his arms clamped about her thighs, holding them to his hips, and his penis, straight as a ramrod, thrust at the base of her belly. With startling skill he nuzzled it at the wet entrance of her spasming vulva, his buttocks clenched deeply, and he slid home into the tightly gripping funnel of her vagina. She gasped with shock, and the pure physical joy of his driving deeply home into her.

'Christ! I'm coming - coo - coming!' Her feet kicked out madly and she convulsed, pressing her face into his shoulder, clutching him while the climax ripped through her.

In the days that followed she was shattered by the sexual appetite he had aroused in her. She felt like she had when they were kids, except with this wonderful, frightening advancement.

'I don't love you,' she said wonderingly, when they met in the flat again after an interval of several days.

'Thank God,' he grinned.

'Since the other day I've done nothing but play with myself,' she said, in the same hesitant tone. 'What have you done to me, you bastard?'

'Never mind. Mike will be back in a few days. You'll just have to make sure he fucks you more often.'

'You won't ever tell him?' she pleaded, her eyes wide. 'He wouldn't understand.'

'Do you?' Again, that grin. She shook her head, still looking vaguely scared.

But it didn't stop them going to bed. This time they undressed slowly, watching each other all the while. She came to him nervously, reaching out tentatively. Their embrace was gentle, as though uncertain of the other's reaction, but then they were straining together, mouths devouring, tongues probing, bellies and thighs bumping, and he was on top of her as they stretched out.

'You want it like this?' he asked, sliding down her body, parting her, to kiss at her lower belly.

'For a while,' she moaned, lifting her knees high, spreading herself wide. When she wanted him inside her and clawed at his shoulders desperately, she found his prick, though soaking wet, was soft, the foreskin covering the helm in a wrinkled pucker. Her fingers slid in the coating fluid as she struggled to rouse him. He shrugged her off, knelt, and jerked fiercely at himself, towering over her lifting, beseeching belly, and he was hard in seconds. He fell on her, thrust deeply home, and they rotted, banging their bodies together, and came within seconds of each other.

'It's never been like this. Never,' she wept afterwards, clinging to him, feeling him sliding out of her, and holding him tightly.

'I bet you say that to all the boys,' he chuckled.

She was thinking of that now, as she stood in her sexily outrageous dress, thinking with that instinctive inner sense of shock about being fucked by these two men, as she had been in the past few days, ashamed of her comparison yet helpless to stop it. Her cousin, God damn him, won hands down. How could that be, when she didn't love him and was crazy about Michael?

She loved the tall, dark blond man, looking so troubled. She felt a warm affection, recalling the look of astonishment, then horror, when he'd first seen her dress. 'You can't wear that!' he'd gaped.

'I have to, darling,' she said, going to him, putting both hands on his arm, while he stared pop-eyed at the spectacle of her rounded breasts and little areolae peeping saucily through the misty cloth at him. 'It's expected of me now. I told you, everything's going to have to change for me with *A Woman's Touch*. I've got to become a screen sex symbol. They insist on it. '

'From the back it looks as though you've got no knickers on,' John piped up. 'Your arse looks entirely bare.'

She glowered at his insufferable grin, and wound her hands firmly through Michael's arm. 'Thank you very much,' she said tightly.

Chapter Three

Felicity shivered at the sensation of Stella's long fingernails scratching lightly at her midriff, then her belly. She lay back amongst the soft cushions of the couch, her right leg slightly raised at the knee, the other straight, her foot pressing against the upholstered arm of the sofa. 'Please, Stella... don't. I'm scared... I've never—'

'Shhh, my angel. You'll love it, I promise. Just lie still.

Leave it all to me.' Those full breasts, the large areolae and erect nipples darkened by the cosmetic, standing out against the creamy paleness, hung over her until she could feel their soft warmth brushing against her own, lesser, rising rounds. The fingers slid beneath the elastic at Felicity's hips, slowly pulled down the black satin briefs, determinedly easing them past the restriction of hips and buttocks against the cushions. Felicity was aware as never before of her nudity when those hands slipped the tiny garment down and off her feet. Even though she closed her eyes, she could see vividly the dramatically highlighted slopes and angles of her frame, the carefully trimmed triangle of her pubis, shadowed against the pallid hollow of belly and thighs, bathed in the warmth of the light spilling over them.

Stella's moist lips covered hers again and held her mouth softly, possessively, until Felicity was ready to fight for her breath. She gulped as the mouth moved, fastened instead on her right nipple, suckling it into the warm wetness, the rolling tongue, and her shoulders lifted, arched upwards as she lost the control she had been fighting to cling onto through these last endless minutes. 'Jesus, Stella,' she cried urgently, squirming under the pinning weight. 'Christ, I can't... don't...' Her cry rose sharply as a hand touched the inside of her knee, swept up over the smoothness of her thigh to its confluence with her belly and the moist centre of her desire. The fingers touched the folds of damp tissue and her hips jerked, lifted, shocked and roused beyond measure.

'And cut!' Ally's voice rang out crisply, just as Felicity's thighs and scrabbling hand clamped over Stella's wrist. The fingers fluttered, caressed her again, and again Felicity yelped. She suddenly found herself sobbing, unable to stop herself, and her naked partner leaned over her tenderly, holding her.

Felicity tried to wriggle free. She was agonisingly aware again of the lights and the crew, and that all seeing lens. 'You - you touched me up!' she gasped, in genuine horror. 'You assaulted me!'

She managed to sit up at last and drew her legs up to her chest, her shoulders bent forward as she crossed her arms over her breasts. She was trapped by Stella, still sitting by her side on the edge of the couch. She squinted up against the bright lamps, the tears channelling through the thick make-up. 'Can I have my robe, please?'

She felt as though she was burning up, striving to cling to the shattered threads of her dignity. Viv came forward swiftly and handed her the towelling robe. 'Do you mind?' she fumed at Stella, who smiled easily and, at last, moved so that Felicity could swing her feet down to the floor and pull the robe on. Stella was standing over her, superbly unselfconscious about her nudity. The sandy fleece of her pubis was inches from Felicity's hot face, and she averted her eyes hastily. Stella's dresser appeared and held a robe out while the blonde shrugged into it with a casual ease of movement.

'That was magnificent, ladies!' Ally crowed, reaching out to pat them simultaneously on their shoulders. 'We'll break there. Have an early lunch. You've earned it.'

Felicity made a great effort to stop her tears. She wiped at her face with the back of her hand. 'You can't print that,' she said, hating the shocked, adolescent squeak she could not keep from her voice.

'We might have to edit a little,' the director said breezily. 'But it was superb. Exactly what I wanted. Bless you, my children.'

'She - she practically raped me! She actually...' her choked words faded away. Felicity felt the tears spring to life again, felt both ridiculous and degraded by the whole business. 'I didn't realise we were making a porno movie!'

'*Baby*...!' Ally's cry was a drawn out protest. 'It was beautiful. It was sheer magic. You wait till you see it. It was art, darling. Poetry. There won't be a dry eye in the house.'

'Or a dry crotch!' one of the crew called, to guffaws from the outer darkness. Ally shuddered dramatically and rolled his eyes heavenwards in that characteristic gesture which denounced them all as Philistines.

Felicity walked off to her dressing room, trying hard not to flounce. Her mind was a whirl of conflict. What a jerk they would all think her, losing it like that. Like some bloody little Julie Andrews getting her wimple in a twist. But really! Stella had no right to feel her up like that. Right there, on set, in full view of... God, it could be sixteen million viewers. Not that they would ever let it go out like that. Of course not. It wasn't a hard core blue, after all. But she still did it. It was there, in the can for plenty of people to lech over, even if it did end up on the cutting room floor. And that bunch of pervs that called themselves a crew. They'd never stop talking about it now. She'd heard them before, going on and on.

She sat in front of the long mirror and smeared cream thickly over her face. Viv came in and pulled a sympathetically rueful face. 'Did I make a fool of myself?' Felicity asked abruptly, and Viv shook her head at once.

'Not at all. It was all highly charged stuff out there. I don't know how you do it, honest to God. Not even for a fortune.'

'I'm not making all that much,' Felicity quipped gamely.

The door opened with no preceding knock, and Stella stood there, looking contrite. 'Sorry, sweetheart. I couldn't tell you before.'

'What? That you were going to grope me for real for the benefit of the ratings? You realise you blew the whole thing? My lines, the rehearsal- the whole thing just went out of my head! The lot! We'll have to do it all again.'

'No, sugar, we won't. Ally says it was great. It was just what he wanted. He says we can dub out the odd word, if need be.'

A deep suspicion entered Felicity's mind. She wiped her face with a tissue, turned, and stared at the blonde woman with dawning accusation. 'Did you... you knew, didn't you? And so did Ally. You planned it! Touching me up like that! Didn't you?'

The question came out as a harsh screech. Stella gazed coolly back at her. 'Viv, would you get me a sandwich, please? One of those chicken salad things. There's a good girt'

Viv knew she was being dismissed, and hurried out. Felicity felt that childish surge of petulant anger again. 'I didn't know Viv was your dresser.'

'Oh, for Christ's sake, Felicity. Come on, let's cut the crap. We can't go on like this.

Pussyfooting around, pretending to have the hots in front of the cameras. You're gorgeous, baby, and you know it. Let's give it a real try, eh? You can be Kathy. You *are* Kathy. And I'm Stella.' She laughed softly. 'It's neat how they picked my real name, eh, Kath? Give it a go, kiddo. I swear you'll love every minute.'

As she spoke she came close, caught Felicity by the lapels of her gown and pulled her to her feet. The hands moved, pushed the cloth aside, baring Felicity's shoulders and breasts. She pulled the cord at Felicity's waist and the robe fell open to reveal the nakedness beneath. Felicity was suddenly incapable of movement. The hands moved again, pushed the robe free altogether, and it fell to curl about Felicity's feet.

Stella was smiling, tenderly, triumphantly, as she put her arms around the slender figure and drew her closer. Felicity felt the rough material of Stella's gown against her flesh. Tardily, she began to struggle, half-heartedly, not even turning her head to avoid the kiss Stella planted on her mouth. Their tongues wound together. Stella held her until Felicity thought she would faint. Her entire body shook and her insides felt hollow. She was panting and quivering when Stella finally released her, and she gulped in great sobbing draughts of air. She stared at the smiling figure, her dark eyes brilliant with tears, helpless in their naked appeal.

'See?' Stella purred triumphantly. 'You'll love it, sweety. You know you will!' She turned, with that deep chuckle, and walked out, leaving the naked and trembling girl still standing there, unable to move.

'I tell you, John, she's a raging dyke! She's done nothing but try to get me into bed since we started. Though God knows why! She's ravishing me all over the set, with the whole fucking crew cheering her on!'

John stretched out on the luxurious sofa, watching her move agitatedly about the living room, drink in hand. She looked even more appetising in the simple outfit of dark brown tank-top and slacks of the same colour. They fitted skintight over her slim flanks and John could discern no trace of a panty line. But then, he knew from recent experience that she generally wore G-string briefs, the rear thong nestled invisibly in the crack of her cute little behind.

'I don't know what Michael will do when he finds out,' she went on, coming over to sit beside him, half turned towards him with one leg tucked underneath her. 'Probably tell me to get lost on the spot. You'll never guess what Stella and Ally's latest idea is.' Her eyes were huge as they regarded him over the rim of her glass. She paused a little for effect. 'They only want me to come - to have a real orgasm for them, on camera!'

A grin spread over his face. 'How?'

'What do you mean, how?'

'I mean how,' he insisted, laughing aloud. 'How are they proposing to blow your top? Is it to be self-induced, or what?'

'No. Stella will actually do it. Get me all worked up, then they'll move in and film the last bit - the critical bit.' In spite of her shock, she could not help a small snigger herself. 'Just Ally and the cameraman, they say. As if that makes any difference.' The snigger was replaced by a frown. 'She's absolutely determined to have me. If she can't get me on her own, she'll do it in front of the camera. I'd no idea she was such ales.'

'Oh, come on. You must have had an inkling.'

'No. Honestly, I swear.' She leaned forward and punched his arm. 'And stop laughing!' she pouted. 'It isn't funny! Just because you're a swinger—'

He caught hold of her wrist and held her. 'Hey. Watch it. Don't jump to conclusions, coz. Shouldn't you be telling all this to your beloved? He'll have to know sooner or later. He's the one you should be baring your heart to.'

'I can't face him these days. I haven't seen him at all since Wednesday. And he's away again all next week. Thank goodness. That shows you how bad I feel at the moment.' She stopped twisting to escape his grip and let herself droop towards him, so that their brows met. 'Anyway, be nice to me, John. You're the only one I can talk to. I need comforting, old chum. Don't be nasty to me, eh?' She purred, moving her face against his, her lips nuzzling in tiny kisses about his mouth and chin.

'Why don't you try it?' he grinned, squinting at her. 'You know what they say - don't knock a thing until you've tried it.'

She lifted her head, momentarily diverted. 'What? With Stella? Get lost. I'm not lest'

'How do you know? You might love it. Have you ever tried it?'

She blushed a little, remembering certain childhood experiences with school mates she'd never divulged to him. She shook her head vigorously. 'Tell you what,' he continued, in that same teasing tone, 'just imagine I'm Stella, right? Or any other girl who takes your fancy.'

She snorted in laughing protest, but he pushed her down on the sofa and began plucking at her slacks. He found the zip and opened her flies, revealing the little triangle of black silk which just covered her mound. He moved, leaning over her, beginning to nibble gently at her, and let his hand slide down inside the briefs, stretching them as his fingers stroked the wiry curls adorning her lower belly, then found the damp flesh beneath.

She felt the spark of excitement kindling at once and shivered, stretching her feet out, slipping off the light sandals, her toes digging against the pile of the carpet. She could feel the tight silk cutting her as his hand worked more vigorously, and her labia swelled and parted a little. Crazily, her mind reran the scene on set once more, then switched as her imagination got to work. She was shocked at herself to find that the figure she visualised was an older woman, the crisply attractive Yvonne Lightman, her agent.

'Don't,' she moaned, closing her eyes, sinking back into the cushions, her feet stirring in helpless little kicking movements. His hand was dragging the pants down off her pubis, which was on view now. His curling fingers were working, inside her, and she was growing ever more wet and roused at this powerful stimulation. She could feel her trousers scratching at her hips, and she lifted her buttocks slightly when he tugged at them, aiding him as he slipped them clear of her flanks. He left them dragging like bonds midway down her thighs, and she whimpered, ashamed at her melting hunger, the wetness, and the squelching of his fingers inside her. She felt helpless and humiliated by this undignified sprawl, lying back, her pants down at her knees, her knickers at half-mast.

'Undress me properly,' she gasped, and impotently hated his mockingly victorious laugh.

'I'm going to gobble you all up, little chicken,' he murmured.

She felt him pushing her thighs open until her legs were straining against the slacks, which did indeed cling like restraints, so that she imagined herself to be in bondage to the mystical figure consuming her. The fingers moved with wicked knowledge,

13

seeking the most intimate responses of her secret flesh. Then he slid to the floor and his head dipped. His tongue glided over the pale flesh of her thighs, and then lapped at the salty fissure into which his fingers delved.

'No!' she wept, lost on the frenzied rush of sensation that swept her along to its shattering crescendo.

Chapter Four

The silence throbbed with a charge of erotic excitement. A shaft of brilliant white light arced down onto the marble centre of the room, following exactly the contours of the four-pointed black star. Beyond the pure whiteness of the light was an impenetrable blackness, yet there was the sense of unseen presences; watching... waiting. Even the slim figure at the centre of the spectacle, whose eyes were covered by a black velvet mask, sensed it. Until her frightened mind was occupied with the ritual that was unfolding about her.

She was a coloured girl. The close-cropped head was bare, the face half hidden by the mask. Her long neck was also bare of any adornment, and protruded from a long black cloak that reached the floor and hid the rest of her completely. At either side of her two similarly clad figures held her lightly by the arms, leading her to the central point of the star. At the tips of each of the four extremities of the star stood other cloaked figures. The one corresponding to the compass designation of north stood on a dais about two feet high. Unlike the others, her enveloping cloak was a rich scarlet.

All the participants were female, their heads, with hairstyles of various lengths and colours, bare. The blindfolded initiate was positioned facing the figure on the dais. At a signal from the scarlet clad form, the two women at each side of the coloured girl removed her cloak, with a single dramatic pull. The material fell to her feet.

Her slim body was naked, the skin a burnished coppery brown, the small breasts generously nippled. The scrub of pubis looked insignificant against the smooth planes of the belly and thighs. She stood with her feet slightly apart, gazing blindly ahead. Though she made no conscious movement, her body betrayed her nervousness by its tiny tremors.

When the figure on the dais spoke her voice was amazingly deep, resonant, almost masculine, yet exuding a sense of powerful sexuality. 'Do you now avow your wish to become a daughter of our sacred band? Answer.'

'I do.' The reply was scarcely audible, a husky whisper. 'Do you swear on your life that you will obey our tenets, and do you swear to keep the secrets of the society?'

'I do.'

Further ritualistic questions and answers followed, the latter being given in the same hushed monosyllables. Then the scarlet leader declared, 'Daughters, prepare her for the ordeal.'

With a balletic fluidity of movement and timing, the three figures at the outer edges of the star, and the two escorts of the initiate, slipped off their cloaks to reveal their own nakedness. They came forward and lifted the dark girl off her feet, then positioned her face down on the cold marble, her pinioned arms and legs following exactly the lines of the black shape beneath her. Four of them remained kneeling, holding her by her outstretched wrists and ankles. The fifth advanced to the foot of the dais and picked up a short handled whip, with three slender lashes in soft black leather.

Her arm drew back, then the wrist flicked and the tails of the whip fell across the flexing buttocks. There was a smothered cry, and the captive girl squirmed and then lay still.

'Do you swear obedience?' the voice from the dais intoned.

The prisoner's voice cracked on a sob. 'I dub - do.' The whip cracked again, and a dark thin line appeared on the brown skin of the behind, the curves of which were lighter than the rest of the twisting body, almost a pale mushroom at the crown of the dimpling cheeks where the marks of the whip were most evident.

'Do you swear undying loyalty?'

Again, the sobbing affirmative. The whip hissed again across the burning flanks. The girl was sobbing audibly now.

'Do you swear secrecy, above all else?'

The response was loud and shrill through the sound of her weeping.

'We accept you, Deborah, into our sacred order. We take you unto us. Come, daughters, let us make her one of us.'

Someone was already tending the abused buttocks, bathing with a cool cloth the angry red tracery of the whipping. The velvet mask, soaked with tears, was now removed, revealing the young face which, smeared as it was, was clearly seen to be beautiful. The five naked figures turned her gently over and spread her again along the shape of the star. Thus her beauty was exposed in every splendid detail, but was soon almost hidden from view as the five girls knelt and bent over her, caressing and kissing until the remnants of the sobbing were transformed into moans of soaring passion.

This loving went on for a considerable time, the only sounds being those of the slurping assailants, and the increasing cries of the figure pinned beneath them. Cries not of pain but of mounting hunger for fulfilment. Only when these had almost reached their crescendo did the majestic figure move from the dais. Her five acolytes parted at once, exposing again the lovely girl who lay, spread wide, weeping in her need. The cloaked figure knelt, then lowered herself slowly over the girl. As she did so she opened her cloak until it lay like a rich blanket covering both their bodies, the folds undulating as they commenced the rhythmical movements which seemed to imitate the thrusts of sexual intercourse.

The leader's long black hair, rich in its glossiness, spread like the scarlet cloak, masking the face of the supine girl, hiding the sealing kiss which bound them together as tightly as the bodies writhing beneath the red folds, until at last there came a frenzied increase of plunging movement and a smothered cry, trapped in a captive throat, to mark the climax.

The cloak ceased its wild tossing. Everything was still.

The only sound was the uncontrolled sobbing of the girl still hidden from sight, and a faint sighing exhalation of breath which came from the outer darkness.

Later, in an elegantly lit drawing room on the floor below, a select group were eating and drinking and chatting easily, lounging on the luxurious furniture and being tended by the same beautiful girls they had watched perform the ritual of initiation in the mystical upper room. Most of the men were elderly or middle aged, though not all.

They were all wearing monogrammed robes and displaying, with equanimity, their nakedness beneath. The girls were naked, too, but without benefit of robes or any other covering. All that is, except the tall figure who had led the ceremony above. She was at least six feet tall, her square shoulders indicating her athletic build which in no way detracted from her startling beauty. The face was flawless, the dark eyes magnificent, the deeply glossed lips full and temptingly feminine. The magnificent features were framed by brilliantly black hair hanging down past her shoulders. The body was clothed in a dress so tight it appeared like a second skin. It was cut low, so that the upper half of her breasts rose above its deep red which glittered with a myriad of sparkling diamante. She could move only because the garment was slit up the left side to the hip, so that her leg showed in all its glory. The outfit was completed by four inch heels which raised her even further so that she soared over the rest of the company, both male and female.

'Magda, that was divine. The most beautiful spectacle we've witnessed in a long time.' The gravelly voice belonged to the host for the event, Lord Burnopside. He came forward and Magda raised her hands to meet his, her long fingernails perfectly shaped and coated in the darkest magenta shading. He planted a respectful kiss on her lips, formed to receive his homage.

'Yes, she's a gorgeous creature, isn't she? She's a very worthy addition to our ranks.' Their eyes looked across to where the coloured girl who had figured so prominently in the ceremony was the smiling centre of attention in a large group near the glowing logs of the living flame fire.

'There's none of them can hold a candle to you, my dear.'

Her chuckle was deep, infectious. 'What an interesting choice of metaphor,' she said appreciatively.

'You know what I mean, damn it,' he went on. 'Ever since we've known each other you've known what I've wanted. You know you drive us all crazy, you witch. I'd give you anything you want to have you... properly.'

The dark eyes regarded him with cool amusement. 'Why, Lord B, you know I'm a virgin. How could I be the Grand Mistress of the Whores of Babylon otherwise? It's a responsibility I take very seriously, as you know. Besides, the girls are so much more beautiful than I. And younger.'

'Nonsense, Magda,' he replied. He was not being gallant. The elite society, whose patron he had so willingly become, fascinated him. The notion of these lovely girls, carefully culled from all walks of life, often having the binding rules of the secret order as their only common element, dedicated to a sexual life which demanded obedience to every dictate of their Grand Mistress, had appealed irresistibly to his libidinous nature. They were not prostitutes. They were fully aware of what membership of the Whores of Babylon entailed, and entered into membership as ardent volunteers. And there was not one of them as intriguing or thoroughly desirable as their magnetic leader - the one who had taken the shocking name of Magdalene; so shocking that none outside the select circle knew of it. And even those of the fellowship always referred to her as Magda.

He had known her for several years. Like all the other men of this exclusive society, he had never known her to have sexual intercourse. He had never even seen her naked, and neither, as far as he knew, had any other of his male acquaintances. All her passionate pleasure was reserved for her own sex, and even that, as portrayed in the powerfully erotic initiation ceremony, literally cloaked from the male eyes which gazed absorbedly at the spectacle from the hidden outer darkness.

But her activity was not confined to homoeroticism.

Now, she saw his excitement, the gleam that betokened his aroused appetite, a gleam reflected in the gazes of all about them.

'Have you anything else for our diversion?' his lordship asked, with a gesture towards his colleagues.

She nodded, as he knew she would. 'Yes indeed, my lord. I was hoping perhaps you or some of the other Masters might help us out. You remember we decided Barbara should be given to Sir Mortimer Durrance for the summer? She went with him on his cruise to the Med. I don't know if you've heard anything, but things didn't work out. She was a very silly girl. She caused an awful lot of trouble. For someone who has been a Daughter for almost a year now, it's very disappointing. And a bad example for the others. I've had her brought back here. I think her punishment should be rather special. Public. Tonight would be ideal. In front of the Masters - and the Daughters, too.' She nodded at the girls scattered about the comfortable room.

'Very good, my dear,' Lord Burnopside answered smoothly. 'Whatever you suggest.'

'I'll have her brought in now, if you're ready, my lord.' The weeping girl in question made no effort to resist as two others swiftly undressed her, peeling off the dress, the lacy black underwear, the dark stockings and heeled shoes, until she was as naked as they were.

She was led forward to one end of the long dining table, the highly polished surface of which shone like a mirror. At Magda's nod Barbara .was thrust face down over the table, shivering at the cold contact against her breasts and belly. She turned her head sideways to rest one cheek on the gleaming surface, her brown hair masking her despairing expression. Her arms were spread out wide. Magda had produced two sets of silver handcuffs, linked by a looping metal chain. Bracelets were fastened over the girl's wrists, then secured beneath the tabletop so that her pinioned wrists remained spread, her pale upper body held flat to the table's surface.

Her taut buttocks flexed, the little rounds hollowing deeply. Magda moved forward and ran a hand in a gentle caress over their outline. Then she quickly smeared them with ointment from a small jar, so that they shone in the light that fell upon them. 'There! That will save you from being cut, I hope.' Her lovely face bent low, her lips brushed against the pale neck of the captive figure. 'Take your punishment like a true Daughter,' Magda murmured, with another light kiss. 'And then you will be forgiven.'

There was a sharp intake of breath and the muscles tensed in the girl's long legs, which were spread wide apart to take the chastisement she knew was about to come.

Magda produced a short-handled whip of black leather.

It had many thin thongs. 'Please, Grand Whore Master,' she declared, passing the instrument to Lord Burnopside.

He slipped the folds of the robe back from his shoulders in order that he might perform more freely. The iron-grey covering of hair at his chest and the thick hanging shape of his prick showed through the dark material. He stepped forward and measured his distance.

The whip hissed as it curled through the air to strike with a satisfyingly sharp crack on the quivering flesh. The blow was a shade high, the thin red line appearing at the very top of the buttock divide. The slender back jerked, the play of the shoulders under the pale skin delightful. The bare feet lifted, did a little jig of agony before they settled again, and the figure waited, still, except for the involuntary trembling.

They could hear her weeping, but she had not screamed. He struck again, aiming carefully, and there was a ripple of appreciative murmuring as the lashes fell squarely across the centre of the bottom, whose cleft was neatly bisected by the horizontal stripe of red. Soon others were crisscrossed over the writhing rounds, and the girl's cries were more desperate, though he'd still failed to elicit the pure scream he'd hoped for. Like most of the other males present he could feel the rising and stiffening of his penis. He was breathing quite heavily. 'Good girl!' he growled, with reluctant admiration. He passed the whip to another male, a much shorter, plumper figure, who took it eagerly.

He lashed with enthusiasm but with less skill, and the girl's head moved wildly, lifting from the table, and her legs danced in wilder frenzy, for the blows fell indiscriminately across the backs of her thighs, leaving their crimson tracery of weals. Barbara was sobbing fiercely; gut wrenching sobs that shook her whole frame. But still she had not screamed at the fall of the blows.

'I'll make the bitch sing!' The speaker was a florid-faced individual, with a freckled bald head and professorial, silvery wings of hair at his temples. He seized the handle of the whip, which was now unpleasantly slippery with sweat, and flicked his wrist savagely. There was a muted gasp of collective sympathy from the watching girls, for the snaking black lashes fell above the scarlet pattern of the abused bottom, and landed on the lower back and the base of the spine. The unfortunate Barbara gave a smothered whimper and her hips writhed madly, her belly and her upper thighs grinding cruelly against the hard surface of the wood. He struck again in the same spot, and this time his victim could hold back no longer. Her shrill cry of torment rang out.

Magda stepped in close to the tall man wielding the whip, so that he had no room to draw his arm back for a third time. 'And so you have,' she said evenly. She was even taller than he was, and her eyes met his and held his stare. 'You made her sing. Congratulations.' There was no doubt of the contempt and reproof in her rich voice. 'I think she's been more than adequately punished.' She turned away from him and nodded at her waiting attendants. 'Untie her.'

Full of tenderness now, the naked figures unfastened her. Barbara wept convulsively, shaking, largely with relief, but her public ordeal was not quite over. She slumped in the girls' arms as they turned her to face their mistress. 'You have been punished,' Magda said. 'What have you to say?'

The weeping figure sank to her knees, then prostrated herself until her forehead touched the carpet. She moved her tearstained face forward until her brow rested against Magda's shapely ankle. Her lips planted a kiss on the soft material of Magda's shoe, at the pointed toe. 'Thank you, Mistress,' she managed, fighting against her weeping. 'I'm sorry. I'll try not to fail you again.'

Another nod to her acolytes, and the forlorn figure was picked up and led out of the room.

There remained one more task for Magda to perform, this time of a more private nature. Safely in a small study she slid the bolt on the door, and led Lord Burnopside to a leather armchair. She pushed the craggy figure down into it, revelling in her power to command and, with a sinuous ease of movement, which in the skin hugging dress required great dexterity, knelt between his slack knees. His robe was already open and his flaccid penis was weeping at its tip. She took it gently in her fingers and massaged it until it grew and stirred, lifting to her caresses, and then she bent and licked the drop of fluid away.

She felt his legs quiver, his feet scraping softly on the thick carpet. He sighed. Her lips opened, formed a sensual O, and slid over the red helm. She drew it deep into her moist heat, then her lips slid down the shaft until she had taken him almost entirely within her. Soon he was rearing stiffly and groaning as his hips swivelled and his belly lifted in supplication, begging her to bring him the ease his drumming blood was demanding.

She played him with captivating skill, prolonging his' pounding excitement and bursting need until he was whimpering for mercy. At the last second she pulled her mouth away and let him jet his come over her uplifted face, and he wept, shuddering in release. She stood and turned away to the desk where the necessities for cleaning herself lay to hand.

Some minutes later, when he'd recovered sufficiently, she said conversationally, 'What about that little popsie of an actress? Any progress there yet? What's her name? Felicity something... I must say she sounds and looks heavenly.'

He sighed. 'She is. But I'm afraid we'll have to tread carefully there. She's going to be enormously famous when *A Woman's Touch* hits the screen. Or should I say, explodes on the screen? Stella tells me she's working hard at getting into her pants - I mean, for real.' He chuckled. 'She's already done it on camera. I've seen the rushes. As soon as I can get hold of a copy we'll have a look at them together, eh? They're utterly delightful, I promise you.

Chapter Five

'Come on, darling, have another drink, for God's sake! You must show me you've forgiven me properly for my little plot in front of the cameras the other day.' Stella tipped the bottle and the wine gurgled into Felicity's glass until she squealed as it almost slopped over the brim. Stella grinned tipsily. 'You've got to admit though, sugar, that it's the hottest scene this side of Lady Chat's daisy decked pussy!' The golden hair was a dishevelled mass. The top buttons of the loose white shirt were undone, showing the deep cleavage of those splendid breasts and the tiny satin bow at the V of the plunging bra which encased them. She had flung the slacks carelessly aside, and her long tanned legs were fully displayed as she lolled back in a wide chair.

Felicity took another swig of the fruity wine. Her head swam. She was pissed, she acknowledged, but it was a pleasant feeling. She was rather proud of herself at the amount she had already drunk. Not without showing its effect, she conceded, but at least she hadn't thrown up or passed out... yet.

'I ought to go,' she muttered, feeling an irritation once more at the way she had allowed herself to be persuaded to come back to Stella's discreet town pad for 'one last tipple'. 'It's late.'

'Relax,' Stella crooned. 'Your boyfriend's away again, isn't he? You can crash here if you like.' Her face assumed an expression of mischievous complicity. She giggled. 'I won't tell if you don't.'

'I'm not gay!' Felicity squeaked in indignant protest. 'How many times do I have to keep saying it?'

Stella unfolded from the depths of the armchair and swayed over to where Felicity sat. The golden figure, looking enchanting in the loose white shirt, dropped to her knees in front of her. 'Listen, kid,' she rasped, her voice deepening. 'Just who in hell are we kidding here? You can say it as many times as you like, sweetheart, but you know and I know different! I've been in bed with you, sugar. I know!'

'You don't!' Felicity felt the colour flaming her cheeks, and her voice shook with the threatening tears. 'We might have to - to kiss and cuddle and all that, but... but—' Stella's fingers dug into her legs, just above her knees. 'Get off me! I'm going—'

'You're not going anywhere, sugar.' Stella's tone was calm, gently teasing.

Felicity could feel the tears gathering in her eyelashes. 'Let me go, please. I want to leave.' Her voice came in a wavering whisper.

'You're a stubborn little bitch, aren't you? You're going to have to be taught a lesson!'

'What? How dare you - get off! No! Don't!' Felicity squealed in surprise, then alarm. Stella was laughing, as though the whole thing was still just some kind of prank, but she was pulling at Felicity's arms, and suddenly they were grappling in earnest and Felicity was out of the chair and they were sprawling on the floor. And all at once her strength seemed to have deserted her. She was lying full length with Stella's pinning weight across her midriff. Her head was spinning as she twisted feebly in the other's entrapping grip. She began to sob, feeling foolish and humiliated. 'Will you get off me?' she panted, her teeth clenched.

'You know what silly little kids need?' Stella answered, also panting with the effort. She rolled Felicity over onto her stomach. Felicity's feet waved in the air as she kicked out. She felt her heeled shoes fly off. She wished fervently she'd worn her jeans instead of an insubstantial miniskirt, which Stella was now lifting off her behind to expose the tiny dark brown thong which was all she had on underneath. It left her buttocks bare, for its narrow band had disappeared in the cleft.

She yelped, with shock as well as sharp pain, at the resounding slap Stella delivered to her bottom. A vivid red handprint stood out on the pale, quivering flesh. Another slap, and Felicity screamed shrilly. 'How duh-dare - oh! Ow! Please - nuh-no!'

Stella spanked her hard; swift, open palmed blows which rained down on both clenching cheeks and spread a glowing fire over their hot surface. The screams subsided to a harsh sobbing. Felicity felt the intense bum, and lay trapped under the pressing weight, her feet tapping rapidly on the carpet. She felt ridiculous, and degraded. Yet at the same time, most shameful of all, she felt the corresponding wicked throb of excitement deep within her sex at the chastisement. She was weeping freely when the spanking ceased. She didn't move, except to massage her stinging behind.

'You silly kid,' Stella breathed. 'Can't you see I'm absolutely crazy about you? Why do you have to torment me like this?' As she spoke her nails scraped Felicity's sensitive skin as she plucked at the elastic of the tiny briefs, and peeled them down over her slender hips.

'Don't,' Felicity whispered, still sobbing, but making no attempt to stop Stella as she slid the damp little triangle of silk down her legs and off her bare feet.

'God, I love you,' Stella moaned, stretching out and pressing her body against that of the delicious girl beneath, so that they made contact from head to toe. Her parted lips sealed Felicity's. Her tongue thrust into Felicity's warm wetness, and they kissed a long consuming kiss of passion. Stella's hand moved, drawn as though by a magnet, to Felicity's flat belly, the small patch of pubis, and the soft wet divide beneath, which flowered open in helpless and glad surrender to this loving invasion.

Her legs bent in a rhythm of response to that caressing stroke, the fingers which unerringly knew how to love, how to draw the melting fire of absolute fulfilment from the palpitating flesh they laid claim to. Felicity still sobbed, still whispered, 'No,' when Stella released her mouth, but the word was meaningless. Her pale thighs were moving, opening, yielding, lost in the wonder of the beating need being roused in this wonderful embrace.

She felt her mind spinning off, felt the strength of her bodily hunger taking over completely. 'I love you,' she gasped. Their tears mingled. Felicity shuddered at the feeling of utter completion as Stella's fingers slid into the tightness of her sheath, took her over, brought her to that awesome splendour, the orgasm building, slowly, inexorably, to flow throughout her until she stiffened, her body arched, and she shivered from top to toe.

She had no idea of how long they lay there, clinging together, a tangle of limbs and locked mouths and clutching hands, before she felt Stella guide her fingers down to that waiting moistness. Felicity felt the wet patch of silk outlining the vulva, and now it was her turn to kneel, to savour that wonderful thrill of love and power, as she eased down the white knickers, undid the remaining buttons of the white shirt, slipped it from the acquiescing shoulders, and unhooked the dainty bra, so that the magnificence of Stella's nude body was revealed. Hastily, Felicity shrugged off her own few remaining clothes, to know the joy of sharing this feeling, of soldering their naked flesh together, before she experienced for the first time the ecstasy of bringing the shattering fulfilment of loving to a partner, which was every bit as wonderful as receiving it oneself.

Some time later, they had no idea when, they picked themselves up, left the scattered bits of clothing lying there, and arm in arm, unwilling to break contact even for a second, made their way to the bed which enclosed them in its magic. Stunned at the ferocity of her reaction to Stella's loving, Felicity pushed aside for the moment the cloudiness of the thoughts waiting to claim her for the undeniable bliss she had found in the exquisite body which mirrored so closely her own.

Felicity stared down at her own hand, which looked tiny and fragile in the firm grip of the palm that encased it. And yet the soft smoothness and the immaculately styled nails with their exotically dark polish, were the essence of femininity. As was everything about this alluring figure whose steady dark gaze disturbed and thrilled her so much. She towered over Felicity; the square, creamy shoulders, uncovered in the simple figure-hugging black gown she wore, seemed almost twice the width of Felicity's slender frame. Even the hair, of identical raven blackness and in a simple style so similar to her own, was so much more abundant.

Felicity felt a little shiver of excitement at the sight of her tight, silk covered crotch. Magda was still holding onto her, and Felicity felt helpless, unable to move or speak. Her giddy mind span back to the passionate loving she had shared at Stella's studio flat by the river. Had the golden girl touched some hidden depth in her which, having

21

lain dormant all these years, had suddenly now burst to such electrifying life? Had she all along had these overwhelming lesbian tendencies buried within her?

She was blushing like a schoolgirl and felt absolutely ridiculous as her frantic brain whirred in the effort of searching for speech. 'You are completely gorgeous,' that rich, deep voice murmured. It was as if she had touched her, caressed her in some secret spot.

'Thank you,' Felicity stammered inadequately, her face burning.

Still holding her by one hand, the other long arm slipped around her waist, Magda led her over the square of richly patterned carpet to where Lord Burnopside was talking to another group. 'She is absolutely heavenly,' Magda purred. 'So much more stunning than her pictures. Isn't she?' The group around his lordship muttered their agreement, laughing politely, to Felicity's further mortification.

'Don't,' she flustered, even more adolescent in her confusion. 'Please - you're embarrassing me.'

'Come on, sugar,' Magda purred, 'you must be used to guys drooling all over you. And gals, too,' she added, to another chorus of polite laughter. 'If not, you'd better get used to it pretty quick, baby. Especially the girls, after *A Woman's Touch* hits the screen.'

There was yet another burst of mirth.

'I hear they're thinking of renaming it, *A Woman's Crutch*,' quipped a chubby, red-faced individual.

Felicity felt the arm tighten about her waist, drawing her even close. 'Don't be so beastly, Sir Hugh,' Magda chastised. 'I'm sure it'll be lovely, and not at all the sort of thing dirty old men with coats over their knees toss themselves off to.'

'No need for the coat,' Sir Hugh answered, undeterred by the challenge. 'It'll be seen in the privacy of their own sordid hovels. They can stand stark bollock naked waggling their dicks at the screen.'

Felicity was surprised at the respect paid by this collection of wealthy men to the tall figure who was holding her protectively to her side. Especially as the other girls, in spite of their wonderful looks, were extremely deferential, and voiced no opinions of their own, responding only when called upon to do so. So much so that Felicity had soon begun to wonder whether they were employees of his lordship, in spite of their elegant grooming and stylish clothes.

In fact, this whole weekend was turning out to be full of surprises already. For a start, she had assumed that Stella, and the other principals from the cast of *A Woman's Touch*, would all be there. But, much to her new lover's disgust, a last minute engagement over in Paris had cropped up for the blonde star. She had tried to postpone it, but without success. The clincher had been when Lord Burnopside himself had telephoned.

'So sorry you won't be able to make it down to the Hall this weekend, but some other time, eh?' he'd said. 'I really think you ought to do this Paris thing. It'll be a great boost to the show. Make sure we get full European coverage. Our French friends will be dying to get their hands on it. Especially after seeing you on *Spectacle de Samedi*.'

There was only Ally from the cast, as far as Felicity could see. And Ted Davidson, the chief cameraman, whom she had loathed almost on sight, and been given no reason to change her opinion through the months of their necessarily close and intimate association. The knowledge of his steadfastly observing her unclothed body, and even arranging it, manipulating the entangled limbs of herself and her lover like some lecherous puppet master, had upset her greatly at first.

Paradoxically, things had improved once she and Stella had become lovers off screen. Or perhaps Ted's lecherous manner just didn't get her goat any more. Past caring, Felicity had gone along with Stella's idea that they should declare their relationship. Should come out, as it were.

'As long as Michael doesn't find out,' she'd temporised urgently.

'No, just for the crew, angel,' Stella had crooned. 'Any rumours get around outside and we'll swear it's just PA trying to gain some kudos. But it'll be one in the eye for Tosser Ted and his merry band.'

So, that day they had both appeared on set without their robes, arms linked in a manner that went beyond the suggestive. 'Felicity's decided at last,' Stella announced, with a dazzling smile. 'If you can't beat 'em, join 'em.'

And that would appear to be that. Felicity still worried a great deal about Michael, though. As circumspectly as she could, she had tried to prepare him for the explosive release on screen in the coming November.

'It's pretty searing stuff,' she'd told him, choosing her moment as auspiciously as she could, as they lay in post-coital tranquillity in his bed. 'They've even got me having an orgasm on screen, God help me.'

He did his best to take it in his stride, but she could see how uneasy he was about the whole thing.

'You won't let it make any difference to us, will you?' she pouted, winsomely. 'It's only acting, darling. This is the real me. Nobody in the whole world's ever seen me except you.' As she spoke, she reached under the blankets and captured his penis, which stirred at once from its limp reclining across his thigh. Her dark head dipped lower, disappeared beneath the sheet, and she felt the satiny touch of his helm leap to meet her kiss. However unquiet his brain might feel about her bodily exposure in public, his prick had not seemed in the least bit reluctant to show its admiration...

Felicity's gaze encountered the coolly amused stare of her cousin, part of the group they had joined. That was another surprise, finding that he was included in the invitation to Burnopside Hall.

'I didn't know you even knew Lord B,' Felicity had marvelled when, two days after Michael had once more vanished into the northern wilds on business for the week, his place in her bed and between her thighs had been taken by John once more.

He'd lifted his head from her flat stomach, and grinned. 'I don't. Apart from meeting him at that launching do for your porno flic. And on the set that time. Perhaps he just wants to keep it in the family.'

'Keep what?' she'd wondered, then gasped as her cousin's skilful hand sought out the sticky folds of her labia and prised them open to insert a wickedly knowledgeable finger into her ready crevice...

She gasped again as Magda's large hand slid over her hip to stroke the contours of her taut bottom within her white jeans. They had been worn as a last minute gesture of independence when, making arrangements over the phone for her and John to be collected by car, Lord B had chuckled, 'And be sure to wear that outrageous little frock you wore at the launch, my dear.'

Too many people seemed to be running her life at the moment, Felicity thought mutinously. She was still inwardly smarting at the way Stella had taken total control since they'd become lovers. She was showing all the tendencies of a bossy paramour, even down to selecting Felicity's underwear for her. However, the frock in question was in her suitcase upstairs and she would put it on for dinner later. Just now that hand casually resting on her backside and steering her across the room was causing her far more concern.

'Let's go and powder our noses, sweetheart,' Magda whispered. 'Away from all these panting men folk. You'll give them a coronary if you're not careful. We'll let them cool off a little.'

In spite of her embarrassment and uncertainty, Felicity giggled in complicity.

Upstairs, in a large and splendidly appointed bathroom, the tall figure astonished her even further by saying, with an uncharacteristic and enchantingly demure look, 'I say, honey, would you mind just turning away for a moment? I'm full of hang-ups, and I just can't pee if someone's watching. Just for a sec.'

Felicity blushed and obligingly turned away, trying not to look at the blurred reflection which showed up in the comer of her eye from one of the long mirrors. She heard the soft rasp of silk sliding over skin, then the startlingly loud sound of rushing liquid hitting the pan. Another rustle of adjusting clothing, then the flush of the lavatory.

'There!' Magda gave a throaty little laugh. 'You can look again, sugar.' She was respectably covered in the black dress. She stood at the washbasin and nodded at the toilet pedestal. 'Your turn. I won't peek either, I promise.'

'Oh, don't worry, it won't bother me,' Felicity answered, far more breezily than she felt. 'I've shared too many cramped dressing rooms in various flea pit theatres up and down the country to retain any false modesty.' Nevertheless, she could feel herself pinking as she unbuttoned her jeans and wriggled as she lowered them to her thighs, before sitting on the still warm seat.

She finished and remained seated while she reached down between her thighs and carefully wiped herself with a wad of the quilted toilet tissue. Suddenly Magda was standing directly in front of her, so close that their toes touched and Felicity could not stand up.

'I'm glad about that,' Magda said, her stirring voice deeper than ever. She reached down and took hold of Felicity's hands.

The trapped girl stared up helplessly. 'I'm not gay,' she said, her voice trembling. 'Despite what you might have heard. They're only rumours—'

'That's not what Stella Priest says,' Magda interrupted, and Felicity crimsoned. Tears filled her eyes at her betrayal. 'It's nothing to be ashamed of, sugar,' continued Magda. 'I'm delighted to hear it.'

'I'm not - I've never...'

'Oh yes, you have,' purred Magda, with that treacle laugh. 'And you enjoyed it. But I can give it like you've never had it before. I'll make that blonde tit sucker look like a girl scout who's just found out there's another hole besides the one you piss out of!'

Tears dripped from Felicity's chin onto her T-shirt, where they spread as though soaking through blotting paper. 'Let me go,' she said weakly.

Magda pulled her to her feet, and Felicity felt her jeans and tiny knickers tangled about her knees. Her T-shirt came down to her tummy button only.

'Don't fight it, sugar,' Magda urged. 'Just relax and revel in it.'

Any strength or will to resist drained from Felicity.

Magda took her in her arms and gently laid her down on the cold tiles. She lifted her limp legs and eased the jeans and briefs clear. The thong sandals fell off as she did so.

'Don't... please...' Felicity whispered, gazing up, the tears shining in her eyes. 'I can't fight you. You're too strong.'

'Relax, baby,' the seductive tones murmured. 'Magda won't hurt you. Magda will show you heaven.' She reached behind, drew down the zip of her tight dress, then stood and wriggled to ease it down over her hips and thighs.

Felicity stared up, captivated by the statuesque beauty exposed to her. The long thighs were full, rounded with muscle, yet tapering in perfect harmony with the shapeliness of the splendid limbs. The breasts jutted proudly over her, held in the satin confines of a black bra, the lace edged cups of which plunged deeply to show the pale contours of the upper halves of the gorgeous mounds. The long expanse of midriff led to a small triangle of black briefs which hugged the promising swell of a generous mound.

'I want you, sugar,' Magda breathed, the smoky voice thrumming with powerful emotion. Then the figure swooped and smothered Felicity, who surrendered her mouth to the searing kiss that claimed her. A hand delved and pushed up the flimsy cotton shirt, baring the breasts that had no other cover. The large warm palm cupped them. The thumb and forefinger plucked and rolled at the throbbing nipple, while another hand slid between their warm bellies and embraced the whole curve of her vulva. The heel of the palm pressed against the moaning girl, deliciously thrilling her with its pressure, so that her thighs parted in blind obedience to the needs of her flesh.

The rich dark hair fell over Felicity's belly and thighs as Magda bent, lowered her head in triumph and in homage to the fluid centre of Felicity's blazing hunger, where, timeless ages later, the lapping tongue, the nipping teeth, and those conquering fingers, brought her to a climax that made her body stiffen, then thresh, her heels hammering on the floor in an ecstasy which engulfed her.

Chapter Six

John Keynes eyed the privileged gathering expectantly. There was a hidden tension, despite the relaxed appearance of those around the long dining table littered with the remnants of the excellent meal. On the surface it was simply an assemblage of rich and interesting people, a modem day equivalent of the country house parties of long ago. Their host was charming, the surroundings the height of luxury, the urbane conversation sparkling, the girls lovely.

The girls. That was enough to arouse his suspicion. They were all prick-raisingly beautiful. And all so unlike the thrusting girl power aggressive types which abounded these days. They did nothing, except to exhibit their beauty. They were watchful, as he was, knowing when to smile and when to murmur a suitable rejoinder. And that was it. If they hadn't been so restrained he would have guessed they were high class tarts or girls from some exclusive escort agency, ready to go along with, and as far as, this bunch of influential rich dogs wanted them to go.

There must be something in the atmosphere. Even his coz had been transformed; as quiet as any of them now, sitting there showing off those sexy little tits of hers through that muslin-like dress, and looking as though butter wouldn't melt in that mouth which she knew how to put to such deadly uses. Clearly, she had gone overboard on this lesbian kick of hers. She had been gone so long with that giant Magda bird - the most fascinating female of all, he acknowledged - that everyone had noticed.

Ever since then she'd been as quiet as a mouse. And he could guess why. He could recognise that slightly bemused air, since they'd so spectacularly been getting it together. The vaguely unfocused quality of those dark eyes. Yes, he'd be prepared to bet that, in some secluded corner of this venerable pile, she'd had a good seeing to at the hands and other things of the exotic Magda.

Lucky little her, he thought with a voluptuous quiver as his imagination worked feverishly. The mystical figure was certainly something to get worked up about, on a literally monumental scale. She was not butch; the vulgarity of that word had nothing to do with her unique brand of sexuality. Yet he could not envisage her in any other role than that of dom. And how he would love to play sub to her, he acknowledged, his senses running riot He couldn't wait for the orgy to begin, if that's what they were there for. But was it? Or were they presently undergoing some kind of test, to see if they were fit for the fleshly delights which might await them? He had a feeling that his coz had already passed hers, whether the sweet thing realised it or not.

In the drawing room, where coffee and drinks were served, he found himself standing near the drinks trolley with their host. Lord B was half a head at least taller than John. He slipped his arm easily around his shoulder. 'And how are you enjoying yourself, young fellow?' he said. 'I can't get over how alike you and Felicity are. I took you for twins when I first saw you.'

John laughed. He felt the heaviness of the man's arm resting across him, claiming him. 'Yes,' he said, 'apparently people used to think that of our fathers. Though in fact daddy is almost two years older than Uncle Charles.' He glanced around again; very aware of the magnetism of the man next to him, the sensation of power he exuded like a subtle perfume. John felt both weakened and thrilled by it. 'The ladies are all so stunning,' he observed, revealing something of the wonder in his voice.

'And none more so than your own charming cousin,' his lordship answered at once.

John shrugged slightly, as though in demurral. 'Who's the coloured girl over there?' he asked. 'She's lovely.'

'Debbie? Yes. She's only just joined us - a matter of days ago.'

Joined us? John wondered. He waited for further explanation, but there was none.

'You like girls?' the gravelly voice went on, with a knowing smile that made John's face burn.

'But of course,' he stammered hastily. 'Why on earth shouldn't I?'

'No reason,' his lordship said easily. 'But tastes can be extremely catholic these days, can't they, my boy?' He laughed richly, and squeezed John's narrow shoulders heartily, briefly pulling him into his side. 'You like that one in particular?' he went on. 'I admire your taste. I'll see what I can arrange for you. Excuse me a moment.'

Minutes later, the coloured girl approached him. 'Hi,' she said. 'I'm Debbie. You're Felicity's cousin, aren't you? John?' She smiled unaffectedly at him. 'Would you like to have a look round the house? I'm still learning my way around myself. There're supposed to be some priceless portraits up in the gallery.' She reached out and took his hand in an oddly innocent gesture, and together they left the room.

A little while later she stood facing him, smiling much more explicitly as she leaned back against the closed and locked door, upon which one foot rested. 'Would you like to fuck around a little, John?' she said. 'You look drop dead gorgeous, you know that?'

'S-so do you!' His pulse was racing.

She continued to smile as she advanced towards him and turned seductively. 'Undo me, please,' she whispered.

His fingers were unsteady as he located the zip fastener of her simple flowered dress and drew it down her velvety back. Her shoulders moved, the garment dropped to her hips, then with one more swift movement it fell around her feet, and she stepped out of it. She wasn't wearing any underclothes. She left her sandals inside the rumpled pool of the dress.

She pulled him towards a solid four-poster bed, the heavy crimson drapes of which were drawn around it. He noticed a thin crisscross of dark lines running over her buttocks. 'Who did that?' he asked.

Her delicate shoulders shrugged. 'I was a naughty girl,' she replied, and did not elucidate. She reached up to pull aside the bed curtains, and he stared with deep appreciation at the play of light and shadow on her rippling muscles. Those hollowed buttocks drew his gaze, the pale tan scratched across by those fading lines. Her hips were narrow, the cleft of her behind tightly inviting. From the back, with her slender figure and her close-cropped hair, she looked both boyish and excitingly arousing at the same time.

Hastily he shrugged off his clothing and left it scattered beside her discarded dress. She was sitting on the high bed with her legs crossed, grinning mischievously.

'My, you *are* a pretty boy, aren't you?' she said. 'So slim and sexy.'

He didn't know if she was mocking him, though her grin looked innocently childlike.

He growled at her, seized her by her upper arms and dragged her over. 'I'll give you pretty boy.'

They wrestled. She fought with just enough wiry strength to make the tussle exciting before he pinned her down on her stomach. Her feet kicked up and down rapidly, drumming on the counterpane, those tempting cheeks of her bottom flexing and dimpling. He slapped it, feeling his open palm bounce on the resilient globes, and she gave a small shriek.

'Ow! Please don't, Johnny! My bum's still sore.'

He hit her again and she yelped, pleaded with him to stop. 'Who did it?' he said, his tone suggesting that if she didn't tell him he'd continue to spank her.

'My boyfriend!' she gasped, pouting exaggeratedly. 'Or rather, my ex. That's why I'm staying down here for a while. Magda fixed it.'

'What's her story?'

He released her and she rolled over, lying on one hip and massaging her buttocks with a rueful grimace. 'You're a bully,' she muttered childishly.

'Magda?' she eventually went on. 'I dunno. I've only just met her since I've been here. She seems to know all these big wheels.' He could hear the awe in her voice and feel her little quiver of sensuality. 'She's really something, isn't she? She's wonderful!'

'Is she a dyke?'

Her head lifted challengingly. 'Are you a gay?'

He growled and grabbed her wrists again, and she lay back and gave a squeal of mock alarm. 'Sorry,' she said. 'It's just a rumour I heard, that's all.' She stared at his thickening penis. 'I guess not, eh?' She grinned placatingly.

'I'll give you gay!' he growled again, seizing her in earnest and rolling her over once more, and again she squealed.

'Don't hurt me too much,' she pleaded, her voice carrying a hint of real alarm this time. He noted the 'too much', as though sexual games with pain were not new to her. Which they clearly weren't, judging by the stripes across her bottom. He felt his prick rear and stiffen to full erection.

He slipped his arms around her slim waist and dragged her off the edge of the bed, then turned her so she was doubled over it, face down, her feet trailing on the floor. He fitted himself into her from behind, slotted his penis along the deep cleft of her behind and felt himself throb mightily at the contact. He guided the tip of his helm, pushing into the crack, and felt the exotic cling of it against his glans. He felt her tense and heard the muffled gasp as he stabbed at the entrance to her anal passage. She thought he was going to bugger her, and for an instant he felt a savage urge to do so, revelling in the boy-like slimness, warm and squirming against him. Then he let his prick slide down, felt the tightness ease a little, and the rasp of wiry pubic hair against him as he located the moist and easier slit of her vagina, into which he ploughed deeply. She gasped, perhaps in relief, and those buttocks tightened against him once more. They lifted, spearing her onto him more firmly with jouncing eagerness.

'Yes, lover... yes, yes!' she panted, urging him on until they were bouncing together, white on brown, lunging in unison until he came fiercely, racked by a spasm which made him cry out in an excess of rapture.

In his book-lined study on the first floor, Lord Burnopside was lolling back on the chaise longue. He drew on his cigar, his eyes wrinkled against the blue smoke which drifted about him. He was naked, his legs crossed. His penis, shrouded and shrunken, still seeping from its recent climax, nestled snugly at the conflux of belly and thighs.

He stared at Magda's exotic figure, shown to full advantage in the skintight body shaper which, held by a bootlace-thin strap fastened at the back of her neck, clung like a shining black skin to her breasts, the nipples poking entrancingly in silhouette against the fine material. The crotch was cut so high that the pale crease of her thighs and belly showed at either side, without even one stray curl to betray a bikini line. At the rear the garment was lost entirely in the divide of her buttocks, the proudly jutting cheeks thus exposed. She was busily cleaning her face and hands at the small washbasin in one corner of the room.

'How are our media guests?' his lordship asked. 'All customers satisfied, I hope?'

'I think so, my lord. Ally's bedded down with Sir Hugh and that broker chap he brought along. That prick of a cameraman will be well into Marie-Angele by now. And I think Joanne went along to keep them company.'

'What about our two beautiful babes in the wood? Who's the boy with?'

Magda gave her deep chuckle. 'You saw him and young Debs when they came back from their time-out. They can't take their eyes off each other. It must be young love.'

'I only hope he appreciates her.'

Magda nodded confidently. 'Oh, I'm sure he will. He's like his cousin. They're both swingers. Bi as they come.' Lord B quivered with desire, despite his detumescence. 'What's she really like? Is she as exquisite as she looks?' He reached down involuntarily, cupped his clammy prick in his palm, and pressed it hard.

Magda gave him a broad grin. 'And more. You're quite right about her. I think she'd be ideal for one of us. She's got that waifish look of innocence. She's childlike, but with that hint of decadence, you know. I'm in love with her already.' She laughed throatily. 'I'm not gay!' she mimicked in Felicity's breathless squeak, fluttering her long black eyelashes. 'And there she was, with her pants round her ankles and her little pussy dripping like a wet sponge!' She laughed again. 'I'm off to get really butch with her now.'

'Damn.' Lord B sighed. 'I almost wish I'd never signed her up for *Woman's Touch* now. The publicity's going to be enormous. They won't leave her alone. Or Stella, who's well and truly in her bed now, by the way.'

Magda's confidence did not waver. 'Don't worry. We'll soon have that blonde cow out of there. And that straight twat of a fiance. It won't matter how famous she is. She'll be one of us - trust me.'

'Where are you having her tonight? I'd like to see it.' His lordship's eyes gleamed and his penis stirred from its nest.

'Right. There's no one in the Hunting Room. You get yourself in the cubbyhole, my lord, and I'll bring her along in about fifteen minutes.'

Felicity stared about her at the high, shadowy room, with the gilt framed pictures of the hunting scenes covering every wall. She shivered for, beneath her long silk dressing gown, she was naked. 'It's all a bit overpowering,' she murmured.

'We won't be disturbed here,' Magda said. She bent and lit the gas fire, which looked out of place in the wide hearth with its ornate marbled surrounds. Its rosy glow -and immediate warmth was cheering. 'The bed's not made up, and it'll be damp as hell. Let's get cosy here.' She pulled down the heavy cushions and spread them on the thick rug before the fire. 'Now. Let me look at you. I can't wait any longer.' She tugged at the sash at Felicity's waist, and though she gave a cry of protest, the girl made no effort to stop her. The gown opened, and Magda brushed it from her shoulders. The firelight bathed the slim body, while Felicity stood there, enchantingly modest, her hands moving in front of her loins.

'I thought his lordship was going to have a go,' she said, her face troubled. 'You know. Try to get me to... to sleep with him tonight.'

'And would you mind, sugar?'

Felicity registered her outrage. 'I'm not a tart, you know,' she cried, her voice shrill. 'I don't sleep around. I've a fiance, and we're going to be married...'

'And Stella Priest,' Magda said easily. 'You're shacking up with her, aren't you? Doesn't your boyfriend mind about that?'

Felicity's face and throat crimsoned. She looked at the tall figure helplessly. 'He doesn't know,' she quietly admitted. 'He'd be horrified. I didn't mean it to happen.' She pulled a face of youthful misery. 'It just sort of... I meant it earlier, what I said. I'm not really gay. It's—'

'Weren't,' Magda prompted gently, drawing forth another blush. 'What you really mean, sugar, is that you're hi. You swing both ways.'

Felicity gazed at her. She made a little gesture of uncertainty, her confusion mute this time. The soft glow of the gas lit her slim young body, showing the little dark patch of her pubis. Tears sparkled in her dark eyes.

'You can have the best of both, baby,' Magda breathed sensually. As she spoke, she untied her own robe, and Felicity gave a gasp of shock, for the superb figure was magnificently naked, except for a small black triangle fitted snugly to her loins, from which a thin strap snaked round both hips to meet the equally slim strap which appeared from the cleft of her bottom. From the centre of the triangle, which seemed to be made of shiny leather or plastic, jutted an ebony black phallus, not shaped in the likeness of a human penis, but entirely smooth, without the suggestion of a helm. It curved upward in a slight bow, and was about five inches in length.

'I know we don't need this shit to have fun, baby,' Magda smiled, shaking the black dildo between a thumb and finger in a lewd yet engagingly frank gesture. Felicity continued to stare saucer-eyed at the figure looming over her, and at the glistening phallus thrusting surreally from the black shiny loins. 'But it can be quite a turn on. For you and me.' The seductive tones sank even lower, grew more throaty. 'I like to penetrate, baby. You know, it can be a hell of a thrill. To feel your pussy bumping up against a babe's, to be in her, grinding away.' The strong face took on a suffused, dreamy expression, the eyes heavy-lidded with sensual promise. 'And I know you like being shafted, baby. We can fool around girlie-wise later. Right now, let's ride!'

'No,' Felicity whispered, but let herself be laid back on a cushion, her legs spread wide, before the athletic form lowered itself gently between them and carefully eased the shining dildo into the narrowness of the moist orifice waiting to receive it. Her legs came up around those sculptured thighs and driving buttocks, upon which her pink heels drummed with increasing urgency.

Felicity moaned, her dark hair tossed back and forth on the cushion. The rigid object burrowing away inside her was a source of both acute discomfort and wild erotic thrill. She felt its stabbing invasiveness filling her, skewering her narrow sheath, which spasmed powerfully even against the burning pain. Magda's breasts brushed against her face. She felt the erect nipples rub over her cheeks and nose, and strained frantically to nuzzle and lick at their rubbery hardness. The breasts themselves were firm, sculpted as though of marble, and Felicity's whirling brain wondered vaguely why they should be so solid, and not softly yielding like her own.

Then, suddenly, the pain flared, the torment stepped up, as Magda began to lunge frenziedly, battering her against the power of those muscled thighs, the pounding hardness of the stomach, until Felicity was crying, tears cascading from her, begging her assailant to stop. 'Please - oh please! You're - it's hurting. Oh God!'

Magda gave one last deep thrust that seemed to pierce Felicity through to her womb, and the tortured figure swamped under the possessed fury screamed shrilly. The wonderfully sculpted buttocks bunched, Magda held herself above the writhing figure transfixed beneath her, holding her weight off Felicity. Several inches of the black dildo were visible between them, spanning their heaving stomachs like some weird umbilicus, before, with a convulsive shudder, the powerful form heaved off the smaller.

Magda gave a deep grunt, rolled away from the sobbing girl, the phallus buckled obscenely, before the large hands ripped it savagely from her loins and cast it aside, to reveal yet another covering, this time of snug satin which hugged the outlines of her sex.

'My love,' Magda crooned, gathering the slim figure, covering her again, but this time with a purely feminine contact, all flowing tenderness, hands and lips and body caressing and soothing. The wonderful mouth held Felicity's until she felt her lungs would burst, and her senses reeled.

Then it left her, only to set her body afire as it traced its slow path over her flesh. It fastened on each nipple in turn, suckling until her breasts blazed with arousal, after which it moved with sweet torment down over her quivering belly. It bit and nuzzled and lapped at the conflux of her thighs and loins, before settling on the raw sex lips which still throbbed with the rough penetration they had endured.

But the pain was soon lost in the overwhelming desire conjured by the feathery strokes of the tongue that probed her slippery folds and sought out the beating bud of her clitoris. Felicity shuddered in transported delight, her fingers lost in the thick black hair that spilt profusely over her gaping thighs and her gently undulating belly. The tongue grazed, moved, ate hungrily at her exposed core, until Felicity's buttocks nipped ecstatically and lifted clear of the floor at the climax thundering through her, over and over, until she sank back, drained, every muscle limp. She wept in an excess of relief, and settled with total surrender into the arms and the body which cloaked her in their encompassing love.

Chapter Seven

Felicity guided the patient horse nervously along the woodland track. It was more than two years since she'd done any hacking, and she had never been at ease on horseback. She was beginning to regret her bravado in accepting Lord Burnopside's invitation to ride. Even then, she had half hoped that her supposed afterthought of not having any togs would get her out of it, but his lordship had assured her that they would find something suitable.

And they had.

She was astonished at the snugness of fit, and the pristine condition of the clothes a maid brought to her room, right down to the calf length highly polished boots and the checked riding jacket with its nipped waist. There was even a striped silk tie and jewelled pin to go with the dazzling white shirt.

'You look splendid, my dear,' his lordship grunted, when they met at the back of the mansion.

She had tried not to show her anxiety, and her mount was steady enough, but she was glad that the wooded area on the sloping hill above the mansion necessitated their slowing to a walk. She had also swiftly realised how sore she was after the astonishing love play she and Magda had indulged in.

Now, the rubbing of her crotch against the saddle rekindled her memory of the weird event. Not only the pain was recalled. To her chagrin, she felt her briefs clinging stickily beneath the thick stuff of the jodhpurs. She glanced round. There had been about six of them in the party, but they were all widely spaced now, some of the more experienced having gone ahead and beyond sight. Only Lord B himself was still with her. He moved up to her side.

'It opens up a bit here,' he said. 'We'll give' em a bit of a gallop, eh?'

Somehow she managed to cling on during the terror-stricken minutes which followed. She was too frightened at the time to be aware of the undignified spectacle she must surely present, as she clung on, hanging over her mount's neck, red faced and whimpering with fear, her hard hat hammed down over her nose.

Afterwards, back at the stables, he carefully lifted her down, his hands gripping tightly at her waist, and she marvelled at his strength, despite his advancing years. Of course he was still handsome, in a time worn, craggy sort of way. His silvery hair and moustache suited him. He was attractive in the way older men could be. She wondered at his age, and blushed as she found herself trying to picture him as a sexual partner. He looked older than daddy. He must be well into his fifties - at least, she guessed.

They went through the kitchen garden and in by the butler's pantry. There seemed to be no one about at all, the house strangely silent, but there was a smell of cooking and some noise of bustling activity from the kitchens.

He sniffed appreciatively. 'Ah! Sunday lunch. Always takes me back, that smell. So nostalgic.' He smiled at her in the dimness. 'Come on, young lady. I've some stuff that should help with the stiffness.'

He held her arm as they went up the wide staircase. On the first floor she could hear voices and the click of billiard balls. She wondered where John was. Or Magda.

He was leading her off to the right. 'I had better go and change,' she murmured. 'I'm—'

'In here,' he cut her off abruptly. 'Come on.' He spoke firmly in a no-nonsense tone, and she obeyed him. The room was quite small and very modern compared with most of the guestrooms. It was comfortably furnished, with a low bed against one wall. She guessed it was his room. A modestly sized bathroom opened off it.

'Sit.' He gestured to a round-backed chair, and she did as she was told, feeling her awkwardness growing.

'Give me your foot.' He bent as he spoke and picked up her right one. With a series of tugs he managed to haul the boot off, and then did the same with the other. 'Get your things off,' he said, his voice thickening. 'I'll run a bath for you.'

Her face blazed. 'Please, I'd rather go to my room, if you don't mind.' She hung her head, unable to look at him.

'I don't mean you any harm, my dear,' he said gravely. 'Nor would I ever dream of forcing myself upon you. You know that, don't you?' His crooked finger lifted her chin, and she felt the tears start in her eyes once more. 'I'll run the bath for you. Then I'll arrange for your massage.' There was a slight pause, before the husky voice continued even more softly. 'You know I care a great deal for you, Felicity. As a person. I don't mean just for your looks - though you are staggeringly beautiful.'

She murmured an automatic denial, blushing even more.

He turned away and went through to the bathroom. 'There's a robe on the door there,' he called, and she heard the sound of water beginning to splash into the tub. 'Slip it on, if you'd rather. '

With a sensation of helplessness which she somehow felt had been with her for most of her brief stay, she unbuttoned the jacket, slipped it off and laid it on the bed. She unfastened the belt and stiffly bent to drag off the riding breeches. Hastily, she shrugged off tie and shirt, then bra and pants, before reaching gratefully for the thick woollen robe, after which she sat and pulled off the thick stockings.

'In you get.' He stood in the doorway, smiling. 'Come on, take your time and have a good soak. Then I'll get someone to massage you. You'll be right as rain by lunchtime, I guarantee.'

She stood and edged past him. There was a wonderful fragrance in the air, and the large tub was full almost to the top with a swirl of thick creamy foam. She stood, blushing, not knowing what to do, and he put his hands on her shoulders, picking up the lapels of the robe. She undid the sash and let him take the garment off her, blushing from top to toe and aware of every inch of her nakedness.

He turned away and hung the robe on the hook on the back of the open door. 'Hop in,' he said again. 'I don't think it's too hot.'

Feeling very vulnerable and foolish again, she stepped into the water and slid down thankfully beneath the concealing lather, savouring the frothy caress bubbling up over her breasts. She was decently covered again, only her shoulders and arms showing. She tensed as he leaned down close, but he merely wadded a towel and fitted it behind her head. 'Now you just lie there and relax. I'll go and see about this massage. Don't nod off and drown, will you?'

The mansion felt oddly deserted when the riding party had left. John wandered into the library, moved restlessly along the shelves of books, idly pulling one out now and then and replacing it after only a brief glance.

'Not into outdoor pursuits?' The deep, rich voice startled him. He had not heard Magda enter. 'I can't say I blame you. Neither am I. I prefer pleasures of a more subtle type.'

He felt a tremor that was almost like a frisson of fear. It thrilled him. 'I can believe that,' he said. His throat felt dry, his heart racing. There was something; an indefinable but immensely powerful excitement which seemed to grip him. Magnetic Magda, he mocked, striving to keep a tight control over his feelings.

'You're as delightful as your gorgeous cousin.' Magda's voice was like dark velvet caressing him. He cleared his throat. 'Am I? I shouldn't have thought you would find me quite so appealing.'

'Oh, but I do.' She came to him, and placed a perfectly groomed hand on his sleeve. 'Are your tastes as exotic as hers?'

He was quivering tautly now. 'Oh yes. At least, perhaps more so, if you'd like to try me.'

She laughed, a rippling chuckle, and leaned in close.

He saw the full, vividly painted lips approach, pursing as they came, to settle fragrantly on his own uplifted mouth. The contact was gentle, but lingering. 'Come with me, Johnny. You don't mind if I call you that, you dear boy?'

The room she led him to was high up, on the mansion's third floor, discreetly hidden away from the main part of the building. There were no windows, and the harshly brilliant strip lighting overhead revealed a bare room, with pale walls on three sides. The fourth, opposite the door, consisted entirely of floor to ceiling mirrors. A series of ropes and metal bars, like trapezes, hung from the thick beams traversing the room overhead. At the ends of several of the ropes were metal rings, from which in turn dangled lengths of chain. There was no furniture, but on a wall rack John saw various instruments of punishment, from whips to leather straps, slender canes, and bundled birch rods. The thick carpet was a rich dark blue.

'I want you to undress for me, Johnny.' The dramatically made-up eyes were alight with mischief as she smiled at him warmly.

Again, he found it hard to speak. 'What about you?' he managed.

She chuckled. 'I asked first. Now come on, I promise you'll love it.'

With a feeling of helplessness, which was all part of the excitement that made his prick throb, he obeyed, bending to slip off his shoes, shrugging off his pants and shirt, the patterned socks, and finally, with only a slight pause, pushing down the tiny black briefs. He stood there and forced himself not to cup his genitals, his toes flexing in the carpet with deep embarrassment.

'Come, give me your hands.'

Afterwards, he reflected on the strange power she was able to exert over him, and on his own willingness to allow her to dominate him totally. But as she spoke his arms lifted almost of their own accord. He felt her power, but was incapable of analysing it, indeed, incapable of any coherent thought over the drumming of his blood.

She fitted his hands inside two of the metal rings and bound them tightly. She gave a tug on another rope and his arms were drawn upwards to their full extent. The strain lifted his chest, his ribcage sprang prominently into view and his stomach hollowed deeply. Magda's painted thumbnails ran over the taut chest and flicked at the tiny hardness of the nipples centreing the hairless rounds. 'Felicity's tits are hardly any bigger,' she murmured.

He found it hard to breathe, let alone speak. 'You'd know, of course,' he whispered.

'Of course, my love. Not jealous, are we?'

For a wild second he wondered if Felicity had told her about their lovemaking, but then his attention was powerfully diverted as those strong smooth hands slid down his frame to stroke and cup his genitals. His penis was engorged, hung heavily, but not erect. The long fingers, with their darkly vivid nails, closed around the base of the column, slowly pulled, drew back the foreskin, and he shuddered, his prick leaping under the caresses, the helm swelling and emerging fully. The feeling of helplessness swept through him in a delightful excess of sensation that made him fear he was about to come. The tip of his prick shone with his emission.

'You're bigger than I thought, Johnny boy,' she breathed, working him slowly, while his narrow hips swayed and his tensed belly strained forward towards the stimulation. 'But not that big. Do you fuck, Johnny? Or do you prefer to be fucked?'

His teeth clenched. He felt close to tears, humiliated.

Yet his body throbbed with urgent pleasure. The degrading captivity and his helplessness were all a part of it. 'Untie me,' he hissed, 'and I'll show you!'

'Cheeky boy,' Magda chuckled, as though she were an indulgent parent with a small child. 'A little lesson in manners first, I think.'

John watched wild-eyed as she let go of him and went over to the rack. She selected the bundle of birch rods. 'This for naughty boys, I think.' She swished it through the air as she advanced upon him, staring at his prick, which jutted stiffly now. 'We'd better do something about that first, though. Can't have that going off half cock, now can we?' The deepness of her laughter was like a cutting blow in itself. She put down the birch and came close, until her face was only inches from his. She had to bend to achieve this, and once more John was struck by her size, the proportions of her magnificent body and limbs. He felt his masculinity draining away, even as she held and began to stimulate him again, with long slow strokes, until his throbbing prick was rock hard, approaching ejaculation. He acknowledged that side of his nature that welcomed his surrender.

As he did so an even stranger feeling possessed him.

As Magda's face came closer, and those brilliant lips parted and sealed his in a kiss that seemed to suck the strength out of him as thrillingly as the semen he was so near to spurting forth, her strong features took on a weirdly androgynous quality, so that their roles were reversed. She was the male, triumphant, dominant, and he was female, yielding gladly, ceding to her sexual authority over him.

At that instant, with her mouth clamped to his and her tongue thrusting into his throat, he gave a strangled cry, his frame shook, and he felt his come shoot forth, on and on, Magda's hand milking him of every last drop, while her triumphant chuckle transferred itself through to his quivering frame.

'Oh, you disgusting, wicked boy!'

Half sobbing he glanced down, following her gaze, and saw the pearly thickness of his semen roped over her fingers and wrist, and splashed in darkening stains across the front of her tight red dress. She wiped the residue from her hand on his heaving belly. His prick shrivelled, the brown folds agleam with his fluid. He hung there limply, watching her remove her dress. Underneath she wore a black body, of a shiny silken texture that clung to her curves like a second skin. Dark, sheer tights encased her legs, and disappeared into the high silken crotch of her undergarment. The narrow shoes had slender heels that added to her already towering height.

She retrieved the bundle of rods she had laid close to his bare feet. 'Let's see if we can make you squeal, eh?' she said, menacingly.

He recognised the challenge, accepted it, and his muscles tensed. His buttocks tightened and dimpled. A flame of swift fire rippled over them at the first swishing blow, and he bit savagely at his lips, his breath escaping in an agonised hiss.

Magda nodded appreciatively.

The second stroke was laid exactly over the first, its force making him squirm despite his best efforts, and his hips shook. He gasped at the bum. She struck more quickly and his body twisted, his feet shuffled and he rose on his toes, the whimpering cries forcing themselves out between his parting lips. His bottom was scored with a myriad of red weals, the whole area afire with the severity of the beating, and, at last, with a convulsive sob, his head dropped between his outstretched arms and he sobbed, 'Please! No more! Please stop!'

She did so at once, and he hung there, shamed, his behind throbbing and his chest heaving as he sniffled like a chastised child.

Felicity was drifting off to half slumber when, some time later, she heard someone come into the adjoining room. To her vast relief she heard Magda's rippling laugh, then the tall figure appeared in the doorway, beaming down at her. Magda was wearing what looked like some sort of Greek costume, in a pearly satin, loose about her bust and torso, with wide sleeves and tied with a sash, and ending at mid-thigh to exhibit her long legs to full advantage. She was bare foot.

'Sorry I took so long,' she said. 'I've been getting to know your lovely cousin. Up you come, quick.'

Felicity glanced apprehensively over Magda's shoulder as she rose, the clinging bubbles sliding off her gleaming flesh. 'It's all right,' the deep voice chuckled. 'We're quite alone. Wait, there's far too much soap. Let me rinse you off.'

Felicity stood, her pulse quickening, while Magda plucked up the shower attachment and, adjusting the fine jet of water to the correct temperature, played it over her, lingering over her breasts and the flattened moss of her pubis, then, turning her, the slopes of her buttocks.

Magda held a towel and wrapped the lovely girl in it, and the large hands began to rub and pat and add to Felicity's arousal while she dried her.

In the bedroom another towel had been spread over the bed. 'Lie down,' Magda ordered. When Felicity hesitated, she added, holding up a small bottle of oil, 'His lordship got this especially. It's wonderful for aches and pains. On your tum first, if you please. '

The capable fingers kneaded, pressed, stirred, and generally cosseted and teased every inch of Felicity's tingling flesh, until she was sighing and gnawing at her lip with pleasure and frustration.

Magda grinned. 'Now, just let yourself drift off to bye-byes, baby. I'll wake you later.' The thumbs and fingers dug into the muscles of Felicity's shoulders and neck, bunching and relaxing them, then traced her spine, pressing her soft breasts against the yielding mattress. Down the hollow of her back, pressing on her coccyx, then the rounds of her buttocks. The thumbs dug deep, parted the cleft, opened her most intimate flesh, and she shivered and thrust her belly into the softness of the bed, feeling the flare of her desire. The hands rolled and kneaded the twin cheeks of her bottom.

Felicity was drowsy, her mind drifting, only faintly aware of a pause, the disappearance of those wonderful teasing hands. Then they started again from the base of her neck, following that sensitive path to her behind, again delving deep, and on to the lesser rounds of her calves, her slender ankles and the delicate curve of her heels. Up again...

She gasped, suddenly conscious that the hands were different, harder. She heard a grunt and, at the same instant, she felt those hands spread under her belly and lift her hips, raising her haunches. She smelt the fragrance of Lord Burnopside's cologne, felt the hardness of his body as he knelt behind her, then the stabbing head of his engorged penis as it nuzzled in the cleft of her behind, seeking the entrance to her already wet and spasming vagina. With a few swift strokes he was fully embedded, and then withdrawing almost to the point of ejection, only to plunge slowly to the hilt once more.

She hissed with discomfort, yet the fierce pleasure was far greater, indeed, enhanced by that very soreness. Her forehead was resting on her folded arms, her bottom raised high, his body folding over her like a warm blanket. Those hands came round and cupped her breasts, held and caressed them until they were alive with sensation, and she knew her crisis was near. She was frantic that he'd begin the wild rutting that signalled his coming, and prayed desperately for her own release. But, wonderfully, he continued that slow rhythmic fucking until her climax came, spiralling to its bursting point, shattering through every nerve so that she cried out a long wailing release. And, at the very instant when the last shuddering shocks of orgasm died, she felt his potent discharge flood her with a mighty surge.

In the shadows Magda stood watching, and felt at that exact moment the flooding rush of her own deliverance.

Chapter Eight

Felicity was greatly relieved that Ally and Ted had their own transport, and that they were not heading back to London on Sunday evening. 'I couldn't bear to face the trip back to town in that creep's company,' she told John, with a dramatic shudder.

He knew she was referring to the cameraman rather than her director. As it was, they had the spacious rear seat of the Mercedes all to themselves, the uniformed driver sealed off behind his glass partition. Felicity sought her cousin's hand and clung to it, reminding him of the more innocent days of their shared childhood.

He studied her with a cool fondness. She was lying back, her head lolling on the upholstered rest, her thigh companionably nestled against his. Her face looked paler than ever. She was, as always, wearing her light touches of make-up. Beneath her eyes were faint shadows, not from cosmetics but from the effects of a hectic weekend, yet these subtle hints of decadence only served to make her more sexually appetising. In spite of his own sore weariness, he felt his penis unfurling in the tight grip of his silk underwear. The tenderness of his behind made him wonder if she was suffering in a similar manner.

'You look shagged,' he chuckled, 'if you'll pardon the expression.'

Her dark eyes widened, and he caught that appealingly helpless little girl look that she used so well. *Please be nice to me*, it begged, and was generally very effective. He dropped his teasing manner, moved by her air of abstracted weariness. He lifted her hand and brushed the knuckles softly against his lips. 'Did you have a good time, though?' he asked.

She gave a pathetic little smile. 'Life gets evermore complicated, Johnny.' She gave a little shiver, nestled in close, and rested her head against his shoulder. 'Magda! My God! Isn't she simply magnificent?'

'Is she?'

'I had no idea I was... well... so - so *lesbian*.' She snuggled into his arm. 'And I *hate* that word. Can I be gay, please Johnny? Is it all right for girls to be gay?'

'You can be what you like, my love,' he told her, patting her hand comfortingly, and gazing out at the passing countryside without really seeing it. 'They don't waste any time down at Burnopside Hall, do they?' he reflected.

She sighed and squirmed around until she was stretched out on the seat, her head in John's lap. The chauffeur was probably far too well trained to gaze in his rearview mirror, and in any case, she had her jeans on so there was nothing much to see. 'Sometimes I wish I was in love with you, Johnny,' she said. 'You're the only one in the world I feel I can be really honest with.'

They spent the night together, enjoying a cosy intimacy which was full of nostalgia for both of them, undressing together, sharing a bath and touching now and then - but only in the friendliest of caresses. And afterwards sprawling in front of the fire and television, eating a scratch meal in naked, passive affection.

She stared in amazement at the network of scratches covering John's buttocks. He passed them off as the result of some boisterous play with the coloured girl, Debbie, and Felicity showed no further interest. He was glad. He wondered at his untypical reluctance to reveal the truth, yet somehow, he felt he could not describe his encounter with Magda, least of all to Felicity.

She talked out her own confusion at the recent complications of her sex life. They lay in each other's arms in her bed, stroking now and then, their limbs intertwined, even kissing gently on lips but taking it no further.

'I honestly didn't have any idea that things would start with Stella,' she sighed. 'I suppose I was thick. It was bound to happen, really. All that stuff in front of the cameras. I mean, we were doing it, after all. Kissing... everything except the final consummation.' She gave a bitter little laugh. 'Even that, in the end. They've even got me coming on the silver screen. I wonder if I'll get a Bafta or an Oscar for that, eh? "And now, for best orgasm of the year,"' she intoned, in an MC voice. 'And as if that isn't enough, I have to go and get myself mixed up with that weird bunch down at Burnopside. Oh God! What's happening to me?'

She began to sniffle softly and John gathered her into him, planting light kisses about her brow and her face. 'Hey, come on, Feely. Don't get your hormones in a twist. What have I told you? You can't fight nature, you know that. There's the heart, and there's the cunt and the cock. Separate compartments, my girl. And where the cunt or cock goes, the heart can't always follow. And vice versa, I suppose.'

In spite of the tears still wet on her cheeks, she gave a little giggle. 'We seem to be a bit confused all ways up. Even with our cunts and cocks.'

'You speak for yourself,' he chided, slapping her thigh.

'Tell me, Johnny, please,' she said, earnestly. 'No secrets, eh? You've never truly admitted it. Are you bi? Like I am,' she added quietly, with painful self-revelation.

'I guess so.'

She could detect a certain hesitancy, even though he tried as usual to disguise it.

'I've dabbled in homoerotic delights, as they say,' he went on. 'Let's just say I'm quite open-minded on the subject.'

In the naked intimacy of the bedclothes she pressed on with real curiosity. 'Have you ever been in love? I mean, deeply, truly, madly. Like I am.'

He smiled. 'Only with you, Feely. And I know I don't stand a chance. In fact, I'm so far down the queue it's not worth waiting.'

'Pig!' She reached out, seized his limp prick and gave it a little shake. 'I really ought to ban you forever, you wicked boy! But thanks for letting me get all this off my chest. I don't know what I'd do without you. And you don't even have to queue. You know that all too well, you cocky man. Now come on, time for sleep. I've got a hell of a day tomorrow. Settle down. Mmm... that's nice.'

She turned her back to him, bent her knees, and he fitted himself into her shape. He nestled his stirring penis into the tight cleft of her buttocks, and rocked gently back and forth. It swelled but didn't harden, and they drifted off to sleep.

Some days later, on the set, Stella was foul with everyone, snapping off heads and spoiling takes, until Ally called an early halt. Felicity had a premonition that she was the central target for Stella's displeasure. They had not got together, in their newly intimate sense, since her weekend down at Burnopside and Stella's return from Paris. Stella had asked briefly about her stay at Lord B's mansion, but it was almost as if she didn't want to hear the details, and Felicity wondered just what she'd heard about the place. She was sure that Stella was now jealous of any activity they could not share, just as she was increasingly and dangerously jealous of Felicity's fiance. Her partner of the screen was attempting more and more to take over as her real life partner, and

Felicity was more disturbed by their relationship with each passing day. She would almost welcome a crisis, except that she was not at all confrontational by nature, and would normally go to great lengths to avoid a clash.

Stella was already stripped down to bra and pants in the dressing room. She turned to Felicity as soon as she entered. 'Hurry up and get changed,' she snapped. 'I've ordered a car.' The tone was brutally dictatorial. She said nothing further.

The weather was chilly, and Felicity was wearing substantial cotton knickers, to which she added a prettily embroidered cotton vest, before dragging on her slacks and a thick sweater. She sat and pulled on her black ankle boots and tied the laces. By now Stella was dressed in her smart white raincoat, the belt pulled tightly into her slim waist. She was standing, nostrils flared, by the door.

'Look,' Felicity began hesitantly, 'do you mind telling me—'

'Shut your lying little mouth!'

Felicity stared, then hurried after Stella as she stormed from the room.

The studio car was waiting, the liveried driver holding open the rear door. 'My place,' Stella ordered.

Felicity's stopped on the pavement. 'Look, I've got things to do. I'd better check with Ally. We're not officially—'

'Get in the fucking car!' Stella hissed venomously. 'Unless you want your precious fiance to find out just what you've been up to lately.'

Felicity got in the car.

The uncomfortable silence continued for the duration of the lengthy journey to Stella's riverside pad. Felicity's brain was working rapidly. Obviously, this was about her weekend in the country. It didn't take her long to work out that either Ally, or much more likely, that super turd Ted, had let slip something about her goings on at Burnopside, which was why the woman beside her was figuratively boiling with rage. Felicity experienced her own choking anger at the way the woman obviously felt she owned her. Just because - she winced - they had become lovers. Life was altogether too complicated. Then her stomach lurched as she thought about Stella's threat. Michael must never find out.

Safe at last in the privacy of the long living room, with its row of windows looking out on the river scene, Stella flung off her coat and turned to face Felicity across the yards of luxurious carpeting.

'Well?' she demanded. 'I'm waiting. What's all this about a giant fucking dyke you had the hots over? You cheap little toe rag!'

Felicity was staggered at the fury of the verbal assault, despite being prepared for it. 'I suppose this is Ted and Ally shooting off their big mouths?' she retorted, struggling to keep the guilt from her tones. 'They think everyone who speaks more than a few words to a girl must be trying to get into her knickers.'

'She did more than try, didn't she? Don't bother to lie, you little slut! I phoned his lordship as soon as I got back from Paris. He couldn't wait to congratulate me on the fine job I'd done on you. He practically gave me a blow by blow account of your cavorting with that fucking female Goliath. In fact, to be honest, he sounded so pleased with himself that I wondered whether he hadn't given you a good shagging, too. And I'm still wondering.' Her eyes narrowed.

Felicity, caught off guard by this pronouncement, felt the hot colour sweep up her throat and face.

'You really are a two-timing little whore, aren't you?' Stella resumed, in a voice that registered her own amazement. 'We've only just—'

'Only just what?' Felicity flared up. 'Become lovers? Is that what we are? I don't think so! You wore me down. You seduced me out there, in front of them all. Day by day. We've been to bed together, that's all. Just as you planned all along. You planned it, not me.'

'Oh no! Not sweet innocent little Felicity, Miss Goody Two-Tits! "Oh Stella, please don't stop, don't stop!"' she mimicked cruelly, in imitation of Felicity in extremis of passion. 'You don't cheat on me, sweetheart. *Nobody* cheats on me and gets away with it.'

She advanced menacingly, and Felicity shrank back in alarm. 'Look,' she said breathlessly. 'I'm not going to fight you. I don't fight. I—'

'Tough shit, baby! Then you're going to get the hiding of your life. Something you've had coming a long time, I should think. I just hope that prick of a fiance learns to do the same.'

She caught hold of Felicity by the arms and thrust her down onto the long leather couch. 'Don't you touch me!'

Felicity screamed. 'I'll tell the police. I'm leaving right now, and don't you dare stop me.' She was sobbing. She made to get up but Stella flung her down again. She lay back weeping while Stella, swearing foully, grabbed her right leg and tore at the laces of her boot, dragging it off after some effort. She did the same to its companion, with Felicity lying on the couch and making no attempt to resist.

'Bitch!' cursed Stella. 'Get your kit off right now, unless you want me to pick up that phone and get lover-boy over here right away. I know he's in town, sugar, so don't bother lying.'

'He won't believe you,' Felicity wept. 'He knuh - knows I went to Burnopside. He didn't—'

'I'll tell him all about us, sugar, and I'll make him believe all right. In front of you. We'll see how good you are at lying then. Now make your choice. Right?'

For a few seconds the only sounds were Felicity's anguished weeping. Then, slowly, she stood, pulled the heavy sweater over her head, and unhooked her slacks and shuffled out of them. In vest and knickers, and her thick ankle socks, she stood there, her arms folded across her shoulders, looking like some forlorn school kid in front of her head mistress.

'Over that chair, slag!'

Suddenly another, different atmosphere seemed to fill the room, catching both of them. Felicity gave a little shiver, moved to the leather armchair, stood behind it, then bent over submissively, her long hair falling onto the cushioned seat. She spread her hands to take hold of the leather arms. She felt the clinging material on her midriff, then Stella stepped behind her and swiftly clawed the knickers down to her knees.

'Open your legs.' She kicked at Felicity's ankles. 'Right, bitch,' Stella murmured softly, and Felicity whimpered, her head down, her buttocks dimpling with anticipation of the torment to come.

And torment it was.

These were no love taps. Stella used one of her own shoes, the leather sole bouncing off the resilient curve of flesh with a loud splat, leaving an angry imprint of its narrow shape and a fierce burn that made Felicity yelp in anguish. Instinctively, she tried to spring upright, her legs kicking out against the restricting cling of her knickers. But Stella's left hand, the fingers digging painfully into the nape of Felicity's neck, forced her down over the high chair back. She squirmed and yelped, sobbing, her cries turning to spluttered pleas for mercy.

When Stella paused she was out of breath, and a vivid red glow covered both quivering rounds of Felicity's bottom. The weeping figure didn't attempt to move from her prostrated stance. 'Now, slut, maybe you'll learn. Girl-wise, you're mine, okay? You don't fuck with anyone until I dump you. Right?'

Her left hand continued to hold Felicity down, and her right slipped between those hot buttocks and explored the cleft, and found the moist slit which beat in clamorous welcome to the invading fingers which claimed its narrow sheath. Soon Felicity was stirring once more, showing how much at mercy she was to the sliding fingers driving her to the culmination of the climax which engulfed her.

Chapter Nine

'Lie still, you silly girl,' Magda's deep voice reprimanded. 'Relax. It's worse when you tighten up. It'll be over in five minutes.' She gestured impatiently. 'Joanne, come and hold the other cheek. There!'

The petite, dark-honey blonde figure moved obediently, and with her manicured fingers held the soft flesh of Debbie's left buttock, deep on its inner surface, holding open the cleft while the tattooist pulled back on its twin. Quickly and expertly he completed his assignment, one of the strangest he had known, and added a small letter B to go with the W he had already inscribed on the inner slope of the other cheek. They would be invisible unless anyone should do what Joanne and the artist were presently doing and open the tight divide.

Debbie gave a shaky little laughing sob of relief. She was lying face down on a padded bench, her skirt folded up onto her back, her white micro briefs down just below her bottom.

'There we go, all done,' Magda said lightly. 'Now pull your knickers up. That wasn't so bad, was it?'

Debbie obeyed gratefully, sliding her panties up. She climbed off the bench and shook her skirt down into place.

Magda paid the tattooist, who winked and said, 'Who's the lucky man?'

Magda stared down at him from her lofty height, her wide eyes fluttering. 'What makes you think it's a man, sweety?'

'Now you really are one of us, sweetheart,' Magda smiled, when the three of them were sitting in the rear of Lord Burnopside's car. She turned Debbie's face towards her, and planted a searching kiss on her lips.

Debbie shivered as, at her other side, she felt Joanne's fingers slide up her bare thigh under the thin material of her skirt, until the fingers traced the edge of the narrow silk, then stroked the moist swell of her mound itself. She felt a hot embarrassment at the thought of Reeves, the uniformed driver, watching all this activity through the mirror, but then her mind spun away with the ongoing asses and caresses to her body.

41

Her life had been transformed so completely these past few weeks. It sometimes seemed as though it was all happening to someone else, or happening on some great screen.

She had always seen herself more as the victim of her senses rather than a transgressor. Try telling that to her morally outdated father, though, who had attempted to beat it out of her until she was ready to run away from home. But she was clever, and devious, and so she bided her time and lied convincingly. When she won a place at college she knew it was the road to freedom. Or so she had thought, until she discovered that she had perhaps been right all along; she was a victim.

Her heady liberty was nowhere more reflected than in her sex life. Parties and partners; a long succession of them throughout that first year. She had even considered going on the game, except that it all seemed too cold blooded, and she was anything but that. She might change her companions rapidly, but however briefly each association lasted, and some were scarcely more than a single night, she was passionately involved.

When a girlfriend came up with the information about the escort agency, Debbie felt it was the answer to her wishes. Good pay, as much or little work as she wanted, and all the clients were so well heeled it was unbelievable. Then one night she had entertained a middle-aged banker who introduced her to his cronies, and that had led to Lord Burnopside and a weekend at his fabulous country home. Which led in turn, shatteringly, to the incomparable Magda.

Debbie did not consider herself gay. She had fooled around, aped at playing the fashionable lipstick lezzie role with one of her closest college chums, had even, one drunken night, shared a bed and let the friend fool about literally with her body. She had even enjoyed it, which was why, perhaps, she had shied away from letting it progress further.

But from the first it had been different with Magda. Debbie could not explain it. She had been excited by her long before Magda had made any move towards her. Weeks had passed; weeks during which Debbie found herself spending more and more time in the same exotic company as the commanding figure, in circles so rich and privileged it made her dizzy. When Magda finally initiated the sexual contact between them, Debbie no longer knew whether it was she or the mysteriously alluring woman who had triggered it off.

She revelled in the fem role assigned to her. Magda's powerful physique - the first night, in front of a group of chuckling and cheering male friends and their lovely female partners, she had picked Debbie up easily and carried her up the wide flight of stairs - and her dominant personality, added up to their clearly delineated roles it the relationship.

When she had time to reflect on such matters, Debbie was shocked at her own complicity in it. The tender ministrations, the kisses, exploring tongue and hands claiming every part of her surrendered body, were rapturously received. But then came the other manifestations of their... love? The roughness of passion, the ingenious and shocking array of sex aids which Magda introduced into their love play, such as the series of penetrative devices, from smoothly purring plastic vibrators to veined latex facsimiles of rampant erections, and the strap-on dildos which brought their bodies into writhing, clashing contact.

It was soon after this that there came the most amazing transformation of all- a transformation that still disturbed Debbie deeply when she allowed her mind to dwell on it.

Their activity crossed into the bounds of SM, and Debbie discovered the frightening reality that pain and pleasure could be intrinsically fused as an aspect of love. There had been glimpses of this already, in the more boisterous, light-hearted moments, when Magda would pull the struggling figure over her knee and deliver a few stinging slaps to her behind, and more alarmingly, in those final frenetic cuttings when Magda penetrated her.

It was only at these climactic moments - quite rare moments, fortunately - that Magda gave any sign of being brought to that point of losing the control she could so shatteringly induce in the lovely brown figure delivered up to her. The large form would begin frenzied lunges whose stabbing thrusts translated into pain in the body smothered beneath her, who was drifting back to awareness in a post-orgasmic haze of bliss.

Magda, eyes closed, her lovely face twisted into a grimace of intensity, would grunt and shudder until came that last thrust, the convulsive judder and gasping cry which would herald a climax of some sort, at which she would collapse, a dead weight on the pierced and whimpering frame underneath.

'Why won't you let me make love to you?' Debbie complained one afternoon, having recovered from the ecstasy to which Magda had taken her. 'I mean properly? Why do you never let me go down on you?' Her heart beating unaccountably quickly as she went on, 'I've never seen you naked - I mean, completely naked.' She reached down and touched the tiny leather cache-sexe, with the little embossed silver designs on it, which Magda always wore. The thin strap snaked around her hips, joined at the back in the region of her coccyx where the other strap emerged from between her statuesque buttocks.

She would allow her lover to play with her breasts, and even to lick and suck at the pale pink nipples. The rounds felt, to Debbie's touch, much firmer than her own. But even this privilege was strictly regulated. Soon those large hands would pluck her head away from her bosom, with a throaty laugh of protest and an exaggerated shiver. 'That's enough, sugar. It's too much. I can't bear it.'

Now, Magda listened to Debbie's tender complaint and smiled enigmatically. 'Yours is not to reason why,' she murmured, lifting Debbie's wrist from the region of that embossed leather groin. 'You know I get off just making love to you.'

Debbie pouted prettily. 'You're a spoil sport, you know.'

'There are other ways to prove you love me.' Those magnetic eyes stared, enveloping her in their mystical warmth and closeness. 'To make me happier.'

Debbie felt a familiar weakness, a thrill of both fear and joy. 'I'd do anything for you,' she whispered. 'You know I would.'

Magda stared as though making up her mind on some matter. 'Would you?' she asked softly. Then she got up from the bed and went out of the room. Debbie lay there in the tangled sheets, her heart beating fast. When Magda came back she was wearing her loose Grecian style tunic, and carrying a long box. She took out a pair of handcuffs, whose inner surfaces were lined with a soft spongy material. 'Give me your wrists,' she ordered.

Too astonished to demur, Debbie did as she was bidden, and soon she was manacled. A short silver chain separated the twin bracelets, and to this Magda attached a longer chain. She pulled Debbie to her feet and led her over to the door.

'Whu - what are you going to do?' Debbie asked nervously, as Magda reached up and tossed the chain over the top of the door, securing it to the handle on the other side. Thus, Debbie was pinioned, her front touching the cold wood, her arms raised over her head.

'Teach you what true obedience means, my darling,' Magda breathed softly, moving behind and nestling into her. Her hands played over the shivering brown skin, from neck down to the taut bottom, stroking and hefting the cheeks, which flexed and quivered under her touch. 'We'd better use this for our first lesson, my dear.'

Debbie's eyes widened. She didn't recognise the object at first, then realised it was a gag, with a thick mouthpiece which Magda wedged between her parted teeth. She adjusted the buckles on the leather straps carefully, so that they fitted snugly around Debbie's head.

'We don't want any curious neighbours, do we, Debs?' Debbie was trembling, but she recognised the fierce pulse of excitement within her sex. When Magda produced a black whip, with its short plaited handle and thin rubber strands trailing over her dimpling brown bottom and the backs of her rigid thighs, Debbie was roused by the prospect of such a novel experience.

Until the first hissing, viciously stinging lash fell across her buttocks and hips.

She screamed at the torment, the sound trapped and muffled in her throat. Her behind was on fire, lacerated with a myriad of thin lines of throbbing agony, when Magda stopped some dozen strokes later. The brown body sagged, glistening with the sweat of fear, and she sobbed when Magda tenderly released her and withdrew the choking gag from her stretched and aching mouth. She sagged in those strong arms, which lifted her easily and bore her once more to the bed, where she was laid on her stomach and her wounds bathed, a blessedly cold cream smeared thickly on them.

Later still, when Magda once more made love to her, Debbie thought she had never experienced such consuming joy as her body soared off on its timeless response to those liberating caresses.

Somehow, Debbie found herself accepting her masochistic role, until it became an inseparable part of the relationship. By which time she had met the other girls united in this strange bonding, and knew she was being prepared for initiation into the strange esoteric society of the Whores of Babylon, whose unique doctrines had now taken over her life.

The car took the three girls back through the rich countryside, which was turning in the last old gold and russet hues of autumn, beautiful even on a sombre day such as this. Back in the library of Burnopside Hall a log fire was already blazing cheerfully, and drinks were waiting.

'Let me see,' his lordship commanded eagerly, and Magda nodded proudly. Debbie stepped forward and turned, still with that endearing air of shyness, and bent slightly, presenting her backside to the seated figure, and lifting her skirt to reveal the tiny white knickers beneath. The gnarled hands reached out and slipped the briefs down off her bottom until they hung at the knee. The large thumbs pressed apart her cheeks, and examined the tattoo artist's handiwork. He slapped the resilient rounds firmly before he drew back. 'Excellent. Welcome aboard, my dear.'

Magda chuckled. 'We were wondering whether it might be better to have her done in a different colour. Perhaps something lighter, eh, my little black beauty?'

Debbie flashed her an injured look, but smiled at the burst of laughter which followed the remark.

Up in the capital another bottom was being inspected, but with far less frivolity. Felicity, wearing one of her plain white nightshirts, which was bunched up around her waist, was lying face down over the edge of her bed, while her cousin stared at the enflamed red mass spread over a generous area of both cheeks.

'I can't bear to sit down,' Felicity grunted. Her face looked drawn, her eyes swollen from weeping. 'I can hardly bear to put a pair of knickers on.'

'No hardship, surely?' John quipped, then smothered his grin at the injured look Felicity threw him. Her behind was shiny with the cream she'd been slathering on in an effort to reduce the throbbing soreness.

'Why on earth did you let her do that to you?' he asked, genuinely intrigued. 'Is she really so butch?'

'She's a maniac,' Felicity scowled, wincing as she rolled over and• stiffly levered herself to her feet, allowing the short nightshirt to cover her loins. 'She threatened to spill all the gory beans to Michael. I just had to bend over and let her thrash me. I didn't think it would be this bad, though.' Her troubled gaze fixed on him, the tears close. 'What am I going to do, Johnny?' she appealed hopelessly.

She made two mugs of coffee, then stood while he sat at the small breakfast bar and sipped his.

'Maybe it's time you told Mike everything,' he suggested, with a shrug. 'Get him over and show him your flayed arse. He's bound to sympathise, isn't he?' he added, after a fractional pause.

Now it was her turn to pause. 'I just don't know,' she confessed. 'He can be so straight sometimes. He's been so tetchy about this *Woman's Touch* business all along. I don't know what the hell he'd do if he found out it was for real.'

'Do you really want to marry him, Feely?' he asked, genuinely curious.

She frowned impatiently. 'Of course I do. I love him, dummy!' Then she pulled a face of rueful self-disgust. 'I know. It's crazy, isn't it, when I'm such a libidinous bitch. But he's so different, Johnny. *I'm* so different when I'm with him.'

'Cheers. Thanks a bundle!' He grinned again, then moved in and slid his arms around her.

She pulled away. 'Don't, Johnny. I'm not in the mood.

Anyway, I can't bear the slightest touch on my bum, honestly.'

'You won't have to,' he promised. 'Come on.' As he spoke he slipped his hands on her shoulders, pulling her down towards the tiled floor. He lay under her and slid his hands up inside her nightie, savouring her warm flesh. She was kneeling now, her legs either side of him, and he slid under her until his head was directly under her crotch. He reached up and lightly kissed the puckered folds at the base of her dark pubis. He lapped at the salty tissue. She was leaning forward, gingerly keeping her bottom away from any contact with him.

'Beast...' she groaned, and lowered her belly forward onto that exquisitely melting embrace. Her hips circled, her belly undulated back and forth, her head arched back and her long black hair tossed, brushing across John's arms as he held her slim waist. Feeling her orgasm approaching she reached back, still rotating over his face, and fumbled at the conflux of his thighs. She experienced a sharp dismay at the feel of his prick, already slimy with his copious emission and small and soft. With a hoarse cry she drove her loins forward and ground her wet vulva savagely against his face, smothering him, flooding him with her coming.

Chapter Ten

'Look, things just aren't working out for us at the moment, are they? We haven't spent a night together in ages.' Michael's voice reflected the tension he was under, in spite of the reasonableness of his words. Felicity eyed him in mute dismay across the restaurant table. The bustle of the lunchtime scene gave them a curious anonymity. 'Is there anything wrong?' he asked. 'Between us, I mean. Are you cooling off?'

'Are you?'

'Of course not. You know I'm not. But I never seem to be able to see you. Not alone, anyway. Not properly.' He gestured at the crowded dining room. 'It's not exactly private, is it? And now you tell me you're going to be away for a week. By the time you get back I'll be in Brussels.'

His handsome face took on an almost comic look of childish pique. She felt a swift stab of real anger, mingled with contempt, which was followed immediately by shame. But why was he always so restrained, so nobly decent? She wished briefly that he would blow his top, create a scene. What? her inner voice mocked. Put you over his knee for a damned good spanking? And what a shock he'd get if he did!

The angry redness of her bottom had changed over the intervening days to a rich variety of bruises, a multi-hued tapestry of shades from faint yellow to plum purple. They were the reason why Michael had, literally, seen so little of her. There was no way she could explain them, least of all by telling him the truth.

She wept that evening when she told her cousin about the luncheon date, and the mutually unrequited passion. She peeled off her clothes for a bath, kicking them to the floor as she shed them, then stood, hands on hips, with her back to him, looking at him over her shoulder. She stuck out her bottom. 'How the hell could I explain this to him?' she demanded.

John, who was busy undressing, shrugged. Suddenly he dived across the bed, grabbed her and pulled her on top of him. They rolled naked, wrestling like kids, and she fought on top of him, sitting astride his chest and pinning his wrists on either side of his head. He felt her thighs gripping him, the rasp of her pubes and the soft cushion of her mons rubbing on him.

'At least you still get your nooky,' he panted. 'What about poor old Mikey?'

'He should have ravished me there and then. He should have laid me across the table and shagged me silly!' She was startled herself at the vehemence with which the words escaped. She continued roughly, 'Anyway, shut your mouth, slave! Or put it to its proper use.' She eased herself further up his body, spreading her thighs wider, thrusting her pubic bush under his chin, pressing her dampening slit lasciviously against him. 'Smell me,' she breathed, growing more excited with every passing second.

He could feel her buttocks rocking on his breastbone, and could scarcely breathe for the smothering weight of her pressing against him.

'I'm grotty as hell,' she said. 'I might as well get my rocks off before my bath. Save washing it twice, eh?' But this time, instead of remaining limply pinned underneath her, paying her his unique lip service, he surprised her by heaving upward and flinging her off him. She squealed at the brute force with which he rolled over on top of her, so that now it was she who lay sprawled and captured, her wrists held above her head, her thighs spread by his knees. The dome of his penis jabbed at her belly, bludgeoned its way through her yielding labia and found her wet and eager to receive the stabbing length. He rode furiously, and soon her belly was buffeting against his, her buttocks lifting clear of the floor to meet the frenzy that sped them to the onrushing climax.

'Look, we might as well use this auspicious occasion to make an announcement.' Stella beamed her professional smile at the intense looking figure of the talk-show presenter, Mary Westerman. 'An exclusive for your show, Mary. We're past the watershed, aren't we?' She crossed her legs, generously displayed in the sheer stockings and tight grey skirt which only reached mid-thigh. On their host's other side, Felicity sat in frozen horror as Stella gazed over to her with a look of narrow-eyed passion, and pursed her lips in a clear and intimate kissing gesture. 'Sorry, darling,' she breathed, at her sexiest, 'but I can't keep our little secret any longer. I want the whole world to know.'

She paused. Felicity couldn't breathe. She stared like a mouse in the path of a snake.

'I'm afraid this gorgeous creature and I are more than just screen lovers,' Stella continued. 'You can call this our coming out party, Mary. Felicity and I have been an item since we started filming - months ago. I've never felt like this about anyone in my whole life. Sorry folks.' As she spoke she rose seductively, moved round behind the astonished interviewer and, lifting Felicity's astonished face, firmly planted a lingering kiss on her parted lips. Like talons her painted nails dug deep into the flesh of Felicity's shoulders, carrying their private message of challenge and warning. Felicity remained incapable of movement or protest.

She was gasping, sitting ashen-faced, when Stella at last broke away. A wild burst of cheering and clapping had broken out from the audience. The show, which went out at ten p.m. on Fridays, *Westerman's Week*, was noted for its forthright feminist views and controversial topics. Now that its eponymous presenter had recovered, her sharp features split into a delighted grin. This was a real and welcome bonus. The subject of lesbianism as portrayed on the screen had been given a most unexpected boost, and she shivered with dawning pleasure.

Felicity continued to sit in stunned silence, smiling mechanically and idiotically whenever Mary attempted to bring her into the conversation. Stella handled it superbly, and when Felicity watched the show's transmission a couple of hours later, her grief was intensified by the almost imbecilic portrait of herself she exhibited.

She had made a desperate plea as soon as the studio lights faded. 'You can't let that go out!' she complained, while Mary Westerman stared at her blankly.

Stella was immediately at her side again, the arm this time possessively encircling her waist, while again those secretly pinching fingers exerted their censoring influence. 'Felicity's a little concerned about our going public, aren't you, my love? But I've told her, it's probably harder to try to go on hiding the truth.'

'Of course, you're right,' Mary gushed. 'Listen, I'd like you on again. As soon as we can fix it. This is going to be a very hot issue, take my word for it.'

Her forecast was extremely accurate. Felicity was still too dazed to put up any real fight when Stella led her, their arms linked, out to a waiting taxi and back to the dockside apartment. Their mobiles were bleeping even before they got home. Felicity was imagining Michael, sitting up in his hotel room, gaping at the TV set, unable to believe what he had just heard. That was probably him right now. Which was why she wouldn't answer.

Stella's first call was from Ally. 'My God!' the director sniggered, his camp tones reflecting his awed respect. 'You've certainly put the cat among the fan shit, or whatever! Our noble lords are peeing in their ermine knickers, sweety. You'd better get into the studio first thing. Tell Felicity, darling. I'm sure you two will be snuggling up together tonight, doing whatever it is you deviant dollies get up to for fun!'

'Michael will never speak to me again,' Felicity murmured, too shocked still to cry.

'Nonsense,' Stella contradicted. 'It'll probably put a bit of ginger into him. There's nothing turns a man on so much as the idea that his girl likes a bit of pussy on the side. If not, there's no hope for him, and he's not worth bothering about.'

'Thank you for ruining my life,' Felicity replied bitterly. 'What do you want me for now? Are you going to smack my arse again?'

'Would you like me to?'

At last the tears came. Felicity sobbed, heartbroken. She was too lost, and too much in need of any kind of comfort, to resist Stella's tender advances. The blonde gently undressed her, then shed her own clothes, and soon their bodies were entwined before the rosy glow of the fire, on the soft rug, the thick pile of which Felicity's outstretched fingers were clawing in the excess of sensations exploding through her arched and spread-eagled frame.

The world outside was waiting, however. The studio was buzzing when they dutifully reported at nine 0' clock. One of the first figures they saw was the craggy Lord B. He wagged his finger at them. 'You naughty pair,' he growled. 'You've set the whole place alight, you brazen hussies!' It was evident that he was far from displeased, and Felicity soon realised why, for every newspaper, broadsheet and tabloid, as well as most magazines, from the kind that featured centrefolds where it was possible to take a pubic hair count to those that concentrated on knitting patterns, carried stories about the latest duo.

'We couldn't have had better publicity if we'd tried - and we did,' his lordship chortled. 'You've guaranteed that every adult, male and female, with the faintest spark of pulse left, will be riveted to the screen next month. Well done.'

Felicity discovered there was no way she could retract from this declaration of her lesbianism. In the restrained luxury of the executive suite, she tried in private to explain her dilemma. Lord B listened sympathetically. 'I didn't wuh - want it to huh - happen,' she stammered, unable to stem the tears. 'And certainly not for the whole world to knuh - know about it. I could die!'

By this time his lordship's sympathy had become more tactile, and she was sitting on his knee, cradled in his arms and trying to ignore the substantial lump she could feel pressing into her thigh. 'It's my fiance,' she wept. 'He - he won't understand. He'll nuh - never...'

'There, my dear creature, don't take on so. We'll think of something.' He offered her his spotless handkerchief, and she dabbed and blew obediently. 'But as to making a public denial, I'm afraid that wouldn't do at all. No, it's gone too far. Besides,' he went on gently, crooking his finger under her chin and lifting her tragic young face to meet his gaze, 'that wouldn't be true, would it? You are Stella's lover, aren't you?' Felicity hung her head and remained silent. 'Not to mention your little dilly-dallying with the redoubtable Magda,' he added, to her intense chagrin. 'Perhaps your young man should show a little tolerance for your catholic tastes, eh? Perhaps we could have him down to the Hall some weekend for a few lessons in broadmindedness. That would be a good place to begin, wouldn't you say?'

Felicity tried to imagine Michael's reaction to such an enterprise, and shook her head hopelessly.

'You're a star now,' his lordship resumed. 'Famous all over the world. You'll have to get used to it. And so will he, if he wants to keep you.'

She gave a sudden gasp. While he'd been talking and comforting her, his lordship's hand had crept beneath her jumper and thin cotton crop top, and located her left breast, which it was exploring and playing with in a manner which stirred new feelings in her troubled mind; feelings which were proving a growing distraction. He pulled at the tight clothing until her breast, with its budding nipple erect, poked out from beneath the displaced garments, allowing him to dip his head and caress it with his lapping tongue. She felt the tickling scrape of his moustache on her sensitive flesh.

'Someone might come, my lord,' she gasped, her fingers twining in his silvery locks and holding him firmly to her bosom. She blushed at his deep chuckle, and her unintentional ambiguity.

'Not yet, surely?' he said, his voice muffled in her perfumed cleavage. 'Don't worry, my dear, we won't be disturbed.' His hand left her breast, and he was now dealing with the button and the zip fastener of her jeans, with such success that they quickly gaped open and the white triangle of her cotton briefs showed. His thick fingers negotiated their elasticated waist and delved from above. They teased at the curls of her pubic hair, then slipped lower, to the damp and yielding softness of her mound and the pout of the divide, which was throbbing with arousal. She squirmed, and suddenly she slid off his knee as he rose, dragging his hand with some difficulty from its nest within her underwear.

He gathered her under her arms and lifted her onto the splendid polished surface of the long conference table, and she lay• back among the tooled leather pads and the blotting paper squares, her legs dangling over the table's edge, the hard wood cold on her bruised bottom. Which was soon on view as he eagerly manipulated her tight jeans and cotton knickers down off her hips until they clung in an undignified manner around her knees.

'A lovers' tiff?' he chuckled. 'Never mind, I'm delighted. Whoever was responsible, I'm glad to know that you understand discipline.'

The craggy head dipped and his hands pushed her top up from her flat stomach. The tip of his tongue dipped into the shallow little recess of her navel, trailed across the quivering skin, over the tufted rise of her pubic mound to the now distinctly moist divide beneath, and her tangled legs kicked helplessly. His fingers delicately parted her labia to give him access to the glistening inner folds, their slipperiness betokened the height of her arousal.

There was an agonising pause while Lord Burnopside wrestled with her recalcitrant ankle boots. She lay with one arm crooked over her eyes, shivering and whimpering with desire, and eventually he managed to tug them free. Impatiently, he wrenched jeans and knickers together off her feet, which he left encased in the thick brown woollen socks. At last she could raise her knees and spread herself wide, opening to his devouring mouth, his hands pushing at her thighs, the noise of his lapping loud over her ragged sighs. Her belly began to lift and her bottom bunch in rhythmic urgency.

His fingers played along with his working lips at her running flesh, sought out her beating clitoris, and she was soon crying frenziedly, about to come, pulling at his silver hair and begging for release. For an instant she felt an overwhelming despair as he left her, but only to straighten and to claw his rampant prick from its tight concealment. It jutted, red and engorged, eager for fulfilment. He seized her feet, tucked her legs under his arms and, pulling her to the very edge of the table, drove deep into her pulsing sheath.

Felicity started to come before his rigid manhood had bored fully home.

Chapter Eleven

'Where the hell is she? What on earth are you doing here?'

John could tell at once that Michael had been drinking, from his dishevelled appearance and his slurred speech. It was also indicative of his emotion that he should speak in such an abrupt manner, so divorced from his characteristic friendliness. He looked careworn, his eyes reflecting his disturbed state.

'You'd better come in,' John said, stepping aside. The taller figure entered and stared around at the familiar setting of Felicity's flat. 'Can I get you anything?' John asked pointedly. 'Coffee?'

Michael slumped in the' nearest armchair. John felt a deep sympathy for his obvious confusion and distress. Again, he was struck by the contrast between the seated wreck and his usual suave appearance and polished behaviour. He repeated his question, and Michael blinked up at him.

'Eh?' the drunk mumbled. 'Oh, coffee, please. Black.' He stood, wobbled through to the bedroom, stared at the unmade bed and the untidiness of the scattered clothes and shoes. He weaved over to the dressing table and picked up a pair of Felicity's satin briefs, held them against his face, feeling their cool caress, breathing in their fragrance, and then dropped them hastily, blushing in embarrassment. John was watching him from the doorway.

'She asked me to flat-sit the place for a bit,' John explained.

'Where is she? Tell me. Please!' John recognised the desperation in the deep voice. 'I've been ringing for days. I've rung the studio... everywhere. Can't get in touch with her. You must know where she is. You're so close to her.'

John answered gently, 'I honestly don't know, Mike.

She wouldn't say. She'll be back soon, I'm sure. As soon as she shows up I'll tell her.'

Michael sat down on the bed, elbows on knees, his head in his hands. He groaned. 'She's told you about our row? It was terrible. But honestly - it was all such a shock. Those awful things in all the papers. On the bloody telly morning noon and night. I just couldn't take it. And since then I just haven't been able to get near. She won't even talk to me.' He glanced up at John, his gaze pleading. 'Is it really true? Margot - a lot of people - are saying it's all just a publicity stunt. To promote that sodding film. I can't believe she would...'

John looked down at him with a mixture of pity and contempt. 'Would it matter if she did?' he said. 'She's still your lover, isn't she? I guess it doesn't alter how she feels about you, even if she has got the hots for Stella Priest. Anyway, maybe it's just a one off thing. Maybe it'll wear off now they've finished working together.'

Michael stared up at him in horror. 'But... how can she? She can't love me and... and...' He shook his head hopelessly, and John felt a sudden stab of impatience with his squareness. He had a strong urge to tell him the truth: Your beloved likes to fuck around with a good number, ducky, including yours truly, a six foot dyke, and a white-haired peer of the realm. But he couldn't be that cruel. He suddenly realised that poor old Mikey would never be a good match for his mercurial cousin, and he felt even more sorry for him. The poor sod was way out of his depth.

'Let's have something a bit stronger,' he suggested. 'You're well pissed now. You can kip here if you like. She might ring later.'

This last argument was the clincher, and Michael morosely agreed. They went through and sat in the cosily lit sitting room with a whisky bottle between them.

Michael lost on all counts, John thought compassionately, for he couldn't even hold his liquor too well, though, to be fair, he must have had quite a skin-full before he arrived. Soon his dark blond head was nodding as though too heavy for his neck muscles, his eyes blinking slowly and deliberately, and his speech even more disconnected and rambling than it had been earlier.

'I just can't... I love her, John. You know that?' His face was red and slack. He frowned, trying to concentrate, then smiled. 'You know - you're really like her, John. You two - you're a helluva lot alike. Twins, almost.' He shook his head, which sagged even lower.

'Come on, old son,' John said. 'I reckon we'd better get you to bed. Sleep it off and hope you feel better in the morning.' He tugged at Michael's arm, persuading him to stand. Michael almost collapsed against the slighter figure, who just managed to steady him. Arm in arm they made staggering progress through to the bedroom. The bed crashed as Michael fell headlong upon it. He buried his face deep in a pillow and breathed heavily, inhaling the faint trace of her perfume.

'Oh God!' he moaned, fighting to choke back the tears. 'I love her, John. I love her.'

'Yes, of course you do. Now come on. Help me, for Christ's sake!' John pulled and tugged, succeeded in getting the jacket off, and then the tie and shirt. The shoes and socks were easy. though the long limbs were a dead weight. Then came the problem of the trousers.

Michael giggled helplessly. 'You're undressing me,' he muttered into the soft pillow.

'Trying,' John gasped, struggling to roll the heavy weight over. He undid Michael's trousers and, by dint of some serious tugging and pulling, he fought them down off hips and flanks, and finally succeeded in drawing them off the sturdy legs. A fetching pair of briefs was the sole garment remaining. John stared down at the tempting swell of the tight genitals hidden snugly beneath the taut white cotton. Michael was floundering, like an inexpert swimmer under water, as John drew the sheets down and helped him to negotiate the bedclothes.

'You're all right, John,' Michael murmured, eyes already closed. 'Good chap. You look like her, you know. Helluva lot.'

51

'Goodnight,' John said, and then went back into the living room. He sat and poured another measure of whisky. He was feeling a little pissed himself, he acknowledged with a wry smile. He stared at the comfortable settee on which he was stretched. Here was a turn up for the books, all right. He and Mikey kipping in Feely's flat, both of them horny as hell for her, and she nowhere to be seen. One thing was for sure, he reasoned, the smile broadening, she wouldn't be feeling as frustrated as they were right now. She was down in the country, safely hidden at Burnopside Hall, where there was plenty to distract her. That six foot wonder woman, as well as a host of other delectable girlies, and, if that palled, there was always the randy old dandy himself, or one of his aristocratic chums.

As he drank his way further down the bottle a wicked thought crept into his mind, and stayed buzzing with increasing irritation, like a fly trapped in a bottle. He recalled the feel and the smell of Mikey's helpless body, the vulnerability of that toned frame as he pulled it back and forth, and its clean-cut manliness. Soon his prick was erect, pushing up against the restriction of his clothing with maddening insistence.

Another glass of whisky and a few minutes later, he made his mind up.

Michael's snores filled• the darkened bedroom. His exciting aroma overlaid the subtle traces of the feminine scent of its usual occupant. Tingling in every nerve, John silently stripped and slipped naked into the bed. He fitted himself to the warm back next to him and slipped his hands under the inert anus, his fingers stroking the tiny nipples and pectoral swells they found. Very slowly and carefully he let his hand slide down over the smooth stomach. He encountered the broad elastic band of the underpants, and slid his fingers delicately beneath it. Below the coils of pubic hair the waiting penis was thick, warm and satin smooth. He felt the thick rim of the foreskin shrouding the helm, and felt the length quiver and stir into life.

Michael whimpered and stirred in John's anus, their legs spooned together. 'What? Who... what?' The drugged voice drifted up through the layers of sleep.

John clung to him. His hand, in the tight nest of the briefs, massaged firmly, skilfully, and he felt the prick stiffen and elongate mightily until it strained against its confines and stretched his fist. Michael gave a startled gasp, consciousness slowly returning.

'There,' whispered John, his lips touching the earlobe.

He planted small kisses on the smoothness of the neck, where it met the shoulder, and he felt the form against him give a responsive shudder. 'There there, Mikey,' he whispered again. 'I've got you, baby. Just relax.' There was another quiver of the warm body, then came the sound of muffled weeping. The tense muscles gave way and the crying increased, while, unseen in the dark, John's hand worked its rhythmical magic of release.

John could feel the body twisting, the buttocks flexing, the movements mirroring the helpless little groans and whimpers. John's hand-strokes grew faster and more deliberate, stretching the dampening material. The elastic waistband slid down and the rigid penis thrust above it, rearing in its newfound freedom. The briefs were now tight around the hairy balls. John knew what was coming, and wasn't surprised when the frame to which he clung shuddered convulsively. There was a muffled cry and he felt the violent surge as Michael's come jetted thickly between his fingers and onto the sheets.

Felicity wondered if she were dreaming. She had wanted to escape, to flee from the intolerable pressures that had been brought to bear on her; the nightmare that meant she couldn't go home without running the gauntlet of a horde of voracious reporters. They loitered permanently outside with cameras trained on every window, so that she had to keep the curtains drawn and lived in a twilight or electric world. And on top of all that her own private life was shattered, smashed to fragments, thanks to that golden-haired beautiful bitch who'd seduced her. The row with Michael had been closely followed by another, with the chief author of her misery.

'You can fuck off!' she had screamed, harpy-like, mascara streaming. 'It doesn't matter any more! You've succeeded, you bitch! He's dumped me, just like you wanted. Except that you've lost me, too. I'll never go with you again!'

Her satisfaction at delivering this verbal broadside was short-lived. 'You need cooling off, kiddo!' Stella had replied, and the next thing Felicity knew her hair was seized in a vice-like grip, and she was dragged across the room to the toilet, where her captive head was forced painfully down the bowl and the cistern flushed on her, drowning out her screams of protest. She came up blinded and spluttering, her hair plastered over eyes and face, which seriously hampered her in the attack which followed. She did her best to defend herself and even strike some blows of her own. But as she had always known, she was no fighter, and within minutes she was lying on the floor of the dressing room, her shirt in shreds and her vest a tattered strip around her neck. Stella was well on the way to stripping her altogether, in spite of the skintight jeans, when a posse burst in on them and saved Felicity from further degradation, not to say physical harm.

That very evening a solution had been found, and Felicity was whisked away by car to Burnopside Hall, and an existence which seemed even more fantastic than any her vivid imagination could ever have conjured up.

Within the fine old building and its beautiful grounds she was totally insulated from all the pressures which had turned her life upside down. She marvelled at his lordship's ability to keep the media away from her, at a time when everyone at home and abroad wanted to talk to the two stars of *A Woman's Touch*.

'The only thing is,' Lord B told her reasonably, stroking her hand securely held in his, 'you'll have to go along with the publicity when the first episode goes out in two weeks. You and Stella will have to appear like bed and bosom chums for a wee while. But I'm sure you can manage that. You're both splendid actresses, and I'll make sure she doesn't lay a finger on you in private. In anger or in amorality, eh? We'll set Magda on her if she does.'

It was that strikingly tall figure which was largely responsible for the sense of surrealism which pervaded so much of Felicity's stay at the Hall. As soon as Felicity appeared in the drawing room Magda came to her, arms outstretched, and gathered her in to her wonderful bosom, then planted a kiss on her uplifted mouth of such tender yet rousing passion that Felicity sagged giddily in her arms. And in front of a whole room full of people, too, who applauded the embrace.

'Come and get settled in,' Magda said possessively, refusing to surrender her hold. 'I'll show you your room. We can chat while you have a bath.'

Once upstairs Felicity suddenly felt awkward and shy, but Magda's ease of manner soon had her relaxed again. The large yet beautiful hands plucked at Felicity's clothing as Magda chatted easily, and Felicity was quickly naked and being guided to the foaming tub. Moments later she was trembling all over with desire as those capable hands soaped and sponged her, covering every inch of her flesh as she stood obediently like a child with its nurse. She climbed out into the warm waiting towel, which engulfed her. The sweet torture continued as the hands patted her dry, caressing her intimate curves until she was gnawing at her bottom lip, trying to suppress her need.

'Have you missed me, baby?' the deep voice crooned, seeming to pass down to the very pit of her stomach as she was edged back onto the bed. And she wept for joy when the strong arms parted her thighs and the dark curtain of hair cloaked over her midriff as that head dipped to slake the drumming passions so tempestuously stirred.

The magic never left in the days that followed. At first she was puzzled to discover that the band of lovely girls appeared to be permanent residents at the Hall. Doubts assailed her. Were they simply the most expensive of hookers, employed solely by the wealthy Lord B for his private pleasure and that of his privileged chums? And yet there was something different about them, about their whole bearing and attitude. They were all so unfailingly nice; to her, to each other, to everyone. And above all they each seemed to acknowledge Magda as their leader - their spiritual guide.

At first she could not stifle the inner stab of jealousy at the level of intimacy they all shared with the tall figure. Yet there was no reciprocal resentment at the clear indications that Felicity and Magda were lovers; at the glorious height of a new and passionate attachment. She was accepted. The girls made every effort to make her feel welcome. Yet she was disturbed by a feeling she could not shake that, despite their friendliness and Magda's physical attraction to her, she remained outside their charmed circle.

They were a very tactile bunch, and totally uninhibited when they were on their own, when there were no visitors to the Hall. They would embrace like lovers, would often recline together in the deep armchairs or on the long sofas with limbs entwined and mouths regularly bestowing kisses upon lips or any other available parts of the anatomy. Though Magda did not indulge in such lingering and lavish displays of affection, she would often embrace them upon greeting or parting, and Felicity could not help speculating that her newest lover had shared passions with them as intense as those she now brought to her.

The lovely coloured girl, Debbie, who'd been John's partner for most of the night when they last visited Burnopside, especially intrigued Felicity.

'You look so like him,' Debbie marvelled, when they were out walking on the wooded slopes above the mansion one grey day. Felicity had jumped at the chance to be on her own with Debbie, for she felt she might learn a little more about the strange nuances which bound this odd little group together under the auspices of his lordship. Debbie was the latest member of this close-knit group, but in spite of her ready friendliness, it soon became evident that she, too, was not prepared to divulge anything concrete.

Felicity was forced to bluntness. 'What is it about you lot?' she asked. 'I don't get it. Are you some kind of escort girls? Does Lord B pay you for your services?'

Debbie giggled. 'We're his sex slaves, darling. Haven't you twigged that yet?' Her tone indicated that she was far from being serious. But she soon found another more effective way to deflect Felicity's curiosity.

'You know,' she declared, 'you're so like Johnny, you've got me sticky as hell. I can't keep my hands off you any longer. Come on, there's a sort of tower thing up here on top of the hill. It's a folly.'

Minutes later they were inside the narrow circular building. Felicity shivered. 'It's too cold—' but Debbie's sweet mouth smothered any further protest. When they broke from the kiss she plucked off Felicity's thick jacket, backed her up against the damp and crumbling wall, and then tugged determinedly at the belt around Felicity's slacks. Soon she was naked from waist to knees, where her slacks and knickers were bunched around the tops of her boots.

'That'll do me, cocker!' the coloured girl grinned, as her cold hand slid between Felicity's welcoming, opening thighs.

The fingers teased delicately around the outer surfaces of the rapidly moistening folds, which soon parted to allow an exploration of their glistening inner slopes. The enflamed trigger of Felicity's clitoris throbbed with sweet torment at the caresses that stirred it, before two fingers worked their way into her tight vagina and began to thrust more vigorously back and forth. Far from resisting the invasion, Felicity reached down, captured the brown wrist and urged it to even deeper penetration, her booted feet scraping the dusty floor, her knees stretching the clinging bonds of knickers and trousers as she soared towards the dizzying climax her loving assailant brought to her.

Chapter Twelve

Daylight knifed its way through Michael's screwed up eyes into his throbbing head. His fuzzy awakening view of the world suddenly swam into clear focus. Slowly he realised he was in Felicity's bedroom. Then his jaw dropped at the vision of the slim, smiling, naked figure standing by the window.

'Here,' it said, 'I've brought you a cup of coffee. Are you feeling dreadful? You must be.' John came so close that Michael found himself staring from inches at the neat penis and compact scrotum, the smoothness of the belly and slender thighs. Words failed him as John put the mug of coffee on the bedside table, then moved around to the other side of the bed. He climbed in, the mattress dipping as he did so. Michael felt a foot scrape lightly across his leg.

Oh God! This was some kind of sick nightmare! Surely he couldn't be awake. Not naked in Felicity's bed - with her cousin. Fragments of memory began to swim back. His lonely drunken evening... then sitting opposite John... the whisky bottle... his swimming drunkenness. Then - his mind tried to shy away from the crowding, tormenting thoughts - the touch of hands, pulling him this way and that, dragging off his clothes. The feel of a slim body nestled against him... and then those hands again...

His muscles bunched to propel him out of the bed, when suddenly another realisation struck him, stopping him from movement. He was naked, too. Completely naked. But surely he'd been wearing underpants? His horrified gaze identified the crumpled garment on the rug by the side of the bed. A vivid memory of Felicity's knickers lying in just such a position, tinged with the evidence of her excitement and their love, assailed his mind.

As though tuning in to his mental anguish, John stirred and moved even closer, so that his warm thigh and leg rested against Michael's limb. He was sitting up on the pillows, above Michael, and he slipped his arm with casual possession over the broader shoulders at his side. 'Come on, drink up while it's hot,' he said. 'It'll do you good.'

At last Michael was galvanised into action. Wildly, he flung aside the blankets and leapt out of bed, while John swore as the coffee he was holding slopped onto the sheet.

'Jesus! What's going on here?' Michael cried, his eyes bulging. He was standing hunched, his hands cupped over his genitals. He bent and grabbed at his underpants, felt the crusting semen, smelt its unmistakable odour, and dropped them again with disgust. His hands flew back to hide his shrivelled prick.

'What did you do to me?' His voice rose in his agitation and disbelief.

John laughed mischievously. 'Why? What's wrong? Are you sore?'

'What?' Michael glanced down at his crossed hands, then up again at John, his face reflecting his terror. 'What do you mean? You bastard!' Suddenly his stomach gave a great heave of revulsion and he staggered desperately, doubled up, for the bathroom, where he dropped to his knees over the lavatory and retched dryly for some minutes.

With a deep moan he slumped and folded his arms on the plastic seat, lowered his head onto them, and began to sob.

A spasm of disgust flickered over John's features as he swung out of bed and followed him to the bathroom. So much for macho man, he thought, unable to suppress his mean satisfaction at the crumpled image of masculinity crouched on the floor in front of him. Then the beauty of the naked figure registered, and he felt his penis stir and throb again. He bent, put his hands under those heaving shoulders, and drew him gently to his feet. Michael's chin was on his chest as he cried softly, unable to look at him.

John knew at once there would be no resistance, no violent attempt to prove or defend his heterosexuality. With an arm around the shoulders, he steered him back to the bedroom. Michael moved as in a dream, still weeping like a boy.

'There's nothing wrong, Mikey baby,' John crooned, his own excitement flaring, his prick rising and stiffening. 'Nothing to be ashamed of. It was good, wasn't it? Don't tell me you don't remember. Don't fool yourself. It can be good - you know it can.'

As he spoke, he eased Michael down upon the bed again, and let their bodies touch. He lay on top of him, their bellies and thighs pressing together. He felt his prick heaving against Michael's warm body, felt the responsive quiver in the penis that lay beneath his own; its swelling arousal, their mutual warmth.

Slowly, he let his face approach the red visage under his, saw the sparkle of tears on the cheeks and glistening in the fair eyelashes, saw the wild fear in the eyes, before his lips closed on the warm mouth. Michael's throat worked and his Adam's apple bobbed violently, but John's fingers dug into his hollowed cheeks and held his mouth imprisoned to the kiss until he felt the stiff resistance ebb from the body beneath him, and heard the choking gasp of surrender.

John's hand dipped down between their bellies, found the swollen column it sought, and jerked vigorously. A huge sob shook Michael's ribcage and sent his chest heaving upward. A spasm wracked the supine frame and his legs twitched reflexively at John's knowing strokes. John's head dipped and his feather-light tongue flicked at the hard nipples.

Then on, over the slight dip covered by a fine swirl of hair, down over the quivering stomach, past the recessed navel, to the thick bush and the stiff penis, the helm gleaming purple and fully emergent from his fist. A drop of fluid shimmered at the tiny slit, and John lapped at it.

Michael was moaning softly, his head rolling tormentedly from side to side, his hips and belly lifting in helpless response to John's stimulation. The prick was beating mightily in John's grip now, the head more swollen than ever. He licked at it, teasing the flanged rim where it met the long shaft, until Michael tossed and whimpered. Straining his jaws, John slid his lips over the shining helmet and sucked deeply, taking as much of the throbbing penis as he could into his working mouth. He gagged, fought for air through his nostrils, then released the captive flesh. He relaxed his hold on the rigid column, pushed it back against the pubis and belly, lapped greedily at the ball bag, then up the root of the shaft, back to that engorged head.

Michael began to kick, his feet scissoring just like Felicity's in the throes of orgasm, and his creamy seed erupted with such pent up force that it splattered onto his chest and into the recess of his palpitating navel, hanging in pearly gobs among the dark curls of his pubis. Some of it spilled onto John's chin, and he dipped his head rapturously to lap at the residue that still oozed thickly from the softening cock.

'You gorgeous fucking man!' he breathed, and buried his face in all that sweet and cloying softness.

'What is it?' Debbie's voice trembled with her nervousness. It was the first time she'd been back in this secret room since the ceremony of her initiation. This time, as far as she knew, only she and Magda were present. She was startled to find the tall figure clothed in her robe of office, her splendid figure hidden by the long scarlet robe. Again, the pool of brilliant light fell on that marble circle and the outer edges of the strange room were in deep shadow. 'I'm sorry,' she faltered, her heart racing. 'What have I done?'

'You went out with Felicity this morning, didn't you? Where did you go?'

'For a walk. That's all. I didn't tell her anything. Not a thing. Honestly.'

'Where did you go?'

'Just up through the wood.' She hesitated fractionally. 'I took her to the folly.'

'And what did you do there?'

'We talked.' Debbie felt her face growing warm. 'I - I gave her a bit of a cuddle. And...'

'Is that all? Tell me.'

'I didn't know - we fooled around. I mean - I made love. I just fingered her, you know? She wanted it. She's lovely. I'm sorry, Magda. I didn't know we weren't supposed to. I mean, we all do it, don't we? The rest of us...' her voice faded.

'But Felicity isn't one of us,' Magda said softly. 'She's not a daughter. You had no right to touch her. Not without my permission. And you didn't have that, did you?'

'No. But I didn't know... I'm sorry.' Debbie's tone betrayed her fear. 'I won't do it again,' she added, in a chastened voice.

Magda smiled. 'No, you won't do it again, my black beauty. But you have to be punished. Don't you?'

The dark eyes widened in alarm. Debbie swallowed, and then nodded.

'Right,' Magda continued abruptly. 'Undress.'

Debbie was wearing clothing suitable for the cold weather. She removed the thick sweater and the camisole top beneath, exposing her pointed breasts, then unhooked the skirt and stepped out of it. She wore panties of pristine white. The rich dark tones of her upper body stood out in delightful contrast. There was a narrow band of brown thigh, then the thick ribbed woollen stockings and narrow pointed ankle boots. A few more seconds and all these garments joined the others on the floor. Naked, Debbie stood and shivered, her hands clenched at her sides.

'Lie down. On the star.'

Debbie gasped at the icy bite of the marble. Gingerly she stretched out, face down, and spread her arms and legs out wide, following the black points. She heard Magda move, heard the swish as the heavy cloak was flung back to give her freer access• to wield the instrument of punishment. It was the three-stranded whip. Debbie shivered anew as its thin tails trailed over her flexing behind, and tickled the backs of her thighs.

'Keep still,' Magda warned, 'or it will hurt far more.' The soft whistle was followed by a stinging line of fire right across the centre of Debbie's bottom. It burnt so fiercely that, for all her determination, she was unable to obey her mistress's dictate, and squirmed, sobbing, before she could bring herself to lie still again and spread herself as before. The whip stung again, and every muscle locked in an effort to keep her from threshing around, with a little more success this time, despite the fiery pain. She bit down on her lip until she tasted blood, trying to smother the cry threatening to burst forth.

Three more times the whip whistled and struck, until her behind was aflame with a torment that forced her to move. Her flanks jerked, her knees and feet banged against the marble in her involuntary squirming, and the sobbing became audible. Her hands reached out behind her, moved to touch the throbbing rounds, and snatched away again, for the slightest contact sent darts of fresh pain through her.

She lay there, her body shaken with her weeping, blind in her ordeal, until Magda's voice penetrated her misery. She was aware of the feet planted firmly apart near her head, and the voice coming from the heights above her. 'You've forgotten to thank me,' it said.

'Thuh - thank you,' Debbie stammered at once. The tears flowed, soaking her cheeks, then she gasped as she felt a sudden iciness touch her throbbing bottom. Magda was bending, spraying on a freezing substance that took away the throbbing burn immediately. Then those gentle hands were turning her, and she lay, her eyes filled with tears, and saw the hazy shape hovering over her like some winged angel. The robe was open, its edges held wide around that splendidly sculpted nakedness, which she could not see properly, did not have time to see, before it descended to cover her own eager frame.

Debbie's head swam, and with tears now of transported joy her former suffering was forgotten. Her whole being and body was alive with need. In an instant she relived the magical conjunction at her initiation, the dreamlike splendour of it, which afterwards had seemed too strangely wonderful to be true. She had thought she'd been drugged somehow; could not have experienced what her body had fantasised. But now it was happening again, that miraculous lovemaking which, her giddy mind told her, could not take place. She felt fingers moving, opening her centre once more, as before, then the penetration, not of those fingers, but of another, fabulous, more solid piece of flesh. It was an impossible amalgam of sexes as that gloriously beautiful body covered hers, and thrust onto and into her with shattering dominion.

'Where's Debbie?' Felicity asked after breakfast the following day.

Magda smiled. 'I think she's having a day in bed, sugar.

Not feeling well. Time of the month, eh?'

'Oh, I'll pop up and see her. Sit with her a while. I know how miserable it can be if it's rough.'

'I don't think so, lover.' Felicity stared in amazement at Magda's words. 'Why?' the deep voice went on, mockingly. 'You can bear to be without her for one day, surely? Let the poor girl have some rest. She won't be much use to you anyway.'

Felicity's face flooded with colour. 'I - what on earth do you mean?' she flustered, aware of the guilt stamped on her features.

'I know what you two were up to yesterday,' Magda answered levelly. 'I think we'd better have a little talk.' She opened the door and courteously ushered Felicity out before her. Firmly gripping her above the left elbow, she steered her up the wide staircase and along the landing. She closed the door of Felicity's room behind them, and nodded towards the bed. 'Sit down,' she said pleasantly, and Felicity obeyed.

'You're a promiscuous little slag, aren't you?' Magda continued, in the same light tone.

Felicity blushed deeply, and her eyes instantly blurred with tears. She opened her mouth to speak, then closed it again. She could think of no defence against the accusation. 'I'm sorry,' she eventually muttered. 'I just thought everyone here seems so free... with everyone else.' She paused. 'It wasn't my idea.' She felt more and more like a sulky schoolgirl. 'It was Debbie who suggested going up to the folly. Debbie who - did everything. I didn't—'

'And you put up a terrific fight, eh?' Magda interrupted dryly. 'It was all very much against your will. A case of rapine, was it?'

Felicity shrugged miserably. 'No, not exactly,' she murmured, head down. 'I didn't think you'd mind. You all seem like I said... so close.'

'We are, my dear. We're very close. Which is why nothing happens around here - to the girls, that is - without my say-so. Didn't you realise that?'

Felicity shrugged uncomfortably. She was beginning to wonder if Debbie's absence today had anything to do with yesterday's incident, and she felt a tiny pulse of both fear and excitement begin to beat deep within.

'I asked you a question,' Magda prompted gently, and again Felicity felt reduced to the status of a naughty child.

'I didn't know I had to have your permission,' Felicity replied, with a hint of defiance she didn't really feel.

'You're my girl,' Magda said strongly. Again, Felicity felt an inward shiver of delight at the dominance in that phrase. 'At least while you're here. And so is Debbie. You don't do anything without my permission.'

Felicity gasped at the bold directness of the statement.

She stared up at the tall figure standing over her, but said nothing.

'I think we need a little lesson,' the deep tones went on. 'Lie down on your tum. It's all right; you can leave your boots on.'

Part of her shocked at her own compliance, Felicity found herself obediently stretching out on the bed. 'What are you going to do?' she asked breathlessly. 'You're not going to beat me too?' Her voice carried a trace of bitterness.

Magda chuckled. 'Just a little, baby. We've got to teach you obedience.'

Felicity was too amazed to put up any real resistance when she felt her arms captured, and a pair of cuffs slipped over her wrists. They were softly padded on their inner surface, and linked by a short chain that Magda padlocked to the bed frame behind the pillow. She began, tardily, to twist a little in protest as Magda plucked up her short jumper and unfastened the waistband of her jeans. She hauled them down off her hips, then rolled the tiny black briefs down off her bottom.

A large hand explored the dimpling cheeks, caressing, stroking, the fingers delving into the tightness of the cleft until Felicity was writhing once more, though not with any thought of escape. Magda leaned close, her lips touching behind Felicity's ear. 'Love taps, my darling,' she crooned. 'Be a good girl and show me how brave you are.'

The bed rocked slightly as she stood up. Felicity's bottom clenched and she began to whimper. 'Don't hurt me,' she pleaded feebly. 'I can't stand it.'

The first blow landed with a loud splat. It stung, and she yelped, stiffening instinctively. The second blow fell almost immediately. The instrument was a slipper, the pliant sole raising blotchy outlines on the quivering rounds until they were soon a rosy red. Though Felicity flinched at each burning slap, she remained otherwise still, her loins thrusting into the yielding mattress, her face buried in the pillow to smother her cries.

The pain burned steadily, and she knew it was over. Strangely, the tears flowed more freely then, her sobs growing more tempestuous. To her surprise, and dismay, she heard the door open and close, and she lay alone in the bright room, weeping, arms pinioned above her head, her behind throbbing painfully.

Chapter Thirteen

'Where the hell have you been?' Stella hissed, keeping her voice low so that the crowds bustling round them would not hear. 'People have been looking everywhere for you.'

It was the first time the two had met since their disastrous clash two weeks ago. Lord B had been right when he'd said they would need their skill as actresses when they were next exposed to the public gaze. The strain of appearing not only bosom friends but lovers was already, after only minutes, beginning to tell. What made it worse was that they were doing an interview and some intimate photo shots for *Liberelle*, a recently released women's magazine which no one was sure how to pronounce but which most people, and all with-it females under forty-five, had heard of.

They were using one of the interior sets at the studio, one that figured famously in the screen epic and was most appropriate to the tone of the article; the bedroom shared by Kathy Weldon and Stella Mann. Several other agencies had been brought in on the pic shoot, though the interview was exclusive to *Liberelle*. That had been bad enough. But now they were required to change into the flimsy nightwear which had featured so much in the film, with the hard bitch from the magazine leering and chatting cosily all the while.

'I'd like a shot of the two in bed,' she announced dramatically to the room. 'Starkers, if that's all right.'

'Why not?' Stella beamed. 'It wouldn't be the first time,' she flashed a withering glare of warning at Felicity, 'and it certainly won't be the last.' She laughed lecherously, and Felicity fought to keep the revulsion from her face.

They slipped off their negligees and slid under the covers, Felicity only too well aware of the ogling cameramen itching to snap them. The *Liberelle* woman deftly arranged them, fluffing up pillows and lowering the sheet until their breasts were fully exposed.

'We've got to have your titties, darlings,' she brayed, while the male photographers grunted their approval. 'Our readers would never forgive us. In fact they'd like a lot more - well, wouldn't we all, eh lads? But then again, I'd like to keep my job,' and she tittered affectedly.

Felicity felt Stella's arm slide around her, drawing her into an embrace, and cameras whirred incessantly.

It was Ally who finally got rid of them all. Felicity refused to budge until everyone had left. She dragged on the pearly negligee before she got out of bed. Though it covered her from shoulders to feet, its translucence barely hid the naked beauty beneath. But it would do until she got back to the dressing room.

In its spartan privacy she quickly hauled on her clothes, glad to be decently covered under Stella's appraising stare. 'You certainly went to ground all right,' the blonde pursued vindictively. 'Been sharing a love nest with your giant dyke?'

Felicity tried not to let her emotion show. She answered lightly, 'How did you guess?' Stella had planted herself in front of the door, and Felicity stood in front of her. 'Do I have to call security?' she asked acidly. 'I promise I'll sue you for assault this time.' She flinched in alarm as the lovely face thrust close to hers.

'You're a cold little bitch!' Stella hissed. 'Is that it then?

Don't you feel anything for me? You can just walk out, like this?'

Felicity was surprised at the depth of emotion she saw in Stella's countenance. The blue-grey eyes filled suddenly with tears, and she looked almost pathetic in her hurt. Even the voice suddenly dropped to a husky, pleading tone. 'Can't we start over?'

'No,' Felicity replied with brutal softness, 'we can't. We never really started, Stella. It was you. From the beginning you went out to get me.' She smiled bitterly. 'And you succeeded. Just be content with that.' The smile was translated into a brittle little laugh. 'I suppose I ought to be grateful to you. You taught me a lot - about myself, I mean. I'll never be the same again. You also ruined my real love relationship. I won't forget that... ever.'

Stella stood like a statue as Felicity walked around her, and out of the room.

But the furore over the screening of *A Woman's Touch* inevitably flung them together in public. And furore it was. Even a head of the Church had a much-publicised view on it. Ratings for the repeat of the first episode and all three remaining parts broke all records, as forecast. It was sold around the world, a series of books were produced and, on the Internet, someone started a lewd comic-strip about the infamous duo. By early December both Felicity and Stella were the world's most revered icons of lesbianism, even though, by the middle of the month, newspapers were reporting their break-up. Indeed, the split served only to refresh the public's eagerly prurient interest in their affairs.

Burnopside Hall became a haven for Felicity. She escaped there whenever she could, and, miraculously, her stays there and her friendship with Lord B remained a well-guarded secret. More and more she felt at home, and more and more she felt drawn to its enclosed society. The world was left outside. Within those secluded bounds she was simply Felicity, one of the girls whose nucleus was the fascinating Magda, to whom she became increasingly devoted.

To Felicity it was the life outside those privileged confines that became unreal. She was still of course caught up in it. And she still spent a considerable time in the company of her cousin during the week, when she was required to be up in town. They continued to amuse and divert each other in their customary ways. But, as they untangled their naked limbs in the glow of the fire one evening, a week before Christmas, John observed, 'You've changed a hell of a lot, Feely, since you got mixed up with Lord B's crowd.'

'What do you mean?' she asked innocently.

He shrugged absent-mindedly, and toyed with her nearest breast until she squirmed away from him. 'It's hard to say, really. You're just different. Quieter. More self-contained, sort of.'

'That's good, isn't it?' she asked. 'And what makes you think it's Burnopside that's made the difference? I don't know if you've noticed, but my life's been turned upside down by this movie. I've become the lezzie of the century. I'll go down in the history books.' She frowned. 'I've lost my lover. My family.'

There had been a very painful scene with her parents only days after the release of *A Woman's Touch*. It seemed their lives had been shaken up too, so that, according to her father, they hardly dared show their faces anywhere any more. It had led to a blazing row, and Felicity's determination that she would not see them again, at least in the short-term future.

'Why don't you see Mikey again?' John said carefully. 'He still feels the same, you know. He's crazy for you...' She shot him a glance that showed how deeply troubled she felt. 'He hasn't tried all that hard, has he? For a start he kept away for weeks.'

'Oh, come on!' her cousin protested. 'You did your disappearing act for a couple of weeks. He was going off his rocker wondering where you were. I told you, the poor sod was permanently pissed.' Although she didn't know it, John's conscience was almost equally painful on the subject of her fiance - or ex-fiance, as he must now be called.

His own part in the shattering of Michael's well-ordered successful existence was no small one. And yet John excused himself; it ought to have done Michael so much good to see at first hand how shockingly uncertain people's sexuality could be, dependent on circumstances - and opportunity. Their brief foray into homoeroticism might have started in a drunken spree, but surely it had made Michael readjust his altogether too conventional and judgmental view of such things?

John had of course said nothing to Felicity about the adventure. Close they might be, but not that close! Besides, she was going through her own crisis of sexual identity; sea changes had been happening to her too, with just as profound an effect. He was not exaggerating when he talked of the transformation within her. She was so much more mysterious; adult, contained. And more fascinating than ever.

He rolled over onto his stomach, positioning himself at her feet. He felt the tickle of the rug's pile on his belly and damp penis, which stirred with renewed sensation, despite his recent ejaculation. He thrust his loins pleasurably into the hardness under him. He picked up her right foot, holding it by the heel in his left hand, propped on his elbow. He lapped gently at the painted toenails, and the toes themselves, which waggled at his moist caresses. She shivered and he tightened his grip on her, so that she could not withdraw her foot. His tongue explored further, more firmly, at the ball of the foot, the narrow arch, the instep, to the swell of the prominent anklebone.

She shivered and jerked against his touch. 'Christ... don't,' she gasped, a hint of pleading in her voice. 'You're a menace, you know that? You'll have me utterly shagged out, and I've a hell of a day tomorrow.'

His thumbs pressed on the fragile structure, massaging, digging deeply, and she shivered again. 'You'll give Mikey another call?' he coaxed, like a hypnotist. He bent and licked again, then let one hand slide up her leg, slowly caressing its contours, until he reached the fullness of her satin inner thigh.

'I'll do no such thing,' she chided, then groaned again. 'Bastard,' she panted raggedly. The backs of his fingers were brushing, light as feathers, across her labia, which were rapidly responding and dampening yet again to his wicked moves.

His fingertips traced the divide and nuzzled subtly within, and she grabbed at his wrist and pulled him into her softness, grinding herself against him in abandon. 'You will,' he murmured insistently.

'Oh fuck... why does everyone tell me what to do all the time?' she moaned. Her hips squirmed and she wriggled down towards him, her head falling back among the cushions, her legs parting while she held him to her, pulling his fingers deep inside her beating orifice.

Michael knocked her wrist away from his loins and rolled over, hiding his limp penis from her. He gave a shuddering sob, his face buried in his folded arm on the pillow. 'Leave it, for God's sake.' His voice was muffled.

Felicity felt the heat of her shame rise to her cheeks. It was all going so horribly wrong. What should have been a wonderful reunion of flesh and love was turning into a nightmare of embarrassment. She scrambled hastily out of bed, snatched her silk robe and pulled it tightly around her. She went into the living room, blushed again at her recall of the abandoned lovemaking she had enjoyed with John on the rug there. She poured herself a drink and knelt by the fire, feeling its bathing warmth on her face and her body through the thin silk.

She was stunned by this unexpected reversal. Was it really because of her? Because he simply could not make love to a lesbian? Confusing images of Magda and the lovely girls at Burnopside kept swimming into her mind. Could it be true, that she was indeed gay? But no - she had very clear evidence that she was not. She knew only too well how ready she was for sex with Michael, and that only added to the bitterness of the tears that flowed down her cheeks.

She heard him stir, then he came out, wearing his unbuttoned shirt and trousers. 'I'm sorry,' he said, in a deflated voice. He too refilled his glass, and then sat in an armchair. 'I don't know what's wrong. Too keyed up, I expect. I've been going through a bad time recently. Not just with us. Work's been hell, too. A lot of problems—'

Suddenly she shook with rage. It welled up inside, almost choking her. With the anger came a rush of contempt for his whining weakness and his inability to satisfy her. When she spoke her words came out in a harsh, cutting snarl. 'You've got problems? What the fuck do you think I've been going through? You were the one who broke things off. If you still don't want me why don't you have the guts to say so?' She was crying, but the tears seemed to fuel her fury. 'It took a hell of a lot to ring you, and now you don't even want me. That's bloody marvellous, that is!'

She felt the wildness surging through her, the aggression stirring her excitement like some kind of foreplay. 'You bastard! I've been through hell lately, so don't come snivelling to me! I want you to fuck me! Understand?' She flung herself at him, seizing him by his open shirt, clawing it open all the way to his navel as she pulled him off the low chair. He was too shocked to resist. The next thing he knew he was lying flat on his back and she was sitting astride him, beating at his bare chest with her fists and clawing at his pants, ripping them open.

She knelt up and dragged them brutally down off his hips, then the tight white briefs that lay beneath. His prick, large but flexible as a hose, hung there between his thighs. Her fingers closed round it and she pulled, stretching it, and he yelped. She jerked her hand up and down, and the helmet throbbed and swelled under her touch, while he made girlish whimpers of protest. The hand moved, her long fingers curved, the nails dragged up the furrowed underside of his balls. Her black hair swung over her face as her head dipped and she nibbled at the stiffening column, pressing it back flat against his belly, holding it with her fingers while she chewed and worried at it. Her tongue licked, the helm reared, and he was as stiff as iron.

She rose a little, still clinging to his prick, and let her gown flow open as she spread her knees wide and descended, guiding him to her sex, taking him inside, feeling the potent shaft surge into her, filling her tightly welcoming sheath. He grunted at each descent of her body onto his belly and thighs, while she rode him furiously to a shattering climax for both of them.

Chapter Fourteen

In the secret upper room, The Babylon Chamber, the arc lights flung down their brilliant whiteness on the marble circle at its centre. Faint blue whirls of smoke drifted up from the shallow metal dishes at the outer surrounds, where the heavy musk of incense burned. From her dais, the scarlet-cloaked Grand Mistress nodded. Her black robed acolytes came forward, carrying a large piece of apparatus, which was a metal frame on a wheeled stand. The frame was laced by strands of broad elasticated tape, which formed a stout but flexible webbing.

They positioned the equipment directly in the centre, on the black star. They then led forward a drooping figure who moved with reluctant obedience. Marie-Angele Carrier, the French girl, was tall, with a mane of rich chestnut hair, which was gathered loosely on top of her head. She was already naked, and the neat triangle of her pubis shone with the same rich redness against the whiteness of her belly and thighs. Her lovely face was stamped with a look of fear, her eyes wild as they moved frantically from one to the other of her companions. Her lips were compressed as she strove to make no sound.

The frame was tilted until it was almost horizontal, and the robed figures helped the girl climb on the webbing and spread herself face down, so her arms and legs stretched out towards the comers. Her wrists and ankles were firmly bound with looped restraints, and she hung there like a pale star, every detail of her body revealed in the brilliance of the light. There were deep hollows in her taut buttocks, shadowed as she clenched them in anticipation of the pain to come.

'Daughter, you have been chosen to undergo the test of obedience, to accept the chastisement on behalf of the Daughters of Babylon.'

Marie-Angele's voice came as a smothered sob. 'I thuh - thank you, mistress, for the great honour bestow upon me.'

Again, the scarlet figure nodded. The frame was tipped once more, so that the captive girl hung at an angle of forty-five degrees, her head uppermost. The muscles on her body could be seen to tense. The frame shook slightly with her involuntary trembling. The first of her punishers stepped forward. Debbie flung back her cloak, revealing the splendour of her brown body as she drew back her arm and delivered the first hissing blow with the three-tailed whip. The webbing strained noisily as the naked girl jerked and a gasp escaped, then a sob, which was quickly bitten off. Her behind flexed. The thin red lines rose, glowing on the abused rounds.

Debbie withdrew into the dimness beyond the circle of light, and another stepped forward quickly. The second blow whistled and struck, the aim as accurate as the first, and more angry lines appeared. A whimper came from the bound form and the webbing creaked again. A third girl replaced the second, struck again, and this was repeated until six lashes had been delivered on the now writhing captive. The French girl was crying, unable to hold back her grief and pain, though the sound of her weeping was muted as she struggled to suppress it.

Magda came down off the dais, into the glare of the light. Gently, she took hold of the crown of red hair and lifted the tearstained face. 'What do you say, child?' the deep voice prompted.

'Thuh - thank you, duh - daughters,' Marie-Angele sobbed.

Her fellow acolytes now shed their robes, and clustered tenderly about her. The icy spray was produced and her burning flesh administered to. Cool wet cloths were also brought, and the livid stripes were gently bathed and dried. Finally, a soothing cream, which made her bottom glisten in the light, was smeared thickly on her throbbing buttocks, and she was released and carefully lifted clear of the frame. Two of them helped her from the circle of light to the outer darkness, while two more wheeled the punishment frame out of sight.

Then the marble floor was taken up by the naked girls, who stood in pairs facing one another, hands on shoulders, nipples rubbing, as though partners for a dance.

'And now, after the test of obedience, comes the test of love,' Magda announced. She stopped at the first pair and held up the object she had taken from the long black box that stood at the foot of her dais. It was about a foot long and of a realistic flesh colour. It was a double-ended artificial penis, complete with twin helms and veined shaft. It was the girth of a turgid erection, and the girls moved, adjusting their spread thighs and hips to accommodate their mistress. Never for an instant breaking their hold on each other's shoulders, the girls thrust their bellies to take the dildo into their eager slits.

Soon the four couples were joined by the latex dildos, and their bellies jerked in unison to the rhythm of their mutual fucking, the inches between them lessening as excitement grew and more and more of the latex shafts disappeared into their vaginas.

The strange, gyrating conjunctions went on for long minutes. Suddenly, the girl with Debbie, a pale blonde of Nordic beauty, gave a wailing cry, shuddered dramatically, and withdrew her end of the gleaming dildo before crumpling to the cold marble floor, her frame still shaking in the dying throes of orgasm. Debbie seized the shaft protruding from her loins and thrust wildly, driving it deep until she too jerked and shivered, and joined her companion on the floor with the instrument still embedded between her thighs.

The other couples hadn't achieved their climax when Magda finally clapped her hands. The enchanting assortment of bodies, shining with perspiration, their breasts heaving, lined up before their mistress, once more on her dais, and stood like an array of Amazons on parade while they chanted their oath of loyalty. They then swung away obediently and ran out of the pale light.

There was a collective sigh, and a ripple of approbation from the unseen audience above.

In the luxurious communal bathroom in the quarters adjacent to the Chamber, the girls were themselves again, beautiful individuals bound by the close ties of love and friendship. Marie-Angele was lying face down on a massage table, a white towel spread beneath her. Her body was still shaken now and then by the convulsive aftermath of her weeping, and the traces of tears still clung to her long eyelashes, but she managed to smile at the heartfelt sympathy expressed by her comrades. Her bottom was marked by the thin red weals, some of which were raised. One of her friends was dabbing at them gingerly, putting on yet more cooling solution with a piece of cotton wool. Even her lightest touch caused Marie-Angele's cheeks to tighten and quiver, while she hissed with the sting of it.

'You buggers. You really whip my arse, hey?' Her French accent was attractively thick. There was a chorus of penitent apologies. Most of the girls were still in the communal showers, turning this way and that under the soothing jets of hot water, washing the remains of their exertions from them. Several were swiftly bringing to a passionate conclusion the sensations that had been aroused by the coupling in the Chamber, their mouths glued together, fingers working, thighs entwined, bellies thrusting.

'Don't worry, Angel,' Joanne smiled, bending to kiss the prone figure on the shoulder. 'You'll get your chance for revenge. We all get our turn on the grill.'

They all turned as the door opened and Magda entered, still in her scarlet robe. 'That was magnificent as usual, girls,' she said warmly. 'Pretty yourselves up, but don't be too long. The masters are waiting in the supper room.'

Within ten minutes the girls had restored make-up and hairstyles, dabbed on perfume, and moved out for the next stage in the evening's entertainment. All except Marie-Angele, who lay, still nude, on the table, where Magda gazed at her in anticipation. 'Now for your reward, my dear,' she growled, and the French girl shivered with pleasure.

She easily picked the figure up in her arms and carried her out into the discreetly lit corridor, and to a small room next door. In it was a single bed and a few pieces of smartly functional furniture. A dim lamp at the bedside cast a subtle glow, leaving the edges of the small room in deep shadow. Carefully, Magda deposited the trembling girl on the bed. Marie-Angele winced at the touch of the covers on her bottom, but she paid no heed. Her body was aflame with the anticipation of joy she knew would be hers.

She drew up her knees and opened her legs wide, while the tall figure knelt between them, looming like a great vampire as that massive cloak spread its richness, blotting out the ceiling, blotting out everything as the wonderful body descended and claimed her. And she was lost, yielding herself up to that resplendent body, while at her loins she felt the live flesh which bridged their thrusting bellies and made them one.

'I sometimes wish I could stay here for ever,' Felicity confessed shyly, her glowing features turned to Lord Burnopside. She felt the sturdy movement of the mare beneath her, and shamefully acknowledged the secret dampness the bouncing canter had induced. She had developed her riding skills considerably since that momentous day of the accident. Her confidence had grown. Sometimes she went out with the groom, sometimes on her own. Occasionally Lord B or one of his guests would accompany her. None of the other girls rode.

She had been glad when she arrived at the Hall yesterday evening to find that no guests were to join them; the first not expected until later this afternoon. It meant a relaxed evening spent with the girls and his lordship, and a taxingly amorous night in the arms of her beloved Magda, who fulfilled for her the combined roles of mother, sister, mistress, and lover, with spectacular success.

It all made the morning ride in the damp grey December air even more enjoyable. She was already looking forward to a hot bath, a good lunch, and the afternoon sleep that would ensure she would be at her sparkling best for the social evening ahead.

She had expected to eat a solitary breakfast. Magda always left her in the early hours, insisting that she must retire to her own bed for at least a couple of hours. Neither she nor the others would appear before nine at the earliest, and were far more likely to have a tray taken up to their rooms. They might well have passed a night as strenuous as she herself had done, for they paired up regularly, she had learned, though always with Magda's foreknowledge.

Felicity was also quite sure that, when she was absent, Magda made use of her girls. She had not plucked up the courage to ask directly, either of the tall figure herself or one of the others, but it seemed so natural. The way she addressed them and embraced them, with long sensual kisses and embraces, made it obvious what her relationship with each of them was. It no longer made Felicity jealous; the only envy she felt nowadays was that they had this wonderful creature to themselves every day.

When his lordship came into the breakfast room in his riding togs, she had been glad to see him. He was, in some ways, the male equivalent of Magda for her, though in the intervening weeks he hadn't made love to her again since that time on the conference table. But the knowledge that they had fucked brought its own intimacy between them, a knowledge that clearly stamped their relationship.

Now, they threaded their way at a slow walk along a woodland path. The smell of mould and wet leaves hung heavily, and there were traces of mist in the distance between the widely spaced trees. Clouds of vapour snorted from their horses' nostrils, their own breath steamed in the chill air, and Felicity was thankful she had wrapped up warmly. Lord B edged his horse alongside her, let it gently bump her mount to one side, off the path onto the leaf mould and clumps of grass.

'Let's pause here awhile,' he said. 'Stretch our legs a bit. It's quiet here.'

At once she felt her heart flutter a little with nervous excitement, sensing some veiled meaning in his tone. Surely, though, he wouldn't want to try anything out here, in this weather?

Obediently, she swung her leg over and dismounted, and he tethered their animals to a stout tree. She noticed there was a wire fence and a heavy five-barred gate, which was padlocked, and beyond it an open meadow.

'How are things going now?' he asked conversationally. 'What are your plans?'

She shrugged, and smiled uncertainly. 'Well, first of all, I want a good long rest. Yvonne, my agent, has promised me some time off. It's been quite hectic since the summer.' He chuckled appreciatively. 'I'll say! And what about your private life? Is that settled now?'

She felt the blush rising, and glanced down at her polished boots. 'Not really,' she murmured. 'Since all that business with Stella, Michael and I - we're seeing each other again, but it's made a big difference. He's having second thoughts, I think.'

'Foolish boy,' Lord B said. 'I've been hearing a bit about your young man. Apparently the city boys think he's a bit of a whiz kid in his trade.'

'Oh, he is,' Felicity concurred enthusiastically. 'He's brilliant. He's the youngest executive his company's ever had.'

'Do you still want him?'

Felicity blinked at the bluntness of his question. She reddened once more and shrugged again. 'I think so,' she said honestly. Then she gave a little jerk of impatience. 'Oh, I don't know any more. I hardly seem to know what I want.' She paused, and added shyly, 'That's why I like coming down here so much. I can't tell you how much it means to me. I love it -love you all. You make things only feel right when I'm here.'

Impulsively, she reached up and kissed him at the side of his moustache, like a daughter kissing her father. She was startled when he grabbed her, crushed her to him, and planted a searching kiss on her parted lips. They were both panting when he released her.

'We're always delighted to have you,' he said thickly, his blue eyes boring into her. She felt dizzy, as though that look was trying to tell her something, and she could not understand. 'Are you in love with Magda?' he asked harshly.

Her face felt steeped in permanent heat as she nodded. 'Everyone is,' she whispered faintly.

'I know all about her lessons of obedience.' His open face, too, was even ruddier than its normal colour, his eyes blazing with desire. 'Do you truly want to be one of us?'

She stared at him, unable to speak, but she managed to nod dumbly.

'I have my own test of obedience,' he said huskily. 'I want you to take it now.'

She glanced around her at the misty scene. 'Here?' she said incredulously. It was his turn to nod. 'Very well,' she managed, her heart pounding.

'Good girl,' he grunted. 'Now get up on the gate.' He lifted her around the waist and she put out her feet, resting them on the third bar, her back to him. He thrust her down and she bent over the top bar, her legs apart, her behind thrust up in the air. She was expecting him to claw at her breeches and haul them down, so she was surprised when she felt him merely lift the flap of her jacket.

'Keep still!' he ordered.

There was a sharp whistling disturbance of air, then a loud crack, and a fiery line burned her backside through the thick material of her jodhpurs and the knickers she wore underneath. The gate shook and her belly squashed against the wood as she jerked and clung on, forcing herself to stay doubled over. She yelped at the next cutting blow and squirmed again, spreading her arms, digging her fingers into the wet wood to maintain her perilous balance. She squealed at the third blow and began to cry. 'Please,' she wept pathetically. She hung there, her hard hat falling over her eyes, the tears streaming down her cold face, her bottom on fire. No further blows came, and he lifted her down. The pain throbbed abominably and she couldn't stop herself from massaging her poor bottom.

She saw his penis hanging free of his breeches. It was long and thick, though not yet erect. She felt his heavy hands on her shoulders, implacably pressing downward, and she sank to her knees in the soggy mould, his prick bobbing mere inches from her face. He removed her hat, dropped it to the ground, and then his fingers entwined in her lustrous hair. Without being told she fumbled off her leather gloves and took his prick in her fingers. It felt alive with pulsing need. She leaned forward and kissed the shining helm softly, fearfully, deeply thrilled by the potent smell of him. Then she seized the root of the stiffening shaft, lifted it, and enveloped the dome with her mouth. It thrust into her, filling her completely, and she slobbered at him avidly, pushing as far down the surging column as she could go. At the last second she instinctively pulled her mouth free as he discharged over her face. Then penitently, she touched her lips to him and absorbed the still pumping fluid into her convulsing throat.

Chapter Fifteen

Michael gaped in bleary, drunken amazement. He could not believe what he was seeing. Felicity had told him just two days before that she'd not be there. She was supposed to be miles away, buried in the country at Lord Burnopside's place with a whole bunch of aristocratic chinless wonders. He had bickered and snapped, and finally they'd had a blazing row, which happened all too easily these days, and she had walked out after telling him he'd not see her at all over the holiday period, and maybe, not after that.

He wasn't going to go to the studio party on Christmas Eve. Certainly not on his own. That show-biz crowd weren't his scene at all. He had only been dragged into it all through Felicity. Trouble was, most of his associates from the financial world were older than he was and therefore tucked up in the bosom of their families, and that wasn't his scene either.

When he rang her flat, just on the off chance that she might not have left for the country yet, he was ready to be suitably abject. Perhaps she would agree to meet him for dinner, or for a drink before she left. When John had answered the phone he'd felt himself blushing, felt that quiver of emotion he didn't even want to classify. Fear, shame - excitement?

'Look, come along to the do tomorrow night,' her cousin had said, his voice warm with persuasion in Michael's ear. 'I'm going to be on my own, too. We can keep each other company. I'd like to see you again, on your own. It'll be good for a laugh.' There was a pause, then the tone dropped and there was a hint of seductiveness. 'You're not still mad at me, are you? I thought we'd sorted that out.'

Michael's face burned. 'Of course I'm not,' he said stiffly, and then laughed awkwardly. 'We were pissed out of our heads, that's all.' He writhed on an internal spit of guilt every time he thought of that weird night - and the morning that followed. He'd felt soiled. He should have thrashed John for taking such disgusting liberties. He should have done something to retrieve his manhood, for God's sake. Instead of shuffling off, unable even to look him in the face, mumbling like a hopeless kid. For an awful second, in the doorway, he'd thought John was going to kiss him again. He'd put his arm around him and hugged him. Not the sort of thing lads did to one another at all. He still woke up sweating about it occasionally. And it festered like a boil whenever he thought about it.

But now, Christmas Eve and not a soul to turn to, unless he caught the train and turned up at home, which would be the biggest humiliation of all, a yearning weakness overwhelmed him. Somehow he found himself agreeing to attend the party.

'I'll see you there then,' John said. 'I'm looking forward to it.'

To the last minute he remained undecided. Everyone there would know all about it - about the split between Felicity and him, about the shakiness of their present relationship. Damn it, that blonde pervert herself would be there, laughing at him with her deviant friends. But loneliness had driven him on. That, and the drinks he'd imbibed which, increasingly of late, he'd found to be an aid to comfort and relaxation.

Stella Priest was there. Glittering, beautiful, defiantly feminine, and with a girl in tow whose spiky haircut and waif-like thinness, together with her drab costume of black T-shirt, black jeans, and ugly black bovver boots, could not have contrasted more drearily with her partner. And yet her youthful, sharp-angled features had their own appeal, one which Michael strongly preferred, and which reminded him quite forcibly of Felicity's vulnerable beauty.

To cap it all there was no sign of John, and with a sense of desperation Michael headed for the bar and hung there on the fringes of umpteen conversations, listening to the riotous laughter and false bonhomie. He was well drunk when he heard and saw a commotion across the crowded room, and there, large as life, was Felicity, swamped at once by a buzzing crowd, making it impossible for him to get anywhere near.

He saw her long black hair as she pushed against the crowd. They were cheering and hooting with laughter, and he stared perplexed. What was wrong with them?

She was pushing hard through the throng towards the golden head of Stella Priest, who seemed to be for once caught off guard, her mouth open, her face tense. Then suddenly they were together and Felicity flung her arms about the woman, pulled her close and gave her a smacking kiss full on the lips. Stella flinched, pulled back, there was an instant tension, and then she was staring, clearly overcome with amazement. She burst out laughing - everyone around them did - and then they embraced again, to thunderous applause.

Sick and furious at that kiss, Michael watched them part again and the dark head glance around, searching for someone.

Him, he realised, as he saw fingers pointed in his direction. Felicity nodded, her face lighting up in recognition. She was making her way through the crowd, who were reaching for her, laughing, touching her slim bare arms, her slender shoulders, so creamy against the severity of the clinging black cocktail dress.

He felt his body tense. He felt trapped, unable to move or breathe in the age it took for her to reach him. Was she going to do the same to him, deliver the same kiss with those lips which had just been plastered against those of her other lover - her lesbian lover? The lover she had assured him she wanted nothing more to do with, whom she could not stand, whom she had never truly loved?

Paralysed, he watched her approach, his drunken thoughts still confused by those grins, the hoots of laughter. Was that why he'd been lured to the party, to be made the fool at the centre of some cruel prank? The dark eyes met his, dancing with that familiar mischief, the lovely face lit by that gamine grin. And yet, what was different about her? His brain reeled, his senses powered by the waft of her perfume as she reached him at last and the luscious mouth closed in, the glistening lips pursed, to meet his... and at the very instant they touched, he knew.

Michael jerked back as though burned, and heard John's husky and mocking voice proclaim, 'Hi. Sorry I'm late, darling. Have you missed me?'

'Fuck off!' Swept by a surge of rage and shame he wrenched away, pushed aggressively against the press of bodies, and fled, the roars of laughter like flails across his back as, tears stinging his eyes, he headed for the distant door.

He managed to get into a tiny cubicle of a lavatory, and dabbed at his wet cheeks in its locked privacy. He was trembling with anger and humiliation, tortured by his sense of ridicule. And, strangest of all, he felt a deep sense of hurt, and betrayal, at the cruel prank played upon him by John. He was shocked by this, just as he was shocked by the secret acknowledgement that what had happened between them in Felicity's bed gave them an intimacy as private as that of lovers.

He was in despair when he re-emerged into the heaving crowd, wanting only to escape so he could surrender to his loneliness and misery. But, to add to his suffering, Stella Priest collared him. She had been waiting for him and grabbed his arm, pressing her breasts against him so he could only stare at that superb cleavage all but spilling from her lacy red dress. 'Come on, *darling*,' she purred. 'Don't run off and hide. Don't be so stuffy. That bastard cousin of hers had me fooled, too. Don't let it get to you. Come and have another drink. It's Christmas, for God's sake. And she's chucked both of us, hasn't she? What the hell!'

Michael, feeling bemused and unable to resist, allowed himself to be dragged back to the epicentre of the party where John, looking so like Felicity, and so desirable in her clothing that Michael felt again that strange dreamlike sensation, was surrounded by a crowd of admiring figures. There were more raucous cheers at the sight of Stella and Michael. She was still clinging tightly to his arm, and he felt a sense of masochistic pleasure in yielding to this collective scorn, as though he'd passed beyond the point of caring - of masculine pride. He simply stood there, the butt of the laughter. His eyes met John's, staring at him from behind their make-up, and he exchanged a look of complicity, of wounded understanding.

Now that he studied the slim figure in the short dress he could see there was something, an angularity, a ranginess that was not Felicity. And of course the chest was flatter, despite the wicked shading he'd cleverly drawn to give the faintest suggestion of a cleavage. Even so, the shapeliness of the legs in sheer stockings, the curvaceous hips, and the immaculately made-up beauty of the face, was far from the drag queen look he would have expected.

The long glossy hair dipped towards him, and the white teeth showed between painted lips. 'Gave you a bit of a fright, did IT John said. 'Don't tell Feely. She'll kill me if she finds out I've been using her stuff.'

On his other side, Stella kneaded his arm. 'Admit it, Mike! He makes a fetching little cow, doesn't he? I bet you wish you were gay, don't you? And I'm beginning to wish I wasn't!' There was another chorus of laughter. She cupped her palm and stroked John's smooth cheek, with just the gesture of affection she used to show to his cousin. 'You really are a sadistic little bitch, you know, giving us both the hots like that. And you won't be able to satisfy either one of us, will you?'

The laughter continued to burst like fireworks over Michael. Stella revelled in the attention all around her, while he stood stupidly, the fall guy for all her barbed comments and her increasingly savage mockery. John had quietly extricated himself, and was soon at the centre of a smaller, more select group. Michael continued to drink, the smile fixed on his face like a death's head, scourged by the flails of Stella's humour and contempt, yet showing no sign of flinching or hurt.

Much later, when the party at last showed signs of breaking up, except for a hardcore who looked as though they might well be there for Christmas morning, Michael followed Stella into the toilets at the end of the large room. There was a row of communal stalls, and a staggering female on the way out leered and raised her eyebrows, but said nothing. When the compartment door had closed on Stella, Michael found a bolt on the outer door and quickly secured it from within, ensuring their privacy.

She came out of the lavatory still smoothing down the skirt of her silk gown, affording him a generous view of her stockinged legs. Her eyes widened when she saw him, but that contemptuous smile appeared immediately. 'I think you've got the wrong room, *Mikey*. This is the little girls' loo. You're not even in drag. Not like our chum. You've got no excuse.'

'You're a perverted bitch!' he spat, the thick hatred welling up overpoweringly. A thrill passed through him at the first sign of fear that flickered in her eyes, though she swiftly hid it.

'Jealous, are we?' she mocked, moving to the washbasin and rinsing her hands. She watched him in the mirror. 'Because I could give young Felicity a thrill she'd never even dreamed of! Because she didn't go for your big manly dick any more? That it? You're so fucking pathetic, macho man! Well, I've finished with her, sonny - you can have her back.' She sneered. 'You'd better watch her, though. Where's she got to tonight, I wonder? She's got a taste for things you can never give her, big boy. I hear there's a dyke down at Burnopside who's built like a brick shithouse and who our little Felicity can't drop her pants quick enough for!'

She made to pass him, treating him to her coldest, most withering stare. 'Excuse me. I've got rid of mine. I guess you're still full of it.'

Michael gave a low snarl as she went to edge past him. He seized her golden hair and ran her across to the cubicle she had just vacated. His fingers dug maliciously into her scalp as he forced her down onto her knees. She screamed, but in the distant hubbub, no one heard. He thrust her head down into the toilet bowl, yanked at the handle, and doused her in the gushing water. 'Felicity told me you once put her head down the bog,' he said, his chest heaving with the exertion. 'Seems to be quite effective for hysterical females!'

He let her up a little and Stella coughed and spluttered, her lovely hair darkened and flattened to her skull, and plastered in seaweed-like strands across her face. He thrust her down again, bending over her, one hand at the back of her head and the other pressing on her shoulder. 'Keep still, and keep quiet!' he hissed.

Gasping and crying she ceased struggling, her head pinned down in that white bowl. He let go of her, paused to see if there was any sign of resistance, and then scrabbled at the hem of her crumpled silk dress. He dragged it up over her lovely raised behind. His rough fingers clawed at her little white knickers, hauled them off her buttocks, and down her stockinged thighs.

She whimpered as she felt his rigid prick jab into the crease of her bottom and thrust against the tightness of her anus. Then his hand was round at her front, fondling her belly, her pubic bush, then lower, guiding the tip of his penis into her vaginal opening. He was surprised to feel the gripping welcome as he drove deeply home into her clinging sheath. He plunged hard, savouring the thrill of her buttocks squashing against his groin.

And though Michael fucked her aggressively, concerned only with his own hectic satisfaction, Stella savoured the throb of her invaded vagina, the novel sensation of her helplessness, and the thrill of being so deeply penetrated. And when she felt the copious eruption of his sperm, her own excitement swiftly drove her to the wild crescendo of total release.

Chapter Sixteen

Michael had little idea of how he came to be standing on the rug in front of the newly flickering fire in Felicity's living room. Yet he was amazed at how sober and sharply alive he felt as he stared down at the fascinating form crouched at his feet. John had bent to light the fire. The short black cocktail dress had ridden up to the top of his thighs, and Michael gazed at the shapely limbs, so comprehensively revealed that he could see the dark patterned tops of the sheer stockings, and the flash of pale thigh beyond. That startlingly realistic hair framing the delicate angularity of the face, and the flawless fragility of the bare shoulder, really made it seem as though it was Felicity herself kneeling there before him.

John glanced up with a mischievous grin, interrupting Michael's tipsy reverie. 'You're a hell of a lad when you've taken drink,' he said with admiration. 'Fancy pushing old Stella's head down the bog!' He laughed heartily.

Michael felt a surge of exultation and pride. True, he thought, with cruel pleasure. He was a lad! And how! And now Stella Pervy Priest knew just how much of a lad he was. He had expected an uproar, screams of rape and God knows what else, when he'd zipped up his trousers and left her lying there, crumpled on the toilet floor. But she'd come out minutes later, looking damp, true, but with make-up repaired and dignity intact. She said not a word to anyone about what had happened. In fact, she'd been quieter than she'd been all evening. Not that he'd hung around for very long after his amorous assault.

John must have been watching Michael closely. Next thing he knew the androgynous beauty was guiding him out and into a taxi, and here they were, back in the privacy of Felicity's flat, his mind and body a prey to all kinds of wild fancies as he stared down at the figure coiled at his feet.

'Sit down... come on.' The bare arms reached up, hands outstretched, and Michael found himself responding, folding beside him in the comforting glow and warmth. His judgement seemed curiously suspended. The dress, the perfume, the make-up, the too perfectly feminine beauty, made John seem like a different creature altogether, a recreation of the lovely girl Michael was hopelessly in love with. Then John reached up, and with a dramatic tug, pulled off the wig, and then kicked the dainty high heels from his stockinged feet with a groan of luxury.

'That fucking thing was so hot,' he said. 'And how on earth girls go around all day in these things!' He flung the shoes from him with a chuckle, and massaged his toes through the gauzy tips of the stockings. Bemused, Michael could see the distinct outline of the darkly painted toenails. 'Undo me, please.' He knelt up, his back to Michael, his slender neck bent as he bowed his head, and the sense of unreality washed once more over the taller figure. Michael reached with unsteady fingers to oblige - just as he did for Felicity. And that white neck and those exquisite shoulders excited him just as much.

The pale back came into view as the black material parted. There was a built in bodice to the dress which made a bra unnecessary, so that John's back was entirely bare down to his hips, where the dress's division ended. John stood, wriggled the garment down over his hips, and stepped out of it. Michael gazed up at the black French knickers, with the wide band of lace at the legs, and the dark self-supporting stockings. He felt his penis swelling mightily against his clothing. Hating himself but unable to prevent himself, he reached up and ran his palm over the smooth satin of John's crotch. Within the shimmering black underwear the shape of John's penis rose up, the outline of the helm quite clear, and the tight curve of his balls hugged by the soft material. Michael traced its length to the bulbous tip, then back, down that growing shaft to the root, where he could feel John's springy pubic hair beneath the sexy material. He could feel the warm dampness, and smell the powerful odour of arousal.

John was still standing over him, smiling down, whispering hypnotic words of encouragement that Michael could barely hear. His legs were only a little apart. His thumbs flipped the elastic waist of the knickers down a little, and his prick emerged, hanging in a curve over the dipping edge of the black garment. It was not erect, but thick and pulsing, and the shining helm was exposed. A drop of fluid glistened at its tip. 'Suck me off,' John breathed, edging his hips forward a little in invitation.

Michael shuddered, but knelt up, and rubbed his forehead against John's glans, feeling the slimy smear of the fluid on his brow. He buried his nose in the damp swell of the balls, still hidden in the tight nest of black silk, and breathed deeply. 'I'm not queer,' he groaned, feeling John's quivering thighs against his cheeks.

'There's nothing queer about this, Mikey,' John whispered. His fingers played affectionately with Michael's ears, and he stroked the crisp blond hair. Michael felt the long false fingernails rasp against him. 'Come on, lover,' the voice crooned, in a seductive whisper. 'Suck cock. You'll love it.'

Michael felt he would come himself at any second. With a sense of drowning he drew back his head and let the dome of that warm column pulse against his eyelids. He rubbed his face against it before, with a delicious quiver of fear, he poked out his tongue and licked timidly, tasting for the first time the salty nectar of another man's emission. Knowing there was no going back, he opened his lips wide and took the helm inside, working at it clumsily, feeling it swell to fill him.

He almost gagged as John pushed slowly forward, holding Michael's head firmly, but careful not to scare the novice away by unleashing the unbelievable passion he really felt building in the pit of his stomach. Sensing Michael's turmoil, John withdrew a little to allow him a moment to grapple with the emotions and sensations he knew would be spinning through his head and body. 'Are you all right?' he whispered, gazing down at his rigid cock - more rigid than he'd ever known it before - bridging the gap between his aching groin and those tightly pursed lips. His question was rewarded with a tentative nod, the innocence of which almost made him come there and then. 'Okay,' he breathed, and then carefully pressed his hips forward and watched that rigid cock disappear completely.

With his mouth full Michael was fighting to breathe, his face enveloped by humid flesh, soft silk and springy pubes. He reached up with both hands and pressed against John's lightly muscled stomach, but was secretly swamped with disappointment as John withdrew completely. As the prize was snatched away from him Michael lapped at it desperately, rubbing his sweating face against its potent length, sucking and licking.

Then the fingers clutching at his blond hair tightened convulsively, lifting his face and holding it still. 'Jesus!' John cried, and Michael thrilled with revulsion and excitement. He kept his eyes tightly closed, the prospect of witnessing his own debasement still too much to accept, and discharged into his own underwear as John's thick seed spilled over his cheeks and open mouth, and all over his upturned, worshipping face.

'Oh, please - no,' Felicity whimpered helplessly. 'Please don't...' She was stretched out on the low table in the library, with many pairs of hands pressing her down lightly, yet enough to make any resistance useless. Not that she had the strength or the will to put up a fight, however token. Then why was she weeping as she felt the last scraps of clothing drawn from her body, the cups of her bra plucked away, the wispy briefs slid and rolled down off her hips and over her limbs, to leave her naked, spread-eagled on the hard surface?

Were the tears because she was, at last, being made to acknowledge the ultimate surrender of all her pretences, the rules of so-called decency and decorum she had professed to in her young life? She had known all along that one day the enchanted company and lifestyle she had embraced so eagerly at Burnopside would lead to this orgiastic moment of truth. And now she realised that the very shame of it, the thought of those eyes fixed on her helpless nakedness - not only his lordship, who after all was already a familiar lover, but the lecherous Sir Hugh, and Admiral Fitzgibbon, and that beaky old senior judge with his scrawny turtle neck and salacious eyes - thrilled her to the core, and added to the sexuality flowing through her at the touches of the lovely girls who had made her their prisoner.

Mouths, hands, and fingers assailed her everywhere; her arms and legs, her throat, her breasts and belly, her thighs, and her feet. The fact that Magda was not one of her assailants but merely looking on with fond approval added to her incredible excitement.

She was near her crisis when, with cruel abruptness, all those caressing hands and tongues were withdrawn. The restraining holds vanished and she sat up, the tears streaming, unable to keep her shivering limbs still in her desperate need. 'Please,' she whispered brokenly, staring about at all those merciless eyes. Her gaze sought that of the commanding figure in the wonderful long gown of deep green.

'I'll take her up, your lordship,' Magda said, and Lord B nodded. Sobbing pitifully now, the naked figure slipped off the low table. 'We'll use the Green Room,' Magda announced, then crooked her finger at Felicity. 'Come on, sugar.'

Felicity glanced around, all the old inhibitions of modesty sweeping back at the awareness of her nudity before all these people. 'You won't need any clothes,' Magda added, with her deep, sensual chuckle. Head down, Felicity walked quickly over to her, terribly conscious of every staring eye.

Outside the library the tears increased. Magda held her by the hand and led her up the wide sweep of the staircase and along a discreetly lit, thickly carpeted landing. 'What's going to happen?' Felicity asked.

In the impressive Green Room Magda nodded towards the four-poster bed, with its heavy drapes gathered in bunches about the pillars. 'On you get, sweetheart.' Felicity's head was spinning. Was it simply going to end with her and Magda making love in these august surroundings? Was her public ordeal over already? She had not expected to be let off so lightly, and Magda's next move suggested she was right in her caution.

'Spread yourself on your back, honey,' she ordered. 'Arms and legs out wide. That's it.'

A blush invaded Felicity's face at the exposed vulnerability of her position. Tasselled velvet cords hung from each post, and Magda used them to secure Felicity's wrists and ankles, pinning her spread-eagled.

'What's going to happen?' she pleaded, afraid again now.

Magda sat beside her on the edge of the high bed and, reaching down, wiped her wet cheeks carefully, then let her large hand cup in a loving caress that lovely face. 'You agreed that you'd be mine, baby, didn't you?' Magda reasoned gently. 'That you belong to me. You said so. You swore you'd do anything for me - didn't you?'

'Yes,' Felicity murmured, pouting like a reluctant child. 'Didn't you mean it?'

'Yes.' Again came that small whisper of confession.

'Because if you didn't, tell me now and I'll let you go. I mean it. You can have a ride back to London and there'll be no hard feelings - no recriminations... okay?'

'Nuh - no!' Felicity blurted desperately. A sob shook her breasts, which were lifted and flattened against her ribcage by her position. The peaked nipples quivered. 'It's just - I'm scared, Magda. You - you won't hurt me, will you?' She thought of the whippings this fascinating woman had delivered; the agony of them, so different from the squirming spankings of their love play. They had not been many, these more serious chastisements, but they still frightened Felicity. Not least because of her own ambivalent feelings towards them; that shameful masochistic frisson of pleasure they gave her, the thought of surrender, and the burning proof of her love for this wonderful creature. And she thought too of that strange episode in the wood, and those three quite vicious cuts Lord B had given her with the riding-crop; so vicious that even though they'd been delivered through the thickness of her breeches and underwear, the angry red lines had marked her bottom for days afterwards.

When she was away from Burnopside, away from his lordship and her beloved Magda, this new side of her character unsettled her immensely. What was it that made her go to them so willingly, to embrace pain - real pain - in her desire to be loved by them? Would she become addicted to pain the way people became addicted to drink or drugs? Is that what they wanted of her, with their tests and talks of obedience, and dictatorial use of her body?

'Whatever happens, happens because we love you,' the compelling voice went on. 'You believe that, don't you?'

Felicity registered the 'we', not 'I'. Who *was* that 'we'?

Magda and Lord Burnopside?

Magda and the girls?

Everyone in this enchanted world?

'Yes,' she whispered. 'I believe you.'

'Good.' Magda knelt, the rustling silk of her gown spreading about her. Her long black hair swept against her shoulders as her head dipped, her face came close, and they kissed, a long slow kiss of passion, until Felicity was writhing instinctively, straining against the bonds. Magda's warm hand nestled between Felicity's sprawled thighs, cupped the mound with its soft fleece, pressed on the throbbing wetness, then moved away, and Felicity's body shook in another sob of hunger and frustration.

'Sorry, my love. I know you're ready to blow your top, but I've got to keep you on the boil. That's part of the test.' She kissed the parted lips again, more gently and briefly this time, before withdrawing a little. 'Don't worry. Your time will come, as they say.' Again, the rich rumble of laughter.

Felicity felt her head being raised. A black velvet eye mask was slipped over her head and adjusted, sealing her in all-embracing darkness. Her heart thudded. She murmured in protest, and felt the springs dip and rise as Magda climbed off the bed.

'Be good,' the voice whispered, fading towards the door. 'I know you will be.' There was one last chuckle, and then Felicity heard a soft click as the door closed.

'Magda!' she called sharply, but she knew she was alone.

She lay there, tied on her back, limbs stretched apart, staring up into the impenetrable blackness. She had never felt more helpless, Or more vulnerable. She was deeply afraid. But she could not ignore it; she was fiercely roused. Her whole body, every fibre of her, quivered for satisfaction. She felt the tug of the velvet cords as she tried instinctively to draw in her limbs, to close her legs, to bring her hands down to touch the centre of her need, the maddening pulse of sexual hunger at her loins. God, this was cruel! She ached with the need to caress herself, to bring the relief her screaming nerves demanded. She began to sob, her body tom by convulsive shudders of grief.

It was a long while before the fit passed. She realised she was cold, despite the heating from the old and inefficient radiators in the room. The cords didn't chafe as long as she lay still. Would they leave her there all night?

Her mind drifted.

She tried to conjure up the faces of those downstairs. She tried to recall previous Christmases.

This was undoubtedly the strangest Christmas Eve she had spent in her entire life; tied naked and blindfolded on a bed in a lord's castle. It was the hot stuff of a teenager's fantasies. Except that no one was there to make her fantasies come true.

She didn't know whether she had actually slept, but suddenly she was jerked to full awareness, straining her ears. There had been a noise. The door opening? She thought she could sense someone's presence. 'Magda?' she whispered. 'Is that you? Who's there?' She waited, there was a creak, she thought she could hear a soft rustle, like cloth moving. 'Who's there?' she called again, beginning to panic. 'Who are you?'

She whimpered as a cold hand grabbed suddenly at her breast, crushing, squeezing, the thumb brushing against the tender nipple. A man, surely? Another clammy hand seized her other breast, equally brutally, and she gasped in shock as much as pain. Then a naked body was on her, covering her, and a searching slobbering mouth sealed hers, smothering the scream in her throat. A hand scrabbled at her belly, prised open her labia, a finger prodded into her, to the wet sheath of her vagina. Other fingers opened her and brushed across her clitoris. They rubbed until she involuntarily lifted her hips, gasping under the smothering weight and kiss.

'Who is this?' she wept impotently when she could again speak. She felt the tears soaking into the velvet of the mask. 'Please,' she sobbed, quieter now, wilting under the onslaught. She could feel an erection resting on her belly, and then the stranger's hips lifting as he clumsily sought to enter her. 'Untie me,' she begged. 'It'll be easier...'

She cried out at the sharp penetration, the sudden plunge deep into her clinging sheath. She groaned shamefully, knowing she was already roused to her former excitement.

She fought instinctively to raise her legs, to wrap them around the lunging figure on top of her. She knew she was coming, arched her back, and screamed aloud, her cry dying to a long wail as the orgasm raged through her.

Chapter Seventeen

Felicity woke, swimming up from the depths of a sensual dream, jerked to full consciousness by the awareness that her wrists were still secured, her arms sprawled out above her head. She moved, felt the unrestricted freedom of her legs, and remembered the relief of someone untying her ankles, allowing her to draw up her knees, lift her thighs, and encompass the rutting body between them. She was aware of the heavy warmth of the duvet which someone - Magda? - had tucked securely around her after the ordeal, and after someone had wiped her sensitive sex with a cool antiseptic tissue.

How many had fucked her? She was still not sure. Five? Six? She wasn't even certain whether it had been the second or the third who had released her ankles, when she begged him to do so, explaining how uncomfortable it was for her. Once her legs were free it had been much easier. In fact it shamed her to remember how excitement had overtaken her once more when one of her invisible assailants, the fourth perhaps, had spent a long time kissing her helpless frame; her breasts, her stomach, her knees, until he reached the puffy lips of her sex, sticky with the discharges previously pumped into her.

The wicked tongue had teased until she was again straining at her bonds, her body arched, sobbing for release that came, eventually, in the shape of another gliding cock. Even that was a connoisseur's performance. Not exceptionally long but wickedly skilful, it moved in such a way that drew the maximum of sensation from her heaving form, withdrawing until she could feel the very tip between her vaginal lips and she whimpered with the fear that she would lose it altogether, only for the bliss of that steady drive to fill her once again.'

The man came even as her own climax was dying its shuddering death. After that she wasn't sure whether it was another one or two that used her. She felt little, and they were soon done. She seemed to lie alone for hours in a trancelike state, feeling strangely proud and somehow vindicated. She had passed the test, of that she was certain, and she lay in an exhausted stupor.

She tried to decide if and when his lordship had fucked her, and was mortified to find she didn't know. Was he the first? She shivered as she wondered if one of her partners had been the venerable judge, the ancient turtle. She couldn't recall any particularly horrendous contact. Surely she would have known such a withered frame? She felt the heat of embarrassment as she mentally relived each bout, thought about the penises that had been driven into her. She could not really differentiate between them.

With such bizarre reflections occupying her thoughts she drifted eventually to sleep, still tied, still blindfolded, in that strange and silent room.

When the mask was removed the light stabbed into her eyes so mercilessly she could not open them for several seconds. When she could, there was her beloved Magda, and the room was bathed in the brightness of electric light. Through the still drawn curtains a dull daylight seeped. Magda at last untied her wrists, and Felicity whimpered as the blood flowed back into her cramped muscles.

Magda picked her up and carried her through to the adjoining bathroom, stood her in the tub, and turned on the shower. The soothing flow of hot water comforted and caressed. Magda had slipped off her robe. She was wearing the black embossed cache-sexe, which she didn't remove as she stood behind Felicity. Felicity could feel the tiny scratch of the metal on its leather as Magda enfolded her in her arms, the large hands slipping round and cradling her breasts in their tender hold.

Felicity revelled in her own surrender, standing inertly while her mistress soaped every curve of her weary body, before lifting her out and drying her. Then Magda sat her on the bidet and allowed the bubbling stream of tepid water to play around the tender lips of her sex, soothing further. Finally, she wrapped her in a long white towelling robe and carried her along to her own room, where she laid her in the bed and curled up beside her, holding her in her arms until Felicity drifted off towards another, more contented sleep.

'Did I pass?' she murmured dreamily, quivering with joy at the lips that lightly kissed the hollow of her neck.

'With flying colours, my angel,' the deep voice breathed, its warmth yet another treasured caress.

The stabbing pain in Michael's head was his first acknowledgement of yet another night of drunken abandon. He opened his eyes to see John standing there, holding a tray with a mug of coffee, a glass of orange juice, and some toast on it. He was wearing Felicity's flowered silk robe. Michael vividly recalled her in it, how it showed her body with misty enchantment through its sheer darkness. Now it hung negligently open on John's slim frame, revealing his nakedness. Michael's gaze was drawn to the neat dark triangle of hair and the small prick hanging beneath. A consuming shame speared through him at the memory of its throbbing potency, the texture and taste of it in his mouth, and the thick issue that had anointed his face and hair.

His jaw clenched. He wished he could hide, and wished the whole of the previous evening had not happened. He had a childish urge to crawl under the bedclothes and pretend he wasn't there.

'Happy Christmas,' John said cheerfully, moving to the side of the bed. 'Here you are, rejoin us in the land of the living.'

Largely because he could think of nothing else to do, Michael struggled up on his elbows, took the proffered glass, and muttered a shamefaced reply to the seasonal greeting. He drank the juice greedily, and sighed with pleasure at its coldness. He was surprised to find that, apart from his throbbing temples, he did not feel too bad, but then remembered how comprehensively he had vomited - after... after...

In the early hours of the morning, after a steaming shower, Michael had stood for long seconds in Felicity's bedroom, staring vacantly at the bed. Then a great weariness overcame him. What did it matter now? He was a queer, a poof, a queen - he broke off the litany of self-abuse, climbed into bed, and listened to the sound of John's ablutions.

With his usual matter of fact manner, John came in some minutes later, climbed in beside him, and switched off the lamp. Michael lay with his back to him, and once more he felt that smooth form fit around him, adapting to his curves. He felt the small prick nestle against his buttocks.

He swallowed hard and fought the sudden urge to weep again. 'I don't - I'm not a bugger—!'

'Neither am I,' John had interrupted. 'Not tonight, anyway.' The warmth of spearmint-scented breath tickled Michael's ear as John chuckled softly. Michael felt the fumbling hand reach round and delicately pick up his limp penis, which stirred at once to the still-alien touch. 'But it's your turn for a bit of fun. That was wonderful back' there. You don't mind if I toss you off as a little thank you, do you?'

His hand was already moving, gently, rhythmically, and Michael's traitorous prick stiffened. Mortified, he made a strangled sound, then whispered, 'I can't... I haven't - got anything.'

John chuckled again. 'You don't need a condom for this, you know. You won't catch anything off me.'

'No, the mess, I mean—' Michael stammered, and John tutted patiently.

'Don't worry, sweetheart. I'll wash the sheets tomorrow.

Now lie back and think of Santa.'

That afternoon, after an excellent Christmas lunch cooked by John, and many more drinks, they were both drunk again. 'Let's have a fancy dress party!' John exclaimed, and pulled Michael by the arm through to the bedroom. He flung open Felicity's drawers and wardrobe, and selected a variety of articles, from the flimsiest of G-string briefs, to the slinky bodies, the camisole vests and cotton panties, and the plethora of tights and embroidered stockings.

'Christ, you'll ruin them!' John sniggered happily, watching a transformed Michael as he struggled with a bra which would not fit his broad chest, and a pair of navy blue tights which he hauled on somehow, over a pair of her red lacy knickers. John was wearing a shiny satin body-shaper of a delicate pearl shade, when they went back into the fire-lit living room. They sprawled on the rug, with freshly charged glasses of brandy.

Michael's prick was hard. It stuck out, stretching the thin material of the knickers and the tights. He stared across at John, whose own genitals could scarcely be seen under the hugging grip of the high cut garment.

'You know, you look bloody sexy,' Michael said solemnly, and John flashed him a come hither look, and pursed his lips in a kiss.

'Why, thank you, kind sir.'

'You - you did last night,' Michael went on, clumsily. 'I really thought you were Felicity. You look good - in her gear.'

John smiled. 'So did you, in a different way.' He stared pointedly at the shape of Michael's bulging prick. He knelt, then crawled over, lying in front of him on his stomach, his narrow feet waving in the air. 'Let's have a peep, shall we?' With a hooked forefinger, he pulled at the elastic of the tights and the red knickers, and succeeded in dragging them down a little at the front. The engorged head of the penis leapt into view, red and gleaming. 'Hello...' he purred in mock surprise, 'what's all this then?' and, leaning closer, he took it gently between thumb and forefinger and kissed the weeping tip. He flicked out his tongue, tasting the slimy liquid at the slit. 'Yummy...' he grinned. He pulled a large cushion off the sofa and pushed Michael back onto it.

The taller figure made no attempt to stop John as he eased the tights and knickers down, carefully drawing the clinging articles off the long legs and feet. Then he parted Michael's legs and knelt between them. He massaged the tight scrotum that hung between Michael's thighs and gently pumped the impressive erection that spear up from his groin. Still a little concerned about pushing Michael too far too quickly, John squeezed an experimental fingertip between his firm buttocks and pushed gently against the tight opening that hid there, and noted that the only reaction he drew from the form stretched before him was a sharp intake of breath. Thus encouraged, his head dipped, his mouth opened, and he greedily swallowed the throbbing prick entrapped in his fist. As the tight anus opened just a fraction for his gently persistent finger, he savoured the promise of what he now knew was to come.

Michael gasped and his belly lifted as the sucking warmth enveloped him and the fingertip prodded between his buttocks. He felt his desire surging. He tried to hold on, savouring the pleasure, but soon he cried out, shuddering, as he ejaculated fiercely. All the while John's mouth stayed clamped over the spewing length, his throat working, suckling sounds filling the room as he swallowed the thick fluid.

When they had both calmed a little John rose and moved away, leaving Michael, his face hidden in the crook of an arm, his body, rosy and desirable in the firelight, shaking with his quiet sobs.

The water ran in the bathroom.

John came back, naked, and knelt beside the still supine figure. 'Now, best bit of all, Mikey,' he whispered gently. He pulled the arm away. Michael's face was blotchy, his eyes and cheeks smeared with tears. He gazed up helplessly, and then John was moving, turning him over, and Michael shivered at the cool touch of the fingers delving deep into the taut cleft of his behind and the iciness of the perfumed cream John smeared there. The knowing fingers probed, and found the hidden bud of Michael's anus.

'No... no...' Michael whispered, appalled, yet allowing John to turn him, his bottom thrust up in the air, his forearms folded on the soft cushion. 'Please,' Michael begged.

'I've never done this. I've never wanted to do this. I swear it. Please don't...' He was weeping, and shaking. John knelt behind him, between his trembling thighs. Michael could feel his own limp prick, still seeping after his recent discharge. It felt tiny, shrivelled, inside its shroud of foreskin. The dome of John's eagerly erect penis nudged and rubbed up and down Michael's lubricated valley.

'You'll just *love* it, darling boy,' John breathed, his lips kissing at the back of the bowed neck. His hands dipped, and guided his rearing penis to the virginal tightness waiting to be pierced.

Chapter Eighteen

'What's Lord B's name?' Felicity asked curiously. She stretched her legs under the warm covers. She felt like a cat, cosseted and cosy in this comfortable nest. Magda herself had brought up the late breakfast tray, and sat now watching her eat, with a maternal satisfaction.

'Why? You'll never use his name. None of us do.' Felicity pouted. 'He's my lover. I've never had a lover with no name before.'

'You've had plenty of lovers without names,' Magda teased gently. 'Or have you forgotten already?'

'I know their names,' Felicity contradicted, blushing slightly. 'I just don't know who was who.'

'How do you know they were our guests?' the mocking tones continued. 'Perhaps they were all strangers. Or the staff. Or the local football team. They could have been anybody.'

For an instant Felicity stared at her in wide-eyed alarm, then pulled a sulky face once more. 'You're teasing me! You're a beast!'

'Am I?' Magda reached out and tweaked Felicity's nipple playfully. 'Yes, I suppose I am. But you still love me, don't you? But how much, I wonder?'

Felicity stared at her, caught by the reflective seriousness in her voice. 'How could you?' she murmured, in genuine reproach. 'I thought I'd proved that already. I thought I'd passed all my tests.'

'Ah.' Magda shook her head mysteriously, then the eyes held hers. 'Are you really willing to do anything for me?'

Felicity' felt suddenly as though she were some kind of specimen, pegged down by that merciless question. The tide of colour flooded up from her throat, and her voice shook with emotion. 'You know I am. You know what I did the other night. I'm not just some kinky tart looking for kicks, you know.' The unsteadiness increased and there was the catch of tears in her words. 'Why won't you believe me?'

Magda stared for what seemed an age, deep in thought. 'What about Michael?'

Felicity shrugged uncomfortably. 'It's all sort of gone wrong. Anyway, I'm going to tell him. As soon as I go back to town. It's all over between us.'

'Are you sure?'

Felicity nodded firmly. 'I'm sure.'

But Magda's next question made her gape in open-mouthed astonishment.

'And what if I don't want it to be?'

Felicity blinked. 'What?'

'What if I prefer to have you wed to Michael Sinclair? He's a decent upstanding citizen. An ideal husband, to coin a phrase. It'd be an outstanding match. Beautiful film star, financial wizard.'

'I don't understand,' Felicity said uncertainly, not sure if she was joking. 'Why would you want to get rid of me?'

'You don't have to understand,' Magda answered. 'You'd still be mine, wouldn't you? Even if you married Michael Sinclair?'

'How could I be? Not like now...' she gestured at the bed and her naked body. 'Michael wouldn't put up with this. Look at the fuss he's made about Stella. Anyway, I doubt he'll have me now.'

'Is he really such a straight old square?' the deep voice drawled. 'It's really quite cute, in this day and age.' She stood up quickly. 'Never mind that for now. I've a job for you. Get up, have a shower, then put these on. Don't dawdle. You've got to be out by eleven.' She went over to the chair, upon which lay a bundle of clothes, and brought them over to the bed. 'Chop chop!' She clapped her hands, and Felicity obediently swung her legs out of the bed.

'What the hell's all this?' Her voice squeaked in startled indignation at the ribbed and laced black corselette, with flounced frills of organdie at the high cut away legs, from which the long ribbons of suspenders dangled. There was also a pair of sheer dark stockings, and shoes with tiny bows and spiky four-inch heels. The white blouse had a high ruffled neck and long puffed sleeves, gathered in frills at the wrists. The high-waisted skirt was flared, and made of a heavy material in a dark tweed, and came almost to her ankles. 'Is this fancy dress?' she asked. 'On the outside I look like a Victorian schoolmarm and underneath a saloon girl from a B-movie Western.'

She yelped as Magda slapped her with playful force across the top of her thigh. 'I've told you, baby, yours is not to reason why. Go and get ready before I tan your arse for you!'

As she showered, then dressed in the strange outfit, all under the amused gaze of her mistress, Felicity's mind raced in a variety of bewildering emotions. Uppermost was the anxiety, the fear that hollowed her stomach unpleasantly. What on earth had Magda planned for her? Could it be another gang-bang? She was privately astonished at how quickly both her spirits and her body had recovered from that experience.

Never in her life had she had more than one man make love to her at a time. And certainly not six in the space of a few hours! She had thought she'd be prostrate for days afterwards, that she would hardly be able to move, let alone contemplate any sexual activity. Yet the very next night, under Magda's passionate domination, she had proved how wrong she had been in her assumption.

Worse, she had thought, would be her shame at having to face those privileged men who had used her so mechanically. Even a prostitute would be hard put to deal with six such clients in one night, she thought, though she had little idea of the realities of commercial sex. It suddenly occurred to her that, if she had met anyone of those fat cats individually, on her own territory, she could have charged hundreds, if not thousands, for her favours. She really was a star now, just as Magda had said. Yet at the Hall she was nothing. A staked-out piece of meat; prime, it was true. And they had used her as such, pumping their seed anonymously into her cunt; a mere vessel for their bodily gratification. And it was that which had secretly thrilled her more than anything about the whole bizarre incident.

She had dreaded facing them the next day, had crimsoned like a schoolgirl when she was led into the drawing room, Magda's arm firmly around her waist. But they had all behaved with their polished gallantry, just as before. No one made any reference to how she'd been used in the Green Room, and amazingly, she herself had come to accept it as though it had happened to someone else, or had been one of her erotic dreams.

Now, dreamlike unreality took over once more as she contemplated herself in the long mirror. The demureness of the high blouse was offset a little by the misty hint of the dark underwear beneath the fine material. The cups of the corselette thrust her breasts up. When she twirled in obedience to Magda's command, the skirt flared out, in spite of the heavy material, and gave a glimpse of her white thighs above the stocking tops, the flesh dissected by the narrow straps of the suspenders.

Magda went downstairs with her, and to the door near the kitchens. The car was waiting. Reeves, uniformed as always, was standing by.

'What about a coat?' Felicity asked.

'You won't need one, darling.' Magda leaned forward and kissed her, quite chastely, on the lips.

Felicity stared in growing trepidation. 'Aren't you coming with me?'

Magda laughed and shook her head. 'No, my sweet. You're all on your lonesome this time. Just remember- do exactly what you're told to do at all times. And don't speak unless you're spoken to.'

Felicity felt empty and lonely, like a child being sent to her first day at school. 'Where am I going?' she asked helplessly.

'You don't need to know, my pet,' Magda answered, and patted her cheek. 'Run along now.'

Reeves smiled, held the rear door open for her and, her feeling of helplessness growing, she climbed in.

She arranged the wide skirt decorously about her as the Mercedes pulled away round the mansion and onto the long drive. She caught Reeves' eye in the driving mirror and smiled at him nervously. 'Where are we going?' she asked, leaning forward a little.

'That's a good start isn't it, miss?' he said flatly. 'You heard what Miss Magda said.'

Felicity flushed a bright crimson and sat back, humbled and a little angry. She stared at the rich parkland slipping past. It was ironic how she was treated here. Even by this - this servant! Now more than ever she was a household name, as famous, perhaps, as any young woman in the land. At the pinnacle of her fame. But that was in the outside world. Here at Burnopside everyone behaved towards her with such contempt. No, it was not contempt. Far from it, she admitted. There was a tender familiarity, but it was as if she was of no more account than Debbie, or Joanne, or Marie-Angele, or any of the other girls. And she wasn't, she acknowledged, deeply ashamed of her brief flare of angry pride. That's why she loved it there. Why she wanted to stay.

The car was passing through the wide pillared gates and into the leafy lane that led to the busy road - to the outside world. With a shiver which betokened both her fear and her thrill, she realised that the special aura of Burnopside was being extended, that she was passing beyond its bounds not as Felicity Keynes the star of *A Woman's Touch*, but as that other compliant persona who wanted only to love and obey.

She leaned forward again and put her manicured hand lightly on the uniformed shoulder. 'Please,' she murmured. 'I'm so sorry, Reeves. Forgive me. Please don't tell Miss Magda. I really am sorry.'

He winked at her in the rearview mirror. 'That's all right, miss. Sit back and enjoy the ride.'

It wasn't until they had almost reached their destination that Felicity recognised how close they were to Heathrow. A few minutes later they were pulling in to the forecourt of one of the large airport hotels.

Reeves turned round and grinned encouragingly. 'Room two-three-three,' he said. 'Up you go. I'll be back at four. Wait in the lounge for me.' He got out of the car and opened the rear door for her. The gold braided commissionaire was already hurrying forward importantly. 'No luggage,' Reeves told him, and then with a final smile at Felicity, he got back in and pulled away.

In the busy reception area, she paused uncertainly, wondering whether to announce herself at the desk. But she noticed a stout woman muffled in a quilted jacket staring at her. She could almost hear the brain ticking over: 'Is that the woman on the tele...?'

Felicity fled towards the lifts and scanned the room numbers. First floor. She hurried into a waiting lift and was out again in the thickly carpeted corridor almost immediately. It was quite a hike to room two-three-three. She tottered slightly, the slender heels sinking into the thick pile. Her sick anxiety increased with every second as she neared her destination. What, or who, would she find there? What could Magda have planned to test her now?

She took a deep breath, patted her hair, and tapped on the door. A man opened it and smiled at her.

'Felicity?' he said. 'Of course it is. Come in.'

He was the stuff of true romance; tall dark and handsome. Her heartbeat quickened. Another pulse, deep in her crotch, beat disconcertingly, too.

'Would you like a drink?' he asked courteously.

She was about to refuse, then decided her nerves required one. She accepted a brandy and soda and stared around at the impersonal comfort, realising that this was in fact a suite - and a highly expensive one at that.

The man gave her another dazzling smile, came close, and inspected her frankly. 'Do you mind?' He gestured, indicating she should lift the heavy skirt. And she did, blushing furiously and feeling utterly foolish. His upturned palm lifted, and she raised the skirt higher still, until the tops of her thighs and the frilled organdie of her undergarment were on view.

'Splendid...' he said quietly, as though to himself. Felicity let the skirt drop, shocked at her own thoughts as she pondered what it would be like to have sex with this good-looking fellow. Is this what Magda was about, after all? Did she simply want to turn her into a high-class prostitute? Was she, or maybe even Lord B himself, being paid a vast sum for her favours? Were he and Magda no more than pimps, operating an exclusive vice service, using her and the other girls at the Hall?

While her giddy brain was busily trying to assimilate all this, the young man went over to an inner door and tapped respectfully. 'Felicity's here, sir. I'll leave you now. Ring when you need me.'

She was still staring in wonder when he smiled a last time and left the room. Through the netted stretch of double glazed window, planes rose and descended soundlessly.

Felicity was stirred from her daydreaming when the inner door opened and a short figure appeared, completely bald and heavily jowled. He was wearing a singlet, and his belly thrust out like a heavily pregnant woman's, bulging over the belt of the expensive slacks he wore. The bull neck and shoulders betokened considerable strength, though it was a strength largely gone to fat and softened by good living. He moved forward, grinning, and several gold fillings glinted in the pale afternoon light.

His hands were stubby, too, like the rest of him, but there was this aura of power that struck her forcibly. His touch was light but firm on her arm and her waist, guiding her to a low armchair. She sank down, neatly arranging the long skirt and crossing her legs as she did so. The faint rasp of nylon on nylon was like a perceptible tremor of sex.

'You're very lovely,' he said. His voice was thick, husky, with a moderate foreign accent. Italian, Felicity thought. Perhaps he was a big wheel in the Mafia, she wondered fancifully. 'I just wish I had more time. Unfortunately, my plane leaves in a couple of hours. I'm glad you could make it. Would you like another drink?'

'No thank you.' She almost asked a question, then remembered Magda's instructions. In the normal luxury of these surroundings they seemed ridiculous, yet she obeyed. Even here she was no longer Felicity Keynes, but someone altogether different. She flushed at the excitement this thought caused her.

'Right,' he announced, in a businesslike tone. He took the glass from her and put it to one side, and then casually unbuckled his belt and shuffled out of his trousers. His underpants were baggy and loose in the leg. She could see no sign of his genitals under their concealment. 'Over here.' He extended his hand, she took it, and he drew her over to the polished table right by the window. 'Bend over,' he ordered, watching her move obediently, and said with evident satisfaction, 'That's right... lovely.'

Felicity's heart sank. It was to be another beating. She turned her head to the side and felt the cold polished surface of the wood against her cheek. He lifted the hem of her skirt and folded it carefully over her back. She wondered how he would deal with her underwear, having to undo the three hook-and-eye fasteners under her crotch. Should she help him? Should she do it herself? But then she realised he was not going to bare her bottom at all.

'The cane, I think,' she heard him say. 'Is that all right?'

Speak when spoken to. She cleared her throat and stammered uncertainly, 'Y-yes.' Her frame tensed as she heard a short sharp whistling sound as he swiped the instrument of punishment through the still air. Her outstretched fingers clung to the far edge of the table, her buttocks clenched, and she held her breath, waiting in dread for the agony to begin.

'Oh, here,' he said, 'better put this in. Just in case.' He pushed a clean handkerchief into her mouth, and she bit down on it. Which was just as well, for as the first stroke cut deep into her behind, in spite of the flounced lace and satin protecting it, she jerked and screamed, the gag trapping the protests deep in her throat. 'Only a few more!' he warned, his voice thick and unsteady with his arousal. 'Don't move!' Somehow she managed to stay down over the table, pressing herself to its hardness in a feeble attempt to escape the pain, while five more cuts bit into her poor flesh.

The breath whistled through her flared nostrils and tears streamed down her cheeks as she chewed desperately at the sodden handkerchief to suppress her anguish. She was trembling violently, grateful through the haze of pain for the steady burn that told her the caning was over. She felt she couldn't move, though her hands longed to caress the burning rounds.

'Good girl!' he panted, and she felt those stubby fingers fumbling with clumsy impatience at her damp crotch, dealing with the difficult fasteners until he finally succeeded and the piece of material covering her sex fell away.

He lifted the little tail of the garment, folded it onto her back, and prodded her feet apart with the toe of his shoe. She instinctively readjusted her stance a little for him, and then felt his rampant prick probe into the valley of her abused bottom. She felt his insistent thumbs prising her cheeks apart. She groaned into the wet hanky, expecting him to penetrate her back passage. But he didn't. He grunted and said, 'You're not one of them, then? Or haven't they done you yet?' Then she completely forgot the cryptic words as his thick penis bludgeoned through into the receptive moistness of her sex, and buried itself deep into her pulsating sheath.

Oddly, the pounding of his fat belly and his groin against her tortured buttocks was comforting, and then highly arousing, as her excitement spiralled to meet his at the crucial moment. She felt the powerful spurt of his coming and drove back against him frantically, the walls of her vagina spasming, the orgasm bursting upon her with all its consuming finality.

Chapter Nineteen

Michael stared sourly at the Mercedes in front of him in the fast lane, and crept close to the tinted rear window, gunning his motor imperiously. The silver-grey car pulled over to the middle lane, and Michael inched past. The side rear windows were tinted too, so he couldn't see if anyone was sitting in the back, but he could see the liveried outfit of the chauffeur at the wheel, staring stolidly ahead and ignoring the malevolent glare Michael threw at him. Doubtless some loaded foreigner heading for the airport. Perhaps a wealthy sheikh with his four wives and the boot crammed with half of Harrods. He forgot about it at once, concentrating on the road instead, and on his own troubled thoughts.

He was late for the meeting, just as he'd been late into the office, where he'd put in his first appearance since before the holiday break. And here it was the thirtieth. Sir Robert had not been too pleased, that was made blatantly clear. In his opinion holidays were for the plebs. For the first time, while Sir Robert chewed his bollocks off, Michael had thought he spied a hint of compassion in Louise's beautifully made-up eyes, as well as the knicker-moistening lust he fancied he could read there. And his PA wasn't the only one with the hots for him, he liked secretly to imagine. The outer office was redolent with the soft sounds of squelching labia, he liked to think, every time he walked past the girls with his best smile.

But not now. He felt the heat of shame spreading up through his body and squirmed in the comfortable bucket seat, his ultra sensitive awareness sending tremors of recalled pain from the tiny fissure of his anus. As on countless occasions during the past four days, he experienced that feeling of horror, of weak helplessness, at the trauma he had undergone with that wicked little bastard, John.

How could he have let that, of all things, happen to him?

He stiffened, knuckles white on the wheel, and from his clamped jaws an anguished groan escaped. And merged with all the tormenting guilt and revulsion, was the tormenting realisation that he'd loved everything he did and had been done to him. The latent thrill of being helpless, the violation of his manhood, and the unique excitement of passivity while being remorselessly penetrated, which had turned his preconceived notions of gender, of sex, so totally upside down.

He had lain there after the shuddering agony of that withdrawal, and sobbed brokenly, unable to move a muscle except for the involuntary trembling which ran through him. He had lain there, aware of his nakedness, his sense of being conquered, of being possessed by the slim figure who so fascinated him. It should have been he, Michael, who was the macho male role player in this homosexual relationship. He had only allowed John to seduce him in the first place because of the striking resemblance to Felicity. The alluring John, with his dramatic beauty and his body slinky and desirable in her silken scraps of clothing - that's what had tempted him beyond endurance.

So how had he wound up adopting the feminine role? Though it scourged him to recall, it had been so all the way through. He'd lain helplessly while John tossed him off that first time... and the second. And still subservient, he'd been pushed literally to his knees to perform fellatio, to pay homage to that prick jutting so weirdly and wonderfully from the black silk of Felicity's underwear. And all of that had led, inevitably, to the moment of awful truth when he had finally and fully surrendered his body to the spearing pain, and the terrifyingly thrilling climax of his total submission.

He had given up completely, weeping like a newly deflowered virgin, letting John tend and be tender, cleansing and soothing him, folding him to sleep in his arms.

It had been the following afternoon when they eventually rose from bed. Michael had used the excuse of work to escape. 'Call me,' John said, and Michael had nodded, blushing, and fled - fled to a three day nightmare of solitary drinking and weeping and self-flagellation; mental only but stinging nevertheless.

At the meeting, in a complex out along a seasonally quiet M25, Michael impressed no one, and gave several food for unquiet thought by his general air of lassitude, and a lack of that flair which had marked him for discreet fame.

'Under the weather, eh?' one of his cohorts suggested, with a knowing grin.

'Roll on January,' another, more senior, exclaimed sourly.

Michael's mobile beeped softly, and Louise's voice buzzed in his ear. 'A Nicki Lowther's been phoning for you. Says she wants you to get in touch with her, urgently. She sounds very upset about something.'

'I don't know a Nicki Lowther,' he replied quietly. 'In what connection?'

'Private. That's all she said. But she was very insistent.' She gave him the number and rang off. An inner city location. He got away from his colleagues and found a chrome and upholstered chair in the bare outer lobby of the business centre. He stabbed out the number and identified himself when his call was answered.

The voice sounded young and extremely tense, unsteady with emotion. 'I have to see you. Can we meet now? Right away? I need to talk.'

'Look, I'm afraid I don't know what this is all about, er, Miss Lowther. I can't...'

'I'm Stella's mate. Christmas Eve? You can't have forgotten, you bastard. I want to know just what you did to her.'

Scarcely knowing why, he found himself agreeing to drive over to the address she gave him, which was a penthouse apartment in former dockland. He recognised her at once when she opened the door to the luxury flat. She was wearing what appeared to be the same outfit he remembered; the black T-shirt and jeans and those ugly boots.

He realised as he entered that this was Stella Priest's pad, and he glanced about warily.

'Don't worry,' Nicki Lowther said sarcastically. 'There's no one else here. Stella's pissed off to Scotland again. She won't be back until New Year. I'm all alone. So you can have a go at me as well, if you want to.' Her jaw lifted and she glared at him with a childish defiance he found almost endearing.

Nicki Lowther's rather awkward, adolescent grace, and her gamine looks which bordered on the emaciated, had been her passport to a world far removed, at least socially and financially, from her humble North London background. Though even that background had itself contributed to her initial success, for her nasal London twang went along with the grungy image the commercial world was looking for then. Catalogue modelling clothes for a company who aped the more exclusive garments of the catwalks had been her first breakthrough assignment. Then came advertisements for a variety of goods, from wrist watches to sanitary napkins, all of which, the moguls decided, would do better if pushed by this fashionably urchin, unfulfilled look.

More and more people began to know her face, with its sulky pout and angular lines, though no one knew her name, and she soon got her chance to encroach on the outer edges of the really big money. She was taken on as a clothes-horse for a new name among the designers, an effete young man who was himself trying to achieve his own entrance into big-time. The show was in New York, and Nicki swung with great strides down the catwalk with some really famous• names, dressed in the seemingly shapeless swirls of flimsy, semi-transparent materials, the thin straps slipping off her hollow shoulders, showing the pink little pimples of her almost flat breasts, the flowing femininity a striking contrast to the laced leather combat boots.

It was these blown up shots which Stella had first studied, when she was delving into the possibilities of *A Woman's Touch*, long before Felicity's name had even come up for the co-starring role. And it was Stella who got Nicki a small, but possibly seminal, part in the production. She had flirted with the youngster, seen the possibilities of a dalliance, before she had become diverted, then preoccupied, with the challenge of converting Felicity. Possibilities which were revived, then fanned rapidly into flame, when she and Felicity had broken their relationship at the beginning of December.

'I gather you don't remember me,' Nicki grinned, when Michael had somewhat uneasily accepted the offer of a drink. He stood watching the vista of loury rainclouds from the panoramic sweep of the windows, and the tossing porcupine mastheads of the yachts in the choppy marina. 'I was actually in *A Touch*,' she continued, 'but I guess you were too busy watching your girl wrestling with Stella, eh?'

He frowned, summoning up his unpleasant manner at her aggressive style. 'So what do you want to talk about?' he asked bluntly.

'You. And what the fuck went on the other night at that poxy studio do. Did you shag her?'

Suddenly he wanted to hit out, to hurt her. And she looked so vulnerable, for all her bravado, that he knew he could. 'Yes,' he answered. 'I shagged her. After I put her head down the loo. And it wasn't rape. She bloody loved it, believe me! Whatever she might have snivelled on about afterwards.'

'That's the trouble,' Nicki muttered, so forlornly that Michael was taken aback. 'She didn't. She never said a word. But I knew something had happened. She hasn't been the same since.'

To Michael's surprise her head sank and her thin shoulders began to shake. She cried like a desolate child, and he felt his anger dissipate, felt the hollowness of his cheap victory.

He pulled out his handkerchief and offered it to her, feeling embarrassed by the unbridled display of emotion. 'Here,' he said. 'You don't need to upset yourself. I've no intention of going anywhere near her again.'

She took it, dabbed at her eyes, sniffed, and then blew her nose loudly. She handed it back to him, keeping her head down. 'Thanks, but I wouldn't bank on that.' Her flat voice sounded resigned. 'I don't think she'll let it go at that.'

Michael let her keep the hanky, not through any real chivalry, but because he didn't fancy putting it back in his pocket after she'd filled it. 'I told you,' he replied hastily, alarm bells beginning to sound. 'It certainly wasn't rape, in spite of what happened. She didn't fight me off. No way.' He was startled by the tearful, dark eyes which lifted to meet his, naked in their hurt and appeal.

'I know that!' she cried tormentedly. 'You don't have to rub it in, you sod!'

He wondered what on earth she meant. The tears had started again, but she made no attempt to wipe them away. Her frame shook with a convulsive sob, then she made a great effort to stem her fit of weeping.

'Look,' she said, in a surprising contrast of tone, as though she was now making casual conversation. 'Would you like to fuck me... now?'

'Eh?' He gawped at her blankly.

'I think you heard me. Would you like to fuck me, here and now? Do what you like with me. Anything you like at all.'

His mind raced. 'What on earth for?' he said stupidly.

She scowled fiercely. 'What the fuck do you think for? Because you fancy me. Well?' She glared at him. 'I'll even fight back if that's your kick.'

He blushed deeply. Could she know about him and John? No, it wasn't possible. And yet her cute precociousness, the defiant jut of her chin, her boyish hips and breasts, all combined like a taunting challenge flung down to him; a gauntlet to his doubtful masculinity. He felt rage and desire spark simultaneously. 'I'm a man, love,' he spat viciously. 'I don't shag lesbians.'

'You shagged Stella!' She sneered insolently. 'Who knows? I might even like it like she did! And you might like shagging a *queer!*'

'You little bitch!' He started forward; did she know or had she inadvertently hit a nerve? She flinched a little but stood her ground, with that contemptuous smile.

'A bit of rough stuff first, eh?' she goaded. 'That turns you on, does it?'

'Get your kit off,' he said tightly.

The smile remained as she slowly crossed her hands and pulled her shirt off over her head. Beneath it she wore a sleeveless vest, plain white, like a boy's. She sat on the edge of the long sofa, and spent an age unlacing her boots and tugging them off. Then she stood and pushed down the clinging jeans. As Michael expected, her briefs were very plain too; white cotton like the vest. It was all she wore now, save for the thick woollen socks of speckled grey, which hung in folds about her ankles.

'Very sexy!' he sneered, and felt a mean sense of triumph as he watched her look down at herself, and the redness that spread up from her slim throat.

'Bastard...' she whispered, and, quickly as she could, pulled off the socks and underwear and stood before him naked, her hands clenched into fists, stiffly at her sides. Her breasts were extremely small, with tiny immature nipples. Her narrow hips were in keeping with her wiry frame, and he stared at the curve of her mound, devoid of hair, with only the faintest suggestion of a shadow to indicate that the pubis had been shaved. The upper peak of her labial lips stood out, the smooth swell of the tight divide lacking any substantial folds of tissue, thus enhancing the impression of youthfulness.

'How old are you?' Michael demanded involuntarily.

'Old enough,' she snapped. 'I've been around, don't you worry. I know what to do and what goes where.'

'Do you?' he snarled. 'Right then.' Their eyes met, and held in competition to outstare each other as he quickly slipped off his jacket and tie and tossed them aside like a hasty stripper. Shirt and vest followed. He sucked in his stomach, aware of the muscled curves of his torso, but then he had to stoop and fumble clumsily as he dropped his pants, pulling off his shoes and socks, hopping slightly as he dragged the last off his feet.

She was studying him as intensely as he had her. His prick curved out, thickened in semi-erection, the helm protruding from its ring of foreskin. He was bigger than John, he thought suddenly, then blushed at the idea that had sprung into his mind unbidden.

Her dark eyes were wide now, and he was savagely comforted by the look of fear he could plainly read on her young face. But at the same time he too experienced a wave of apprehension as he wondered whether he would be able to perform; the last few days had been pretty• traumatic, to say the least.

She cleared her throat. 'Do you want to go to bed?' she asked huskily, sounding extremely uncertain. She was still standing rigidly to attention, hands clenched at her sides.

He felt his prick lurch and stiffen slightly, responding to her nervousness. He gave an ugly grin. 'No, this'll do fine. I don't want any dyke's den to fuck around in.' He saw her flinch at his cruel words, and savoured the reaction. He stepped forward and sank into the soft cushions of a wide armchair, lewdly letting his legs loll wide apart. 'You know enough about pleasuring another dyke. But do you know anything about pleasing a man?'

Another dark flush swept over her features, but she knelt at once between his thighs and rested her elbows on them. 'I told you,' she whispered, 'you'd be surprised.' She pursed her shining lips in a blatantly sexual provocation and took his penis between both palms, rolling the column between them. The muscles of the shaft throbbed and it leapt within her touch. The neat fingernails scratched lightly along its veined length, and it beat strongly, the helm swelling to an engorged purple. She bent forward, and Michael suppressed a moan of weakening pleasure at the feathery caress of her tongue. She lapped at the glans, over its spongy surface, tracing the flanged edge where it joined the shaft, then down towards the yeasty bag of his balls. His belly lifted automatically, his prick rearing like a lance, painfully roused and pulsing against her nose and damp forehead.

'Jesus!' he gasped, while she licked at him feverishly, from root to the tip.

She grasped it firmly near its base, and guided the seeping helm to the O of her lips, which slid over the slippery dome and drew him in deep, a gagging snort coming from her working throat. There was a loud plop when she finally slid her mouth up to release him and gasp for air. She swallowed him again, and again his belly rose to meet her and he moaned in helpless joy. He felt once more that insidious surrendering of himself, and the reminder of what he'd done with John evoked a sudden swell of rage and shame that gave him the strength to drag her away from his erection, just in time to forestall the premature eruption he knew was so near.

She cried out in confused alarm as he spun her round and, lifting her bodily, flung her down with her face buried in the sofa, her dipped back raised. He clung like a limpet and eyed the raised and narrow buttocks, deeply pronounced as they tightened in trepidation. In his mind, he saw again the slim desirability of John's supple frame.

His prick reared against the taut rounds and his fingers scrabbled hungrily, pressing them apart. He thrust his column into the divide and stabbed at the tiny anus. There was a muffled protest. He squeezed a hand around her hip, seized her hairless mound and manipulated her sex lips. With finger and thumb he spread them and felt the slipperiness of her inner slopes, and nuzzled his penis into the entrance of her vagina, which gripped him with an uncomfortable tightness. Uncomfortable for both of them, for he heard her gasp, and then felt her instinctive reaction to his deep thrust. He felt that tightness yield, felt himself sink deep, felt the soft embrace of the moist passage. Highly stimulated by the clenching buttocks that nestled into his groin, he drove on aggressively to the explosive bliss of a quick climax.

He withdrew at once from her collapsed body, leaving a glistening trail of fluid across the fold of her buttock and thigh. The cheeks of her bottom hollowed and her hips ground in compulsive rhythm. He watched her hand squeeze between her tummy and the sofa. He watched the elbow pump rapidly. And he watched her fingers in the squelching wetness he had just vacated, until there was a wailing cry and she slumped in sobbing exhaustion, her head buried in the crook of her other arm as it lay limp amongst the cushions.

Chapter Twenty

When Reeves appeared in the foyer of the hotel, Felicity was already waiting for him. She was standing by the large raised circle of a marbled flowerbed with its exotic array of greenery. Her face was pale, and she could not quite hide the expression of pain as she walked, a little stiffly, towards him.

'Can we go right away?' she asked tightly. He smiled and nodded, offered his folded arm with old-world courtesy, and they made their way slowly back outside.

In the spacious rear of the car she shuffled uncomfortably, trying to keep the pressure off her bottom, where the vivid weals of the caning were still burning fiercely. She tried to rest on one hip, leaning sideways, and bit her lip at the throbbing ordeal. Reeves was eyeing her in the rearview mirror. The glass partition was lowered.

'Had a rough time, miss?' he asked sympathetically. When she blushed he smiled reassuringly. 'It's okay, miss. I know a fair bit of what goes on. You don't have to worry, I won't breathe a word. I'm too well paid to risk stepping out of line. But I take a lot of the girls out to rendezvous like this one. And they often come back in a similar state to yours. You can take your things off if you like; make yourself comfortable. There's some stuff in the fridge there - cold cloths and a packet of those wet-wipes. Takes the sting out of the tail, if you get me.'

She blushed even more, but nodded appreciatively. 'I've already bathed my bum once. Up in the hotel room. But it's still sore.'

'What did he use? A belt or paddle, or what?'

'A cane. Six of the best, in time-honoured tradition.' She managed a brave attempt at a laugh, grimacing as she did so. 'And they weren't on my bare bum, either. But God! They don't half sting.' She inhaled sharply and gingerly lifted up the skirt. The corselette was still unfastened at the crutch and draped open, so her bottom was bare. The thin lines of the beating showed in irregular parallel stripes.

She knelt awkwardly on the luxury upholstery, the skirt gathered up around her hips, and dabbed gingerly with the blessedly cool cloth.

'Like me to do that for you, miss?' Reeves asked casually, with that same friendly grin. 'I've had a fair bit of practice.' He chuckled.

'Why not?' She tried to match his light tone as she felt a tremor of excitement, ashamed though she was by it.

'I'll turn off a mile or two on. There's a quiet stretch I know.'

He had obviously done this before, she thought. Her arousal was simmering, in some weird way intensified by the steady throb of pain in her bottom. She wasn't taking much notice of where they were going. She remained crouched, bum in air, the skirt and the flap of the corselette raised over her back, enjoying the sensation of cool streams of air on her nakedness. Presently she felt the well sprung vehicle bouncing over rougher ground, and she saw they had turned into a kind of wooded parkland, with narrow tracks wide enough for one car only. He continued for quite a way, penetrating further into the quiet of the woodland, the wheels sinking into the softness of the damp earth, before he drew to a halt.

She was surprised at the strength of her excitement, despite her recent sexual activity. Ashamed of it, too. What was it about this kind of purely physical sex with complete or virtual strangers that turned her on so? And since taking up with Magda, she found the contrasts between the kind of loving she shared with her beloved mistress and the often aggressive coupling she'd experienced with her male partners more wonderfully stimulating than ever. Which was why, right now, as she lifted her bottom while Reeves dabbed gently at those enflamed welts, she could feel her sex pulsing imperiously in its need for fulfilment.

Would he oblige? she wondered, trembling at the thought. She'd imagined that any such contact would be strictly forbidden. Reeves was so much a part of the unique regime at Burnopside. Besides, he had always been so formal and correct in his demeanour. She had scarcely spoken to him, except to exchange polite greetings and thanks. Yet she knew now that if he made the slightest move towards some sort of sexual liaison, she would not be able to refuse him. And would she be capable of keeping it secret from Magda? She had a strange feeling that she'd be compelled to confess all, even if it meant another painful chastisement. Maybe even because of that, her inner honesty prompted, with embarrassing self-awareness.

She gave a little flinch of pain, though his touch was as delicate as she could wish. 'He laid it on pretty thick, didn't he?' Reeves murmured, with one last touch. 'There we are. That should take the sting off soon enough.'

She remained kneeling on the seat, her behind thrust towards his face. 'Who was he?' she asked, glad he couldn't see her face.

'Can't say, miss,' came the smooth answer. Can't or won't? she wondered. As though reading her earlier thoughts, he went on, 'You don't have to worry about any of this. I mean, me and you, like this. Miss Magda's told me. If ever I have the chance to fanny around with any of the girls, like now for instance, I can go ahead. That's if they're willing.' She felt his hand on the back of her thigh, very lightly stroking its inner surface. 'Are you willing, miss?'

She turned carefully, kneeling still, keeping her bottom away from contact with the seat. 'Please,' she said, with a shy smile, 'call me Felicity.'

He shook his head firmly. 'Oh no, miss. That wouldn't be right. Just as I'm always Reeves. That's as it should be.'

She smiled ironically. 'So, it's all right to fuck me but not to use my name, is that it?'

'That's about right, miss. Now, if you wouldn't mind stepping out for a sec I can slide the seat forward. It makes a very comfortable bed.' He helped her out of the car, and she stood there while he arranged the rear seat into a surprisingly accommodating bed. 'I'll be as gentle as I can,' he assured her while he worked. 'So as not to hurt your bottom, miss.'

'Thanks,' she said inadequately. He helped her back in and carefully laid her down. With great competence he removed her blouse and skirt, then unhooked and unlaced the tight corselette. The wired garment had left little red marks on the undersides of her soft breasts, which he massaged tenderly until she shivered with delight. She wore only the sheer stockings now, but he wasted no time in rolling them slowly off her lovely legs. 'I'd like to see you naked, too,' she breathed huskily.

'Of course, miss,' he replied, as though be found her request eminently reasonable. He knelt tall and methodically removed his clothing, religiously placing it neatly over the front seat. She saw how darkly hairy he was, all over his body, with a touching lack only on his head, the top of which gleamed immaculately. And from the forest of curls clustered about his belly, stood a cock of splendid proportions, already proudly erect and a fiery red at the dome. It quivered, as though in anticipation of the delights to come, at his every measured movement.

'I can see you're ready,' she sighed admiringly. 'Plenty of time,' he said regimentally. 'Old John Tom knows how to wait. Mustn't be greedy.' As he spoke he took her in his arms and dipped his head to her welcoming breasts. His tongue flickered around her tingling nipples, and she writhed gently and moaned her encouragement. She reached dreamily for that rampant prick, feeling it pressing against her thigh. But he grasped her wrist. 'Relax, miss. This is for you. You've done your work for today. It's time you were treated to a bit of pampering, I reckon.'

Felicity lost the power of coherent thought as he made considerate love to her with his tongue, lips, teeth, hands and fingers, while a thumb expertly strummed her engorged clitoris. She burst into sobbing cries for mercy and release, and wrapped herself tightly around him.

She screamed in torturous bliss as he sank home, sensing every gliding millimetre of the pulsating shaft driving into her rapturous cunt, riding with him all the way to that shooting climax of perfection that took the soldered bodies soaring.

And the car stood anonymously in the lonely forest glade in the damp December dusk.

In an even more luxurious and more traditional make and style of auto, Lord Burnopside settled back in the soft padding of the upholstery and stroked Magda's stockinged thigh with absent-minded delectation. 'Do you think she's ready yet?' he asked.

Magda felt the rub of the discreet ring on his little finger. He wore it only when acting in his capacity as chief of the select group that made up the spear-side of the Whores of Babylon, known as the Whore Masters. All the members wore rings, which appeared to a casual observer to be identical; an oval of jet in a gold setting, with the letters WM engraved in flowing script. But each ring's impression was as individual as a fingerprint. Some of the exclusive membership argued that it was an unnecessary elaboration, for the society's numbers were few and impostors easily identifiable. However, their numbers were growing, albeit slowly, and the current Grand Master, Lord B, envisaged the time, not too distant, when both Masters and Daughters would be too numerous, and in too many locations, to be known at once by their fellow constituents.

Magda was cautious. 'I don't know, my lord,' she answered thoughtfully. 'We'll see how today went. Signor Ricciardi can be a very rough fellow.' She chuckled. 'I think our little Felicity will be shuffling about on her chair at dinner tonight.' Then she was serious again. 'I'm still a little worried,' she continued carefully. 'She's so well known now. It could be a great risk, making her one of us.'

His lordship's fingers dug into her flesh with increased enthusiasm. 'That's the whole point, my dear. She'll be our first disciple out there, in the great wide world. Just think of it. Such a face, such a personality, known to the whole world, and all the time she's a Daughter - a Whore of Babylon!' His voice betrayed the pleasure he derived from such a notion.

'But• there will be so much more temptation to betray us,' Magda argued.

His hand slid up the muscled curve of her inner thigh, to the very top, his fingers caressing the gauzy nylon, feeling the hard edge of the little shield of her cache-sexe beneath. 'We have her with us for another month. She must be initiated by then.'

Magda knew by his tone that no further discussion was possible, and put aside the private doubts that assailed her.

'Now, let's enjoy ourselves,' he said, confirming the end of the brief debate. 'Debbie's such a delightful girl. I know everyone's looking forward so much to seeing her in action. You've done such a splendid job there, my dear. As always.' He pinched the firm flesh and quivered with anticipation.

Soon the car's headlights swept over the bank of trees which led up to the tall gates of a large house, tucked snugly behind high walls and security cameras in the stockbroker belt.

In a room on the ground floor greetings were exchanged, and the select audience, all males except for the voluptuous figure of the Grand Mistress, settled down on comfortable sofas and armchairs, before a wall comprised almost entirely of a window which gave a view of the room beyond. It was as brightly lit as a theatre set, with a wide bed devoid of any covers standing centre stage.

Debbie lay in the small compartment beyond that room.

She shivered as a tall blonde in a white tunic massaged perfumed oil into her brown breasts, and gave a dark nipple a final tweak for luck. Debbie was stretched naked on a massage table, and her svelte brown skin gleamed all over with the slick lotion that added to its lustre. 'He's an absolute stallion,' the blonde breathed in her ear. 'You'll love it.' There was a faint buzz and the girl slapped Debbie lightly across her flank. 'Go get it!'

Debbie went through the door indicated, and found herself in a room so brightly lit that she involuntarily blinked against the glare. A huge bed seemed to occupy most of the space. There was no other furniture at all. The walls were white, and the carpet was white. No windows, no pictures or ornaments of any description. No bed linen, except a dazzling white sheet stretched over the deep mattress. And, on the far side of the bed, an entire wall composed of one huge mirror.

She stood uncertainly, staring at her reflection. She had expected to find the room occupied by the man who was to be her partner. She had no idea what he would look like. She knew she must not speak, unless invited to do so, nor should she take any initiative in the sex play, but merely be ready to follow her partner's lead. She wondered whether he'd be old, and felt an inner dread that it might be someone like Judge Fairlie, with his parchment-like body, who was no longer capable of maintaining an erection and had to be teased and cosseted for hours before he could achieve a climax. Most of the Whore Masters were of an advanced age, and though she'd not been called upon to service any of them, except for the Grand Master himself, which had proved to be no hardship for Lord B was more virile than many a younger man she had known, she was well aware that the duty of a Daughter might well be to provide relief for any or all them.

She was pleasantly surprised, therefore, when the door opened and in stepped a figure with the muscled build of an athlete in his prime. The man was of African race, his hairless skin of an ebony blackness far deeper than her own brown complexion. He too gleamed with a film of oil.

He flashed her a brief smile. Not a word was exchanged as he advanced and took her in his arms. Their lips met, opened, stayed together, while their tongues entwined, and she felt her breasts crush against the chiselled hardness of his body. He scooped her up in his arms, carried her the two paces to the bed, and spread her out, carefully arranging her, before he lowered himself and knelt between her outspread thighs. For a long while he concentrated on her upper body, lingering over her sensitive breasts, gnawing at each erect nipple until they ached with desire, before his mouth and lips traced her quivering stomach and his tongue dipped into her navel. He moved on, over her belly, the scrub of pubis, to the already wet divide of her labia, which he peeled back with thumbs and fingers, exposing her running hunger, the fissure glistening, and the fluid flowing in response to his gentle kisses and licking tongue.

Without warning he swivelled round and knelt over her head. His potent phallus swung rigidly above her entrapped face, and the fecund testicles hung just above her spellbound eyes. She knew what she had to do. She squirmed a little, allowing his dipping head access between her splayed thighs, while she lifted her slender neck, twisted a little awkwardly, and sucked the huge plum of his prick between her moist lips.

They ground against each other until she was moaning around the stalk impaling and stretching her mouth, her face covered with a sheen of perspiration. She felt the approach of orgasm and strove desperately to hold it back. His mouth left her and the rearing prick was snatched wetly clear of her straining attentions. He knelt again between her thighs, took her by the ankles and turned her slightly so that, for a brief instant, she could see herself in the mirror, legs bent back and the whole gleaming area of her vulva exposed.

He folded her back until her toes were on either side of her head, the curve of her loins uppermost. With balletic grace he knelt across her as though she was a fulcrum, placed his hands flat beside her feet, and took his weight on his straightened arms. He eased the bulbous helm inside her, then sank, centimetre by slow centimetre, his erection like a sword ritually piercing its victim through to the vitals. With pistoning smoothness his hips started to rise and fall.

Debbie's toes curled into the white sheet. Her desperate bucking, and the rising urgency of her cries, indicated her climax was near, and then upon her. As the convulsions of orgasm swept through her he began to move faster and harder, thrusting into her remorselessly until he hastily withdrew, scrambled to her side, and held his penis over her like a weapon. He pumped it in his fist a few times, and then his semen jetted powerfully from its tip and spilled in an abstract pattern of shining pearl on the lovely upturned face beneath.

Chapter Twenty-One

'Just a scratch, honey. Won't be a mark left in a day or two.' Magda finished her inspection and tapped Felicity lightly on her rear. She straightened up, and Magda pulled the naked figure down playfully onto her knee. 'Did you come straight back afterwards?' she asked casually.

There was a fatal microsecond of hesitation before Felicity murmured that she had. Even as the fib left her lips she knew she'd blundered.

'I think not, sweetheart.' The strong fingers pinched at her thigh, still playful, but with enough force to make her flinch. The tears welled up in her eyes, and she felt a deep hurt at Reeves' apparent betrayal of trust, and his lies.

'I'm sorry - I mean - we did stop a while, it's true.' Her words came out a little rushed, with the guilty need to explain herself. 'He said - he said he'd soothe my bum for me.'

'And is that all he did?'

'No,' Felicity admitted sheepishly. 'After we... he fucked me.'

'So why did you lie to me, baby?' Magda crooned, cradling her close, and Felicity flung her arms around the broad shoulders.

'I'm sorry, Magda.' She shrugged hopelessly. 'I don't know really. He said it was all right - that you'd said he could have some fun with any of the girls.' She stopped talking, near to tears.

'Are you like any of the girls?'

Felicity sensed the significance of the pause, without properly understanding why it was so. She swallowed and cleared her throat. 'I'd like to be,' she breathed, aware somehow of the deeper meaning behind her words.

'Do you really mean that?' Magda held her away from her a little, staring into her eyes.

'Oh, I do!' Felicity pressed her face against that of her lover, her mouth open, giving herself fully to the passion of the kiss, which left her breathless.

Magda seemed to be pondering her enthusiastic answer. 'Get over the bed, honey,' she murmured, almost absently. 'Lie across the end. Stick your backside up.'

Felicity shivered but did as she was told, her toes trailing on the rug, her behind raised, her face resting on her folded arms. The crumpled sheet was still warm against her cheek, faintly damp and rich with their perfume and perspiration.

'You mustn't lie to me ever again,' Magda said gently. 'About anything, no matter what. You do understand that, don't you?'

'Yes. I promise I'll never do it again. I swear.'

'You won't, my darling.'

Magda picked up a hairbrush from the dressing table. If Felicity had thought the punishment might be lessened because of her ready repentance, and because of the wonderful loving they'd shared in the hours since dawn, she was mistaken, as she discovered with the first resounding splat delivered plumb centre on her clenched rounds. She screamed at the immediate blaze of pain, which raised a blotchy red outline on the quivering flesh. Magda's large left hand encircled the back of her neck and thrust her down forcibly, while the second blow landed, with its cannon crack, and Felicity jerked and howled like a demented marionette. She blubbered and twisted, choking on huge sobs, and the brush continued to fall in rapid succession until her bottom was a flayed and scorching mass of undefined agony.

'Come - down - stairs - when - you've - dressed!' Magda ordered between each swooping strike, and over the wail of Felicity's anguished weeping. And then the beating abruptly ended. 'And put a skirt on - no trousers.'

Felicity lay there when Magda had gone, stretched face down on the bed, her fingers clutching the sheet, soaked with her tears. It was many minutes before the violence of her grief died away. Her eyes were puffy when she did rise and glance over her shoulder at the area of reddened flesh, and gingerly tried to touch the stinging curves, wincing as she did.

What on earth was happening to her? Why was she letting that sadistic creature and this strange place take over her life? She was a star now, famous throughout the land - and abroad. A whole new world awaited her. Hollywood, perhaps. Who knew? Yvonne had said anything was possible for her now. And did she seriously want to give all that up, now on the very threshold of major success, for this? To be part of this mysterious cult, this tight little band of Magda worshipping slaves who surrendered every vestige of free will and independence for her love? She shivered as she realised how powerful was that element in her which answered yes. Even now, the throbbing pain in her bottom compelled her fingers to steal down over the dark fleece and caress the folds of her sex.

She sat on the bidet, easing her discomfort under the warm flow, and washed herself carefully. Then she took time to make up her face and disguise the marks of her grief and passion. She noticed her dark eyes were shadowed, the faint bags underneath a token of the hectic life she'd led in recent weeks. But she decided it added a subtle attraction, a hint of decadent youth that went so well with the role she was playing at the Hall. She dressed in a plain blue sweater, with demure neck and long sleeves, in keeping with the season, but over a bra which made the most of her curves. She also wore a grey skirt of modest length. When she had brushed her lustrous black hair she was pleased at the reflection which gazed back at her. A girlish, wholesome figure of demure conservatism verging on the pearls and twin set, and one far removed from the elfin modernism that marked her persona in the outside world.

The girls and Magda were gathered with his lordship in the morning room. Magda called Felicity over at once, and lifted the back of her skirt to show Lord B her scorched bottom. 'You see? I had to smack our girl, my lord.' She smiled. 'She's very sorry though, aren't you, my dear?'

Felicity's blushes made her feel even more like a little girl as she murmured contrite apologies, even though she'd lost sight of why they were needed.

'Don't get cold, will you?' Magda went on fondly. 'No knickers or tights. In *this* weather.'

'What about that young man of yours?' Lord B asked jovially. 'Is he coming down for the party tonight? He'll see the New Year in with us, I trust.'

'Oh - I don't think so, my lord,' Felicity blustered. 'I mean - we haven't - I haven't spoken to him since before Christmas. Things are a bit... tense... between us.'

'You did ask him, though?'

'Oh, yes my lord. But that was - before. We quarrelled just before I left.'

'Then call him up,' Lord B persisted. 'Get him down here. He'll come if you ask him nicely, I'm sure.'

Despite his jocular smile, Felicity knew it was an order. 'Yes, my lord,' she responded. 'I'll do that.'

'Where are you going?' Nicki Lowther was sulking, pouting so childishly that at any other time Stella would have snorted with laughter. But now when the beautiful blonde stared at her, it was with a look of dark contempt. She was busy fastening her magnificent breasts into a black bra, the satin half cups of which cut away so steeply that, in the low-cut dress she intended to wear, it would look as though the pale fleshy orbs were devoid of any form of support. The only other garment clothing her at that moment was the tiny black triangle of her G-string, hugging her mound and leaving the fuller globes of her bottom on splendid display.

She sat on the edge of the untidy bed and held out a long leg, toes pointed, and drew on a sheer dark stocking. With its companion in place she stood to adjust the darker lacy tops. She glowered at the forlorn figure, whose slight frame was covered to mid-thigh by a crumpled and baggy T-shirt, the tiny points of her nipples evidenced against the white cloth. 'For God's sake get changed,' Stella grumbled, and gestured angrily. 'And tidy this place up! Look at it, for Christ's sake! I've only been away a couple of days and it's like a pigsty. When Margy comes in she'll do her nut.

'What is it,' she added nastily, 'a case of *nostalgie de boue?*'

'Eh?'

Stella gave a dismissive shrug. 'Oh, never mind.'

Nicki's face turned beet red. 'Sorry, but you know how thick I am. We can't all speak fancy foreign languages!' She watched Stella ease herself into the black elegance of the skimpy mini-dress. 'Why can't I come with you?' she muttered, sounding even more like a sulky teenager.

'Because I say so, all right?' Stella rounded on her, her face colouring with rage. 'For God's sake, why don't you stop whining and get off my back?' She saw the hurt on the young face, and guilt assailed her. 'I don't know when I'll be back,' she went on, in a gentler tone. 'If you want to go out, go ahead. Just make sure you lock up.' She left hurriedly, slamming the door behind her, before she should start to feel too sorry for the forlorn figure standing there with tears in her eyes.

In the loud silence of the luxury flat Nicki sobbed and flung herself on the bed, crying harshly, the storm of grief shaking her wiry frame. She knew bloody well where Stella was going. She relived the feel of his brutal invasion of her body, the hard thrusting of his cock, burrowing into her, the weight of his body pinning her down, smothering her, trapping her while he satisfied himself. She shuddered at the memory of that potent discharge, warm, then cold as it trickled from her after his horribly abrupt withdrawal.

'There! Feel better now, you big macho bastard?' she'd snarled, after quelling her own gnawing excitement with her fingers. He'd reacted, rounding on her, bending her over his knees and slapping her rapidly, an open-palmed spanking that left her bottom stinging and evoked yet more dark pulses of desire, despite her so recent orgasm.

Now, through bitter tears, her brain ran a vivid picture of Stella's beautiful body coupling with his, made acutely responsive by the very self-denial she'd imposed only a short while before. 'I haven't time,' she'd said bluntly, cruelly snubbing Nicki's tentative attempts to initiate the beginnings of lovemaking.

And that wonderful slit would be flowering once more, revealing its moist treasures for that swollen stabbing brute of a cock. Nicki groaned tormentedly, her face buried in the sheet. Helpless in her need, her hand crept down between her closed thighs, caressed the slight swell of her mound, feeling the tiny bristles of her shaven hair, and the pulsing edges of her labia peeling back to her touch, wetting her fingertips with their lonely desire. The fingers moved, stoked her clitoris until her hips were undulating, driving her belly against the heel of her palm. The still faintly bruised buttocks lifted and sank, tightening and relaxing. She drew up her right leg, the knee out to the side, thus offering herself more openly to her caresses, the rhythm increasing. Her jaw clenched and she moaned softly, moving slowly towards the still distant peak of her lonely self-consummation.

Michael put down the phone with a mean sense of triumph. Felicity's voice had sounded meek in its penitent humility. 'I'm sorry,' he'd said. 'There's simply no way I can change my plans now. I've promised to be somewhere. Call me when you come back to town.'

Perhaps he would have liked a little more protest, a little begging. But never mind. The hushed tone had certainly sounded anything but uncaring or disappointed. And, by Christ, he hoped she *was* suffering, after all she'd put him through these past few months.

Excitement knifed through him like a sweet pain as he turned his thoughts to the matter in hand. When the bell buzzed and he saw Stella standing there, muffled in a fur against the cold, he had to breathe deeply to calm himself. He took the coat, striving not to show the tension he felt inside.

'Well,' she said, after a sip of the drink he poured for her. They sat on the sofa and her blue-grey eyes held his steadily. He felt an odd mixture of both anger and admiration at her composure. 'Where do we go from here?'

He had to say something, for she paused, waiting. 'Is there anywhere to go?' he asked, hoping there was.

Her eyebrows rose. 'I would've thought so. I don't like being jumped by a man, even on Christmas Eve.'

'I'm sorry,' he said, gaining a little confidence at her calm manner. 'Would you have preferred it to be a woman? Are you going to file a complaint?'

His gibe did not seem to bother her. 'I don't know,' she replied slowly, studying him. 'I'm not sure what happened.' She laughed then and raised a hand. 'Well, I guess I know what happened, I'm just not sure why. On both our counts. Were you just out for revenge?'

'I was - at first.' He felt compelled to be honest. 'When I followed you in there. But then I suddenly wanted you. Wanted - to make love to you.'

'To fuck me, you mean.' His blush deepened. 'Well, don't you?' He shrugged helplessly. She nodded. Her face was very intense. 'I don't know, either. That's why I'm here. That's the first time - in ages - that a man's screwed me.' The lovely features looked suddenly vulnerable, almost afraid. She shivered. 'I'm not sure how I felt... feel.' She stood abruptly, looking down at him as though having made a decision. 'Will you take me to bed?' she asked nakedly.

Once in the bedroom she seemed to wilt. He actually felt her go limp in his embrace. 'You'll have to take charge,' she whispered. She was crying a little, and his erection was beating mightily against his clothing. His hands moved with a new sureness, stripping the little dress from her, peeling away the twin scraps of lingerie and admiring the firm thrust of her breasts, even without the support of the bra. When he was also naked he laid her out on the bed and used her stockings to tie her wrists to the bed-frame. He knelt, her sandy fleece before his face, and dipped to kiss it.

She cried out, her tethered hands twisting vainly to reach for his blond head, and he lapped at her tangy vulva, not with a sense of submission, but of domination. Domination fully realised moments later when he moved of his own volition, lifting her thighs about him as he drove his rigid penis into the tightness of her sheath. He seized her ankles and pressed them up and back beside her pinioned hands, in an undignified sprawl that lifted her buttocks and exposed her mercilessly invaded cunt, which throbbed as madly as the driving prick possessing it. The frenzied whimpering and thrashing that denoted her orgasm followed his ejaculation by seconds.

Chapter Twenty-Two

'Happy New Year, my dear.'

Felicity felt the tingle of the champagne• trickling over her sex, and felt a cold stream meandering up her belly to catch in the folds of the dress rocked around her waist. Her pubes were flattened and darkened by the sparkling liquid. She shivered as the judge's slobbering lips touched her labia, his tongue lapping greedily at the wet divide of her flesh.

From her inverted position, her head resting uncomfortably on a cushion on the floor, she stared up past his knobbly knees, his scrawny hairless thighs, his scrotum, and the jutting little spout of his penis with its puckered folds of foreskin gathered at its tip, shrouding its head. The pot-belly reminded her of poor refugee children she'd seen on TV, with their bulges of malnutrition. Not that that was the explanation for Judge Fairlie's paunch, or the flaps of his breasts that hung like an old crone's.

Two of the girls were stationed on either side of her, holding her upside down against the wall, her legs spread wide. Her limbs were still encased in sheer black stockings, which were attached by black ribbons to the garter-belt. The blue evening dress was bunched about her middle, the hem hanging at her breasts. Her shining dark hair draped over the cushion supporting her head. Only the tiny knickers had been removed before they upended her for this unusual way of drinking a toast to the New Year, which all the naked male guests were lined up to take part in.

The judge poured a little more from his fluted glass, and hastily buried his snout in her soaking mound, snuffling and slurping like an old pig. She shivered, the muscles tensing in her thighs at the shameful excitement his touch kindled.

It was doubly appropriate that she should be squinting up inelegantly from the floor; her world was indeed turned upside down, and would never again right itself, she suspected. Clearly, she did not wish it to, for she had brought about all of this.

She was astonished at the strange new sense of freedom she had. One of the greatest terrors about doing *A Woman's Touch* had been that of exposing herself, literally, to the public gaze. She had from an early age been quite libidinous, with few sexual hang-ups, and always ready to learn something new. But always with one partner only. She had an entirely puritanical dread of exhibiting herself publicly. In fact, until she had begun cheating on Michael with her cousin, she had never had a sexual relationship with more than one partner at a time, fastidiously ending one before she took up with another.

And even then John had not seemed to count, somehow. They were so different together, so closely connected, by blood as well as by temperament. In many ways it had seemed merely a natural progression, to something started long ago in the innocence of childhood, and which should have been brought to a physical fulfilment long before.

But since she had fallen under the spell of Magda, and Burnopside Hall, all her values had been turned topsy-turvy. She remembered the night they had stripped her, all the girls, spreading her out on the table in the library, their hands and mouths fanning her desire to an unbearably sweet strength. In the midst of her giddy excitement she had been terribly conscious of those hungry male eyes fixed on her with priapic hunger, and, though it had shocked her, it had added potently to her feeling of sexual arousal. As now, this weird unveiling of her sexual parts, this ritualistic use of them, so openly spread and exhibited before the salacious audience, thrilled her until she knew she might climax helplessly in front of them all at any minute.

The secret lay in that sense of utter surrender, for with it came the irresistible bliss of freedom. Freedom from any iota of responsibility for anything that happened to her. The yielding of every vestige of Will-power, which made her a slave, it was true. A slave that could be tied blindfold to a bed, an instrument for anonymous pleasure. Or sent by car to present her body to a perfect stranger in a hotel room, and to have him do whatever he chose to her; to whip her, cause her fierce bodily pain, or make fabulous love to her. Or bend her over a chair and fuck her like a farmyard animal, then leave without a word.

But none of it was anything to do with her any more, except on a purely physical level. For she belonged, body and spirit, to Magda, and by extension, to his lordship, who had been the first to taste the nectar between her outstretched legs and use her cunt for a drinking cup. Surely her beloved mistress must know now that she was ready to take that final step, had already given up her body and soul to her?

She looked up at the distorted view of the next in line, and saw the great underhang of belly that proclaimed Sir Hugh. Instead of pouring out his libation over her vulva, he was leaning forward, and she felt his fingers prising apart the cheeks of her bottom, gazing avidly into the valley he was shamelessly exposing. 'Won't she look simply divine?' he purred cryptically, in that slightly plummy voice, and she gawped up at his shrunken prick and fat ball-bag, at a loss. Then she remembered the foreigner at the airport hotel, and how he, too, had opened her up intimately, as though searching for some sign or mark. She was confused, but this was not the place or time to ask about it. Indeed, her mind was soon occupied with far more pressing problems, or pleasures.

She'd had a feeling all day that this ending of the year was to be yet another watershed, perhaps the ultimate test of whether she was truly fit to be a member of this exclusive set. As the grey, sleety dawn of the new year rattled at the windows, his lordship summoned her and Debbie, led them with boisterous arms about their waists, to a fire-lit bedroom and an old-fashioned bed upon which they romped in splendid three-way nakedness.

Felicity was close to coming when Lord Burnopside's florid features were suddenly raised from between her slack thighs. 'I think you're one of us now, my dear,' he said. 'You've learnt so much about true pleasure these past weeks.' He turned to the watchful coloured girl crouching at his side. 'Don't you think so, Debbie? Let's see, shall we? Bring the shackles.'

Felicity's heart began to race as Debbie immediately moved away. His lordship was kneeling astride her. His erection had died, but his prick still hung heavily between her breasts, weeping its sticky juice into her cleavage. His strong fingers played with the soft mounds, teased at her nipples, and she shivered with dread and desire. 'Are you going to hurt me?' she whispered huskily.

He smiled down at her. 'That's what true pleasure means, my dear. That's what we want to teach you; the pleasure of pain.'

Her heart beat wildly as she lay submissively under him, and her limbs trembled. His fingers curled, pressed harder and harder into her yielding flesh. 'You must give yourself up to it,' he urged. 'Let your body go with the pain,' he murmured hypnotically. 'You'll understand-when you're truly ours.' She whimpered, felt as though she might faint, and was shocked by the massive charge of erotic thrill that passed throughout her body.

The cold metal of the restraints bit into her wrists and ankles. She didn't struggle as Debbie fitted them to her. All the rings interlocked. The bracelets securing her wrists were fastened to those around her ankles, so she was hobbled, bent forward, folded upon herself, her backside proffered for whatever use his lordship chose to put it to. She was placed in a kneeling position across the bottom of the bed, her forehead fitted between Debbie's spread-eagled thighs, her brow pressing against the curl-capped base of the brown belly. Debbie's hands pressed firmly on her shoulders, pinning her down.

Blindly, every muscle tensed, she waited.

There was a soft thudding noise, and then a shocking jar as something thick fell across her uplifted bottom. She could not identify it, but in any case she was incapable

103

of constructive thought as the blaze of breathtaking pain flared over her clenching buttocks. She screamed, despite her determination to endure the punishment in silence. Debbie's thighs tightened about her, the hands held her instinctively rearing body, and her cries were muffled in the fragrant female flesh. The fire rippled across her flanks, there was an agonising pause before the second stroke fell, and she screamed again, unable to resist the sweet feeling of release such an onslaught brought her.

She didn't know how many times she was beaten. She gradually became aware of the steady throbbing of her flayed bottom, and the lessening of pressure from the girl holding her. 'Splendid, my dear.' Lord Burnopside's voice was thick with passion. Even he was gasping, short of breath.

She hung there, still folded in her subservience, when they both left her alone. She felt the bed bouncing vigorously, almost toppling her off the side, and she realised his lordship and Debbie were fucking furiously, their limbs occasionally buffeting her as they coupled.

It was over fairly quickly. Felicity whimpered at a light touch on her throbbing flanks, but then came a blessed sensation of coolness and ease, as some icy liquid was sprayed over the crimsoned globes.

Later, Lord Burnopside showed her the whip he had used, with something of pride. It was one heavy, thick lash, of a curious rubbery substance, bound with silk. 'We won't always have to worry about marking you, my dear,' he told her, as though that was something for her to look forward to.

'I think you'd better get your things together and go,' Stella said coldly, facing the tragic looking figure garbed in her customary black outfit and ugly boots. Nicki's young face was red and smeared with her tears. She sniffed like an urchin recovering from a fit of crying. 'That's if you can ever sort them out,' Stella twisted the knife. 'You've turned this place into a tip.'

'Can't wait to get your boyfriend moved in, I expect!' Nicki whined, again sounding so childish that Stella almost smiled, losing the edge of her impatience.

'Probably,' she answered calmly. 'It'll save a lot of to-ing and fro-ing.'

The sense of rejection and frustration were just too much for the youthful figure. Her secret had been festering for days. Long lonely days spent mostly in solitary misery, her grief and resentment smouldering away inside. She had been discarded before the affair had really begun when Stella had fallen for that simpering bitch, Felicity Keynes. Nicki had pretended that all the publicity that came with the launching of *A Woman's Touch*, the endless photos and telly interviews, the sight of their unclothed frames plastered together leering at her from everywhere, didn't bother her. But then, to find her wishes coming so stunningly true, when she had given up hope, to find herself Stella's lover and partner only to be tossed aside once more, after a matter of a few short weeks, was too cruel to bear.

Her desperate effort to forestall that prick Michael Sinclair by interceding, placing her own body between him and her beautiful Stella, had not worked either. He had spurned her too, after that one memorable session here in Stella's flat, just before New Year. Not that he'd have had much time, even if he had fancied another session with her. Stella had made sure of that. The two of them had scarcely been out of each other's sight or arms since then.

Her own hurt was too strong to resist the desire to inflict pain elsewhere. 'At least that way you'll be able to keep an eye on him, I suppose,' she sneered. 'And believe me, you need to.'

The blue eyes narrowed icily. 'And what's that supposed to mean?'

'Just that he's not one to turn down any opportunity for a bit of nooky. As I well know. I've never said anything before now, but he had a go at me while you were away in Scotland. Right here - on the sofa.'

'You lying, twisted little dyke!' Stella roared. And for a split second Nicki questioned the wisdom of seeking revenge. But she summoned every ounce of resolve.

'Oh yeah? He fucking had me, right there.' She stabbed a finger at the sofa. 'Made me strip off and he did it to me. We didn't even make the bedroom. And afterwards he tanned my arse for me, if you want to know. He enjoyed himself on both counts. Why don't you ask him if you don't believe me?'

'You jealous little cow!' Stella gave an inelegant snarl of rage and launched herself at the slim figure, knocking her back onto the piece of furniture where the adulteration to place, sinking talons into the T-shirt and clawing it off the overpowered girl. She knelt over her victim, pummelling and slapping ineffectively, while the sobbing girl kicked feebly and covered her face with her arms.

Stella soon stopped and stood up, breathing heavily. She was convinced Nicki was telling the truth, and was amazed to find her anger was entirely dissipated. Indeed, she felt startlingly good, her body calm, the adrenaline like a relaxing drug. 'You pathetic little kid,' she said contemptuously. 'Come on, get your things and piss off. One thing I'm certain of, sweety - if he *did* shag you, he'll have forgotten all about it long since!'

Later that evening, when Michael arrived, she told him Nicki had gone. 'I threw her out,' she said, studying him closely. She could read the guilt in the slight flush, and the way his eyes darted away from hers. 'Are you sorry?'

'Mm?' He tried to act casually, as though not really interested. But the guilt made him overdo it.

'I just thought you maybe fancied keeping her on, as a kind of substitute. You could always bring her on for the second half if you thought I was flagging a little.' Uncomfortable embarrassment suffused his features and made him shuffle from foot to foot. 'I hear you smacked her backside for good measure. I wish you'd show *me* what a macho man you are!'

He recognised the challenge, and the excitement behind the taunt. And he felt the throb of a new and exultant force flow through him. The new Michael. The decent, gentlemanly prat had gone forever. 'Oh, I will!' he promised tightly.

She fought surprisingly realistically. Soon her dress was ripped, buttons wrenched off, her breasts, encased in a satin bra, were thrusting free. Her shoes were scattered, flying from her kicking feet, before he bent her over his knee, her knickers tugged down off her bottom, which he struck until his hand ached and the pale rounds were rosily hot. He pushed her off his lap and she lay at his feet, still squirming, her clothes dishevelled and her eyes wild. She rubbed her stinging behind and glared up at him through dishevelled golden locks.

'And then you shagged her right here, is that right?' she panted, her deep cleavage heaving invitingly.

'That's exactly right!' He seized her, hauled her roughly upright, then thrust her head down into the cushions. She had stopped struggling. She remained doubled over while he dragged the silk briefs down her limbs and off her feet, flinging them behind him. She sobbed, her rosy bottom uplifted while he fought out of his own clothes, then folded himself over her and immediately thrust his rearing penis into her moist cleft with savage elation.

'No...' she wept, grunting under his impaling thrusts and the rhythmic battering of his groin against her burning flesh. Yet it was his very brutality that set her own desires soaring, and led het on to the ecstasy of the explosive release which tore its way through her.

Chapter Twenty-Three

Felicity was taken to a part of the mansion she had never seen before. It was on the top floor at the far end of the east wing, and isolated from both servants' quarters and the other inhabited areas of the Hall. The bedroom was small, the narrow bed comfortable enough, and the furniture functionally adequate. The most striking thing about the room's decor was that it was entirely white; the chest of drawers, the dressing table and its stool, the wooden chair, and the doors of the built-in wardrobe. Even the drapes and the bed covers and the carpet. The walls, too, were of pristine snowiness, except that a great deal of their surface, on three sides of the room, was taken up with long mirrors. Wherever she turned she could see reflections of herself, as though surrounded by pale ghosts.

For two days and nights she saw no one, except Magda. Her mistress - for she was proud to acknowledge her as such - brought her frugal meals and sat with her for hours at a stretch, telling her in every detail about the society she was about to enter, the secrets of which she had long guessed at but now marvelled over as they were carefully revealed to her.

It was soon after the New Year's party that Magda had sent for Felicity and first told her of the Whores of Babylon. When the petit blonde Joanne had entered the room Magda turned her about and lifted the cherry-red mini-skirt she wore. Magda teased down the back of the white micro briefs until the curve of the blonde's buttocks was exposed, then she opened the cleft with thumb and forefinger. Felicity saw the tiny twin letters standing out against the pale flesh.

'It's not some kinky game,' Magda said, her tone indicating her seriousness. 'If you want out, say so now, before we start. It'll be too late otherwise. You'll be a Daughter forever, bound by all the oaths. You'll belong to us completely, for always. A lifetime of total obedience, total loyalty. Bound for all time. Do you understand?'

Felicity did understand. She nodded, her heart thundering. 'Yes,' she whispered.

The next day, after being given one last chance to opt out, she was taken up to the white room at the end of the corridor. Already caught up in the ritualistic fervour, she undressed at Magda's command, and handed over her clothing. When the door closed after the tall figure, Felicity knew she was a prisoner in the room. She did not even need to test the door to see if it was locked.

Her watch had been removed, and there was no clock, but through the small window she could see a comer of the building and the leafless branches of a copse of trees, so she was able to gauge roughly the natural passage of time. It was almost dark before Magda returned with a tray of coffee, a plate of salad, and yoghurt. She told Felicity about the Whores, and the absolute commitment she was required to make. She explained, too, about the Whore Masters, and about Lord B's supreme role as Grand Master. She smiled dazzlingly. 'And I am your Grand Mistress. You belong to me, and through me to every Whore Master. And to anyone I choose to give you to.'

Felicity nodded, too full of emotion to speak.

Magda made no attempt to touch her during the three days Felicity remained shut in the white room, and Felicity did not try to initiate any sexual contact. On the first night, when Magda rose to take her leave, she smiled and said, 'This is a very special time for you, Felicity. The time to prepare yourself for initiation. The time to examine yourself, to get ready for the new life you will lead, the new person you will become. The beginning of the discipline every Daughter needs to help her live this life. Test your own strength. Don't touch yourself in any sexual way - not even for a moment. Do you promise?'

Felicity stared, trembling. She nodded, but Magda made her answer, the very first of her vows. She had believed as she gave her assurance that the fervour she felt, the heat of the brand new convert, would enable her to see through this abstinence without problem. But the lonely hours, the nakedness, the very sight of her body thrust at her from all sides, day and night, was an ordeal the like of which she had never imagined. In spite of her desperate efforts, her hands would steal to a breast, to the tuft of pubic curls, the curve of her flank, the moist folds of her sex lips, so that she would snatch her hand away with a cry as though she'd touched a hot stove. She was soon exhausted, for she dare not climb into bed or lie down on the counterpane. Whenever she did so she felt an almost overwhelming desire to stroke, to touch between her thighs, to masturbate for the relief her nerves demanded.

She realised, appalled, that she had never known a period of real continence. She had always indulged in masturbation, and self-caressing moves which were purely sexual in purpose. And such behaviour had always been a counterpoint to a satisfyingly hectic sexual association with others. True celibacy she had never known. It was a refined torture that reduced her before long to bitter tears. She pushed her forehead despairingly against her reflection and beat her fists against those of her image, before sinking in exhaustion to the floor, where she remained curled and weeping for an age, before she wearily lay on the bed and sank into sleep.

On the other side of the glass, a few feet from the distraught girl, Lord B studied her compassionately, while Magda crouched between his legs and massaged his prick to a rearing erection. 'Ah, Magda, you don't know how much I want you!' he groaned, his naked body writhing in the chair as Magda's long dark curtain of hair descended and draped over his lifting loins. Her lips milked the spearing erection and drained its potent load until he sank back with a weakened sigh.

When calm had been restored, he studied the sleeping figure on the other side of the glass. 'She's ready,' he decided. 'You've done another wonderful job, my love.' He reached up tenderly for her hand, drew her gently down to kiss those lips which had brought him such bliss, and his dormant penis twitched in his desire for the unattainable perfection of coupling with this unique being.

Felicity's brain was reeling. She did not know whether it was the drink she had been given, or the wreathing incense that pungently filled the darkened chamber, with that one brilliant shaft of white light like a pillar at its centre. The whole setting was so magical, the mystical anointing of her flesh so stirring, she hardly knew if she were awake or dreaming. Under the long cloak, her glistening body was trembling. She prayed fervently that she would have the strength to get through the ceremony, that the emotion would not prove too strong and cause her to faint away before its completion. She waited, tensed through every fibre of her being, feeling the cold of the marble striking up through the soles of her feet.

At last the velvet mask was slipped over her head and adjusted so all vision was blocked. She felt the arms of the others about her, gently guiding her forward, positioning her. The cloak was unfastened at the neck and swept aside. She could sense the brilliant light was bathing her body, and she tried to control her trembling, to keep completely still. From the darkness ahead of her the deep voice boomed out that she knew was Magda's, yet sounded awesomely different. She gave the ritual replies, clearing her throat nervously, anxious to be heard by all the invisible watchers.

The hands were lifting, then stretching her out on her stomach, and she gasped at the contact of the icy marble on her bare flesh. The rounds of her behind clenched, and she felt the grip of the hands at her wrists and ankles tighten. She bit her lip to suppress the whimper struggling to escape.

The bite of the whip across her flanks was an exquisite agony. A scream was muffled in her throat.

'Do you swear obedience?'

She cried out, absurdly pleased that her voice was clear. 'I do!'

The searing sting of pain again, and the next question, demanding her undying loyalty. Her voice was ragged, hoarse, but still quite clear. The slender strands bit for the last time into her quivering flesh, and she jerked against the restraining holds, unable to prevent the first sob from breaking forth, as she gasped her pledge of binding secrecy.

The fire throbbed steadily, then came the blessing of fragrant wet coolness, as her companions bathed the striped bottom, and the mask was removed from her tear-laden eyes. The light was so dazzling when they turned her onto her back that she was still blinded, but she surrendered herself, luxuriating in their ministrations; the kisses, the fondling caresses, which stirred her eager body to a sweet urgency of desire. Lips closed over her nipples, nuzzled at her inner thighs, at the swell of her mound itself and her throbbing fissure, before, with dramatic suddenness, the blinding light was obscured and an outspread shape hovered over her. It descended, and Felicity sobbed with joy at the enveloping warmth of her mistress's wonderful body; the weight of those ripe breasts upon her own, the nipples engorged, the muscled stomach and sturdy thighs.

The cloak wrapped itself about them, sealing them in their own magical world, so that the invisible watchers and her naked companions faded from thought as Felicity yielded in weeping happiness to that body. With a shock of delight her spinning mind registered the wondrous fact that, for the first time in all their intimate relationship, her mistress was entirely naked. The tiny cache-sexe, that embossed triangle of final mystery, was gone. She felt the smoothness of the tapering belly, its conflux with those splendid thighs, and even the small tuft of silken curls to crest that blessed centre of sexual bliss which she'd never touched, never set eyes upon.

And then fantasy fused with spiralling reality. The powerful knees parted her thighs, and she felt strong fingers opening her further still to the last magical secret, for there, at the lips of her divide, a living column of flesh nuzzled and gained entrance. Not a facsimile, not a harnessed instrument of pleasure such as she had known and delighted in in the past, but a living organ of flesh, inches of hardened dome-tipped phallus, which took possession of her, melding its oily fluid with her own secretions of love. She felt the swoon she'd feared rush to overtake her, the drumming of blood in her ears drowning her cries of ultimate fulfilment at the orgasm which sucked her into its terrifyingly shattering power, and which claimed every part of her, from her fragmented mind to her curling toes.

'Good God! Where the hell have you been? Your agent - Yvonne what's-her-name's been going spare. She's never stopped ringing this past week.'

Felicity smiled at her cousin, walked past him into the flat and put down her small case. 'How are you, Johnny?' she asked breezily. 'It's good to see you.' She kissed him lightly on the lips, and broke away before he had the chance to turn their embrace into a more passionate one. She plonked herself down on the settee and looked around. 'The old place is certainly a lot better than I ever kept it,' she acknowledged appreciatively. 'It looks immaculate. Get me a drink, will you? I'm bushed.'

John was staring at the elegant figure in the severely attractive grey suit. She crossed her legs, the short skirt riding up to allow him a pleasing view of her shapely limbs. She pushed the dainty heeled shoes off with her toes, which curled in abandoned luxury. Her black hair had been cut shorter and shaped to her neck, its waved softness enhancing this thoroughly feminine ethos.

'You look different,' he said, bringing her drink, and standing over her admiringly. 'You look like some super brat female exec type.'

She laughed and pulled a distasteful face. 'Oh don't say that, please!'

But she *was* different, it struck him forcibly. Not only her quietly sexy, more openly feminine appearance, but her contained manner. Not subdued, he realised - far from it. There was an assurance, a restrained maturity about her that was entirely new. It was mystifying, and appealing. Yet he felt a twinge of sadness too, for he knew the last fragile link to their childhood together was gone, never to return.

The final confirmation came when, after she had gone into her room to change, she came out again and stood in the living room doorway. His heart and his prick leapt. She was wearing a black bra and black briefs - a tiny scrap of satin and lace barely covering her mound - and a thin web of a garter-belt from which the ribbons of suspenders stretched over her white thighs to sheer stockings. She smiled tenderly at his obvious appreciation.

'You sexy thing!' he breathed, rising and moving towards her. But when he got there she skilfully avoided his grasping arms, and gave him another of those light kisses, mouth to mouth, but which lay somewhere between an affectionate greeting and a promise of passion.

'I think I'll have a quick bath and go straight to bed,' she said. 'I could do with an early night. It's going to be hard work picking up the reins again after such a long lay-off. Night, Johnny.'

She turned back at her bedroom door. 'Oh, by the way. Don't worry about the flat. You can stay on here as long as you want. I don't think I'll be around that often. And if I need it to entertain or anything, you can always blow for the odd night or two, can't you?' Another sweetly innocent smile, and she was gone.

Was it all a come-on? he asked himself briefly, seated once more in the suddenly lonely room. But he knew Felicity was no longer the ingenuous girl he had fooled around with so recently. She had moved on, leaving him behind. And so he sat on in the lamp-lit quiet, sipping a whisky, regretting and already missing the things that had been and were no more.

He was woken next morning by the sounds of flushing and running water, and her strongly tuneful voice raised in song. The bathroom door was unlocked. The shower partition had been drawn across, but he peeked round the end of it, enjoying the spectacle of her gleaming back and the tight curves of her behind. He stared at the fading pink lines crisscrossing her buttocks, suddenly deeply roused by the memory of his own chastisement at the hands of that mystical six-foot Venus. 'Shit! I thought *I* was kinky! Your new chums play rough, eh?'

Felicity was not in the least bit embarrassed. She slid back the glass partition and stepped out onto the mat. She almost touched him as she reached for a towel and began to dry herself. She smiled, and her dark eyes met his levelly, and with amusement. 'Maybe I was a naughty girl,' she purred.

He went to seize her, but his move lacked conviction.

She did not resist, just stood very still, and his hands fell away from her damp arms. 'No fun and games?' he asked, keeping his tone light.

'No fun and games,' she confirmed. 'There really isn't time.' She dropped the towel on the floor, letting him get an unrestricted view of her nakedness. 'Clean up after me, there's a good lad.' At the door she turned back towards him, with a smile that was full of affection. 'But even if there *was*, there wouldn't be, if you see what I mean. The games are over for us.'

She didn't object when he followed her into her bedroom. She just carried on dressing quickly and efficiently, saying nothing.

John couldn't stop himself. 'What do you think about Mikey and your ex-lover?' he said, suddenly wanting to spiteful.

The relationship between Michael and Stella Priest had been blazoned all over the tabloids, and was the source of numerous sniggering articles in a score of magazines. She gave no sign of being disturbed by his vindictive words. 'They're both my ex-lovers,' she prompted gently. She sat at the dressing table and swiftly applied her light make-up. She selected a light and very short skirt of a summery thinness, and over it a more substantial jacket, in keeping with the chill March weather.

'Don't you mind?' he was forced to probe.

She turned to him with her sunniest smile. 'No, I don't mind. I'm pleased for both of them. Perhaps they deserve each other. I'll call later. I don't know if I'll be back tonight. Bye.' She blew him a kiss and was gone.

He flung off the silk robe he had pulled on, and wandered naked into the kitchen. He felt irritably mean, and cheated. And also randily frustrated. He stared down at his penis, which immediately lifted and stiffened. He played with it, stirring his sexual longing further. He went back through to her bedroom, picking up the scattered evidence of her swift departure. The black briefs lay in a tiny crumpled bundle on the floor. He picked them up, held them against his lips, and savoured the tangy, perfumed smell of her.

His erection was aching. A sudden vivid recall came to mind, of Michael's neat blond head at his loins, the feel of his lips around his prick, which jutted from the fragile silk and lace, just like the fragment he held in his hands now.

With a look of cruel determination, he moved towards the phone.

Chapter Twenty-Four

Felicity removed the dark glasses as she stepped out of the elevator. The hotel corridor was so cooled by the softly humming air conditioning that her bare arms, and scantily clad body beneath the gossamer stuff of her dress, were all goose bumps. Her skin was a pale honey colour from the Californian sun, which at that moment was beating down outside in steamy summer intensity. She had been here for almost three months now, filming for an American TV series which would prove far more profitable than her role in *A Woman's Touch*.

She had been extremely reluctant to accept the offer when Yvonne had told her about it, and given her a copy of the pilot. 'Oh, shit! No! Not another lezzy role, for God's sake! I'm going to be typecast.'

'You're going to be a millionaire,' Yvonne told her crisply. 'And out there nobody's going to give a toss what you are, my dear.'

But it was not her agent, or even herself, who would decide what she must do.

'You'll go,' Magda said simply. 'We don't want you fading away from the public gaze. Far from it. And if you're good we'll let you fly back here for a weekend every month.'

To Felicity it was not an opportunity, but banishment. The tears and the passionate farewells were not exaggerated, for she felt desolate at being removed from that special world she had become a part of. 'You're so lucky,' she told the other girls forlornly. 'All I want is to stay here, like the rest of you. Always.' Still, she had to admit there was a kind of thrill in knowing she held such a vital secret when she again moved out into the glare of the public domain.

'It's a series with a gay theme again, isn't it?' Mary Westerman leaned forward eagerly. She had asked Felicity to appear on her show as soon as the news of the signing had broken.

'Well, yes,' Felicity admitted, 'but somewhat understated. At least compared with *A Woman*. It's really a woman cop thing. Two partners who happen to have a relationship. We won't be rolling about naked in the hay with our tongues down each other's throats the whole time.'

'Oh well. Never mind,' Mary said cattily, and Felicity managed to keep the smile plastered on her face beneath the bright lights.

She had made several trips home since the filming had begun, but it was over the phone that Magda had called and given her simple instructions. Just a name, and a number. And that had led to this moment in the luxurious hotel. Her heart was thumping, and she realised how damply excited she was, the thrill heightened as always by that edge of nervousness. She tapped at the door.

She recognised the slim figure, the slightly wizened, watchful features of the man who opened to her. 'Mr Dillman?'

He smiled, and nodded as he gestured for her to enter.

He held up his right hand and twirled the ring on his little finger. It was very familiar to her; she had seen its like on a number of privileged digits.

'You want to see *my* credentials?' So saying, she turned, lifted the back of the flimsy dress, and bent forward a little. She was wearing a white G-string, so he didn't have to lower the tiny garment to open the cheeks of her bottom and observe the little letters marking the inner surfaces.

'There was no need,' he chuckled, 'but never let it be said that I passed up the chance to feel such a cute gal's fanny. And such a famous piece of ass, too!'

She shrugged modestly, and was about to make a witty reply when she remembered she was there as a Daughter, and not as Felicity Keynes, the hot little Brit movie star who was the latest talk of Hollywood. *A Woman's Touch* had been screened over here only a few weeks ago, and was still the subject of sizzling gossip wherever she went.

'I was talkin' to the Grand Master,' Matthew Dillman continued, 'and he said he'd be in touch. And here we are, huh? Just a little job for you, honey, and I know you'll be hot for it. One of my companies got this merger planned. Mega-bucks, sweetheart, and I mean mega! But there's a lot of wheelin'-dealin' involved. We need some financial backin' to see this one through, and we're gonna get it. But we've got this young feller negotiatin' - a true blue Brit, like yourself. We gotta keep him sweet, sugar, and there ain't no one sweeter 'n you.' He leered at her. 'He'd mortgage the moon for us if he thought he could get into your panties, honey. And that's just what we're gonna let him do.' He chuckled. 'Not buy the old moon for us, but somethin' just as big, as far as he's concerned, and that's to lay you. Screwin' Felicity Keynes. Imagine! He'd be ready to cut off his pecker and donate it to science after a night with you.

'It's all fixed, honey.' He held up his right hand, as though swearing an oath. 'All very discreet, don't you worry. Not a soul will know. And he's quite a hunk, so you should enjoy it too. Tomorrow night, here. This is the suite. Limo will pick you up from your place at seven-thirty.'

She nodded, made to leave, but he called her to him. He was sitting in a chair by the window, where the sunlight was streaming in. He drew her close, so that she was standing between his slack knees. He slid his hands up her bare legs, feeling her thighs, then on up inside the dress, cupping her bare buttocks, digging his fingers in tightly. 'Yes, indeedy! You sure are one mighty piece of ass.' His hands slid round, explored the tiny triangle of satin over her mound, his fingers stroking the curls he could feel under the gauzy material. He flipped the elastic down so that her mound was exposed, and let his fingers ferret through all the moist furrows, inserting them inside the dampening divide, seeking out the throbbing clitoris until she gasped and thrust her belly forward.

Slowly, he peeled the G-string down, off her hips, then pushed it down her legs, and she stepped out of it. 'Strip off, kid,' he murmured hoarsely. She lifted the dress, drew it off over her head, and stood there, her body bathed in the shaft of sunlight, until he scooped her up with a roar and fell with her onto the wide bed. Concerned only with his own urgent appetite, he clawed himself out of his trousers and underpants. He grabbed her wrist and guided her hand to his rampant prick, jutting squatly from his shirtfront.

She swivelled round, working the column all the time with slow, vigorous strokes, and crouched, her behind raised, her lips peeling apart to slide over his glistening helm and take all that tangy prick into her suckling wetness. He filled her throat. She tasted his fluids, mingling with her saliva. She felt his mighty surge, withdrew her lips swiftly, and squeezed the root to prevent him ejaculating too soon. Rolling onto her back she spread her thighs and gratefully took his plunging length. The penetration was just in time to feel the powerful flood of his coming, which triggered her own exquisite climax.

Chapter Twenty-Five

'Wait a minute, kid. If we can't have the real thing, we've got to fake it. Right?'

Nicki Lowther grimaced, squinting against the brilliance of the big arc lamp. The squat Arabian looking figure waved his assistant over, a girl as swarthy as he was, but whose long frizzed hair had a sun-bleached copper tint. She smiled at Nicki, who was lying propped up on her elbows on the cushions. She was friendly enough, Nicki thought. And why not? Only half an hour before that coppery head had been planted firmly between her thighs, working away greedily, with a relish which was by no means assumed for the rolling camera hovering over her shoulder.

She'd be glad when she got out of this porno pic, she decided. She moved obediently when the director's hand pushed at her inner thigh, exposing her shaved mons and the divide of her labia, where he was carefully smearing a pearly thick fluid meant to represent the semen of her male co-star, who was sadly incapable of producing the real stuff at this seminal moment. Maybe it wasn't a substitute. Maybe it was the real thing after all, milked from some other worthy donor behind the blinding light.

Nothing would surprise her about this outfit. None of the guys had really prodded her in front of the camera. Some of them had been massively equipped, true, and had got it up where it was supposed to go all right, for a few vital pistoning thrusts, then it was a case of cut and run. Out they went, and the magic died before she'd had a chance to register anything except the shock of their entry.

The girls were better. Especially this sultry gypsy, or whatever she was. Her name was Laila, and there were no problems of faking it there. She had a tongue that slithered about like a snake, together with fingers that knew exactly where to go and which buttons to press. It was the only bit of this sad movie that they hadn't faked, for Hamid had just left them to get on with it and, after a time, Nicki didn't even notice the camera crawling around them.

'I have to do everything round here,' Hamid grumbled, handing Laila the dish of whatever and wiping his hands on a towel. Carefully, he positioned Nicki's limbs, lifting a knee, pushing the thighs a little further apart to highlight what lay between. 'Okay. Now lie back. And look well fucked. Right? Action!'

Well pissed, more like, Nicki thought, as she lowered her head and parted her painted lips, assuming an expression of what she hoped would pass for replete gratification.

Resentment surfaced once more as she showered the sticky goo and the heavy body make-up off in the tiny shower afterwards. It was boiling hot in the big barn-like studio where they made these flies, except for the outside locations, kept to a minimum, which had to be shot in some godforsaken spot at about five o'clock in the chilly summer mornings. She was sure that superbitch Stella had been putting in a very effective oar to spoil her blossoming career. Decent offers should have come rolling in after her appearance in *A Woman's Touch*, even though the part was small. But no. Nothing. She had been forced to go back to modelling, and even then none of the big names would touch her. Which was why she had turned to the nude modelling. Just to tide her over, she had assured herself, but it had gone on out of necessity until it had led to this.

Well, at least she was a star, she told herself ironically, even if no one would remember her face. Plenty of other bits for them to look at!

She was startled when the tall figure approached her as she made her way to the car park and her waiting taxi. 'Can I give you a lift?' it said.

Ten minutes later, in the back of a chauffeur driven Mercedes, her brain was whirling as she studied the charismatic woman who was sitting cosily close to her. 'Oh, yes,' the deep voice purred, 'we know a great deal about you. My partner's very interested in you. We think we could help your career a great deal.' An immaculately manicured hand with dark red nails fell on her black jeaned thigh, and stayed there, the fingers pressing a clear if unspoken message. And the moist flesh beneath the crotch of those jeans responded traitorously.

Before the car was back in the choked arteries of the city itself, Nicki had fallen entirely under the spell of this spectacular creature. She exuded a power, and not just because of her splendidly gigantesque frame or the beauty of that smoothly open face. There was an aura about her, a strength that Nicki felt herself instinctively and willingly surrendering to. She was captivated, entranced, the damp patch at her crotch transformed to a swamp by her emotive response.

'Of course, my dear, it means a lot of discipline. It means putting yourself completely in my hands. Doing exactly what I tell you, without question.' One of those hands had moved now, the long finger crooked under her chin, lifted Nicki's worshipping gaze towards her, those smiling lips parted, honey sweet, close to her own. A shiver ran through the slender form at the words, which were themselves like a caress to that yearning centre.

'Yes, of course,' Nicki whispered reverently. 'Anything you say.'

She would have been deliriously happy to know that her own answer elicited a very similar response between those powerful thighs nestled next to hers. Yet shocked, too, had she witnessed the physical reaction. For against a snugly reinforced triangle of supple leather embossed with silver, a seeping head and stubby column emerged from between brown folded lips and pulsed against its enfolding captivity, while Magda gave an imperceptible sigh of pleasure, and of exquisite torment.

Felicity gladly discarded the disguise of dark glasses and the long blonde wig, as soon as she was safely behind the locked door of the hotel suite. The mystery attached to her assignment smacked uncomfortably of the ridiculous. But, as she had to keep telling herself, she was here as a Whore of Babylon, one of the Daughters, not as her glamorous public persona. Or was she? She wasn't sure any more. This Brit fellow she'd belong to for the night clearly knew who she was. Mr Dillman had made that plain; that it was the clincher as far as this financial gnome was concerned. He would produce the goods for their capitalist venture purely because he had been gifted the famed body of the controversial movie star for one whole night. Clearly, a trip to paradise for this sad prick.

She was curious, as well as apprehensive, just how he would turn out. She had of course envisaged a wrinkled, paunched oldie, a combination of Judge Fairlie and Sir Hugh - in which case she almost hoped he would prove to have a penchant for the blindfold that had covered her eyes during the never-to-be-forgotten multi-bang at the Hall. But then she was sure Matt Dillman had called him a 'young feller' - though she could hardly remember what he had said, after the hectic finale to their one meeting.

She wished it could have been the fatherly figure of Dillman himself she was required to spend the night with. She hoped she might be ordered to service him again some time. He undoubtedly qualified as an oldie. His face, if not his lean body, gave his age away. Not that he made any effort to disguise it. That's why he'd seemed so fatherly to her. She blushed as she thought of the can of fantasy worms coupling with him had opened up for her. But whatever, it had been far more satisfying than dealing with some of the Masters she had encountered at the Hall, and at other discreet places back home.

Tonight would not be like that, she feared. Whoever this guy was, young or old, he sounded a sad little git. She'd had her detailed instructions. Which was why she stood now in the dayroom of the luxury suite, done up like a stripper waiting in the wings; down to front opening black net bra, frilly French knickers, and the lace fringed garter-belt with the requisite black stockings and high heels. All she needed was the drum roll, she reflected, then pushed such disparaging thoughts resolutely from her mind. She brought up the image of Magda, and the magical conjunction of their flesh that had made her hers for all time. She was a dedicated Whore, and she would do her duty.

The bedroom door was open, twin lamps directed like spotlights to the space at the foot of the wide bed, where she was summoned to perform. She took up her position before the dark shape lying propped on a mound of pillows in the centre of the bed. He was fully dressed, as far as she could see.

'Take your clothes off,' he intoned huskily. 'Take your time.'

Jesus! Why didn't he just go to a strip joint? She could not prevent the disgusted thought from entering her mind. This felt truly sordid. Once again she made a valiant effort to banish such admonitory thoughts, and slowly unzipped her dress, shrugged it forward off her arms, then wriggled it down her hips to fall about her feet. She stepped out of it, bobbed gracefully to scoop it up, and laid it on a nearby chair.

The silence was unnerving. She wondered if she should break it. Did he know about the Whores of Babylon? The discipline Magda had taught her prevailed, and she forced herself not to speak. She unfastened the cups of the transparent bra, teasingly drew them apart, and then eased the straps down off her shoulders. Daintily, she turned and dropped the garment on top of the dress, then turned back to face the shadowy figure on the bed. In slow motion she held her breasts in her palms and massaged them in circular motions, and let her fingertips play over her small nipples until they peaked.

She slipped off her shoes, raised one leg to rest her toes on the bottom of the bed, and unhooked her suspenders, before rolling the stocking down with the same, teasing adagio movement. When she had done the same to its companion, she dropped them on the small pile of clothing on the chair. She unsnapped the catch of the belt at her waist and removed the flimsy garment, with its dangling ribbons, which joined her discarded things. All she had left on were the knickers, but as her thumbs hooked into the elastic, the hoarse voice spoke again.

'Wait! Turn around and spread your legs. Hold the back of the chair.'

She inhaled sharply. So, he was going to chastise her. She wasn't really surprised. It seemed to be an expected facet of the duties of a Daughter. She knew how important a part corporal punishment played in the role of a Whore of Babylon, the tenets of discipline by which they were required to live. She had learned to accept it with a genuine willingness, and had even learned how it could enhance the bodily pleasure of sexual acts. Her tearful thanks, while her bottom burned from the attentions of Magda, or Lord B, or one of the other Masters, were entirely sincere.

But here she had believed she was not playing her accustomed role of an anonymous Daughter. She had thought this shrouded individual on the bed was paying for the glamour of possessing the famed star who had notoriously orgasmed on the silver screen. The burlesque strip show had all been part of it, she had thought; the kinky thrill this sad man would get from having Felicity Keynes perform for his exclusive pleasure.

Her knuckles whitened on the back of the chair. She flexed her behind. Suddenly she felt that familiar clutch of real fear. Perhaps it was again the idea of whose arse it was that would give him his kicks. And if that was so, he might well lay it on until her flayed backside resembled a piece of raw meat. She bit her lip, her breathing suspended as she stood, bowed forward, her bottom thrust out.

The first swipe was shockingly loud, a great splat that sent fire flaring all over her taut cheeks. Though it smarted abominably, she breathed a thankful prayer that he was using some sort of flat paddle. Not a whip, or a wicked cane, which could cut so nastily and raise welts that would take weeks to fade.

Still, she was sobbing audibly after the third or fourth loud smack, and hopping from one foot to the other as she tried to remain bent over in the position required for her punishment. It was soon over, though it didn't seem so at first. The steady throb indicated that he'd finished. She hung there, weeping, her hands clamped to the chair back. She was shaking, and felt the secret insidious stirrings of desire the fierce pain had roused. The humiliation of her submissive stance and the vision of her glowing rear stuck out for his inspection added to that beat of sexual excitement.

He had lowered the knickers just clear of her buttocks, and then gently peeled them down her tensed legs. She winced as she lifted her feet to allow him to remove them.

'Stay there! Don't look.'

She obeyed and felt his arms move around her, and then swing her round so that she faced the bed. He was still behind her. She realised he was naked.

He positioned her on the bed, kneeling, facing the pillows, her punished bottom raised high. She braced herself, inched her thighs apart as she felt a hand squeeze between them, searching for the soft lips of her sex. But, instead, the fingers were probing the valley of her bottom. She gasped at the cold oiliness of the cream he was smearing there, and at the invasive finger that pressed into the tight and tiny fissure deep in the cleft.

'No... please...' she pleaded unconvincingly as a bulbous helmet probed between her buttocks and pressed against her anus. She held her breath, waiting, and then her back dipped as he sank forward and her bottom was impaled by a rigid column of flesh.

'You know,' he panted quietly in her ear, 'from the back you look and feel just like your cousin.'

'*Michael...*' Felicity groaned.

Also by Nicole Dere and available as paperbacks from **AMAZON**:

A Desirable Property
Chain of Command
Prisoners of Passion